The Resurrection Man

CHARLOTTE MACLEOD

The Resurrection Man

A SARAH KELLING and MAX BITTERSOHN MYSTERY

THE MYSTERIOUS PRESS
New York • Tokyo • Sweden • Milan
Published by Warner Books

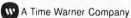 A Time Warner Company

Mysterious Press books are published by
Warner Books, Inc., 1271 Avenue of the Americas,
New York, NY 10020.

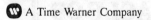 A Time Warner Company

The Mysterious Press name and logo are trademarks of Warner Books, Inc.
Printed in the United States of America

FOR SARAH BOOTH AND RICHARD CONROY

with much affection

1

"Max, are you quite sure you don't want me to go with you?"

Sarah Kelling Bittersohn watched anxiously as her husband picked his way down the front steps of the ancestral brownstone. Sarah's ancestors, not Max's. Kellings had been among the first to fork over their six shillings to the Reverend William Blaxton for a building lot on the peninsula of Boston, to cast their votes for John Winthrop as the Massachusetts Bay Colony's first governor, and to side with him against Deputy Governor Thomas Dudley in the dispute over making Boston its capital. Their side had won, of course. Kellings had never had any trouble figuring out which side of the bread would wind up with the butter.

By now there had been Kellings on Beacon Hill for going on four hundred years; Sarah had been born and brought up here. Even after she'd remarried and moved to the North Shore, she hadn't been able to bring herself to sell the Tulip Street house she'd inherited from her first husband, who'd also been her father's fifth cousin. Her Cousin Brooks Kelling and his wife, Theonia, were living here as caretakers, paying the utility bills and doing the endless repairs so old a place demanded.

It had gone without saying that the Bittersohns would continue using the house as a pied-à-terre whenever they pleased. They hadn't planned to spend the summer on Beacon Hill, though, until Max, a private detective specializing in the recovery of art objects, had landed in Massachusetts General Hospital with a badly fractured leg and an assortment of broken ribs, results of an altercation with two unprincipled persons who'd been reluctant to part from the Goya they'd taken such elaborate pains to steal.

By now, the ribs had knitted nicely and the leg was responding to therapy. Max had progressed from a walker to crutches to a handsome silver-headed cane, once the property of Sarah's Great-Uncle Frederick, who was by now deceased and tucked away in the family vault to the unspoken relief of many and the expressed delight of a few. For the past couple of weeks, Max and Sarah had been taking short strolls together, down Charles Street to the hospital for Max's therapy treatments or over to the Public Gardens, where there were benches to sit on and plenty to see.

They'd even penetrated the Back Bay alphabetically from Arlington to Berkeley to Clarendon, then on to Dartmouth and Exeter. Max wasn't yet up to Fairfield, Gloucester, or Hereford, but his hopes were high. Today he'd decided to solo, Sarah couldn't blame him for that. A man used to striding the world as if he were breasting a forty-mile gale all the way must have found it irksome to be trammeled by sudden infirmity and, possibly, by an overanxious wife.

She told herself to go inside and leave him alone, but she didn't go. Tulip Street's brick sidewalks were part of Boston's history, picturesque to look at but hell to walk on for a man with a cane and a steel-pinned femur; narrow, uneven, and worn slippery by many generations of feet, not to mention a number of dauntless backsides. Written large in the annals of Beacon Hill was the story of the time when the city fathers had got the idea of ripping out the old bricks and replacing them with smooth, up-to-date, easily maintained asphalt. Tradition-minded residents had thwarted these evil machinations by the simple expedient of planting their own bean-broadened buttocks on their beloved bricks and refusing to budge till the vandals went away.

It had been Frederick Kelling who'd led the fight on that historic occasion, carrying the selfsame cane Max was using today. Cousin Brooks had fitted a new nonslip rubber tip to the ferrule; Max was neither slipping nor tripping. Sarah saw him to the corner, blew a kiss when he turned to wave, and went inside.

Max's plan was to cross Beacon and walk across Boston Common to his office in the Little Building, which is in fact rather large. Originally he'd used the office only now and then. Since his marriage to Sarah, the one-man firm had become a family affair. Brooks, a trained ornithologist, and Renaissance man, was proving even wilier at snaring crooks than he was at netting birds for banding. Theonia, half grande dame and half gipsy fortune-teller, lent her multiple talents as occasion demanded. Even Sarah went out on a job when she could spare the time, though her primary concerns were the research and the increasingly complicated paperwork.

They'd all been carrying on as best they could while Max was laid up. As soon as he'd been able to hold a phone, he'd started running up astronomical long-distance telephone bills to his many free-lance operatives in various parts of the world. Brooks and Theonia had been doing what traveling was necessary. Sarah had stayed put to care for Max and their young son, Davy, with the help of henchpersons Mariposa and Charles, whom Sarah had hired as maid and butler during her widowhood, when the brownstone had temporarily been turned into a boardinghouse.

Davy was walking and talking well now, and exhibiting the same investigative zeal as his father. Sarah had decided it was time to augment their staff by a nanny, a secretary, or possibly both; but she hadn't yet got around to interviewing anybody. Max was mulling over the pros and cons, making good time across the Common and not feeling the pain in his leg to any unbearable degree, when his attention was arrested by a steam whistle shrieking his name.

"Ah, my God, the magnificent Max! What is happen to you?"

The sun was in his eyes. No, it wasn't. He was merely catching the dazzle that was being reflected from dozens of tiny mirrors sewn into a white gauze scarf roughly the same length as the one that had strangled Isadora Duncan by getting caught in the wheel of her motorcar. Its ends were floating free and easy in the summer breeze for about a yard and a half behind its wearer. This was a tall, gauntly elegant woman wearing a black sateen walking suit, circa 1912, with white lapels all the way down to the knees and a slit in the hobble skirt to make walking possible though not convenient. Black kid gloves, a rolled-up black parasol, and a broad-brimmed black straw hat of the same vintage, laden with the tail feathers of several game cocks and worn very much on one side, made a smashing climax to the *tout ensemble*.

"Good God!" said Max.

The woman under the hat found his reaction amusing. "Is just me, not even angel of lowest rank, though I strive to improve my image. You see me now as respectable Boston Brahma."

"I do?"

Max had seen Lydia Ouspenska in many bizarre outfits and in the company of many strange companions, few of whom could by any stretch of the imagination have been called respectable. Some were petty thieves, some small-time con artists, some peddlers of inferior or downright counterfeit narcotics. One had been a Grade A, big-time swindler, thief, and murderer. To the best of his knowledge, Lydia had never been a conscious participant in any of their chicaneries; but most of the minnows had used her in one way or another, and the kingfish had very nearly succeeded in killing her.

It had been Sarah and Max who'd rushed the near-corpse to the hospital and sat through a long, ghastly night waiting to know whether the old girl was ever going to wake up again. Now what the hell had she got herself into? Max took a firmer grip on Uncle Fred's cane and groped his way to a bench.

"Sit down, Lydia, and take a load off your parasol. I haven't seen you in ages. Where've you been keeping yourself?"

Max realized too late that he'd made an awkward choice of words. Countess Ouspenska, as Lydia preferred to be known, would never have been keeping herself if she could have found a man to do it for her. During recent years things hadn't been too brisk in the demi-mondaine department. The last he knew, the aging siren had been scraping a meager living by painting antique Byzantine icons and selling them through one of her so-called friends. Being a true artist, Lydia had pulled off some masterful forgeries, but each took a long time to do and her pal had no doubt swindled her on their prices. When last Max had seen her, she'd been thin as a rail and pale as a ghost.

Now Lydia was more svelte than skinny, the desperate hollows under her cheekbones had filled out enough to make her look less like a Käthe Kollwitz charcoal drawing and more like a fashion sketch by Erté. Whether her color was any better would have been impossible to say without excavating, but her maquillage was a work of art in the Byzantine style. Her dark eyes were aglow, she'd had work done on her teeth; she was no longer the wreck of a beautiful woman, but a beautiful woman growing older with grace and dignity.

Lydia furled her scarf and took her seat on the bench with a haughty disregard of pigeon droppings.

"I am keeping myself in Boston but no longer at Fenway Studio. You like my chapeau?"

"The hat's great. The whole outfit's great. You look great, Lydia."

"You sound monotonous, Bittersohn. What has happening to you? And where is your beautiful dragoness?"

"Home taking care of the kid. We've got a son." Max reached for his wallet but Lydia grabbed his wrist.

"You show me baby pictures, I scream for cops and claim molesting. Is too depressing, the handsome Max turning to *bon bourgeois* papa with child on knee and maybe soon hair falling out. Where is *beau boulevardier* Champagne Charlie of yesteryear?"

Max Bittersohn had worked his way through high school, college, and graduate school; he'd been working ever since. His hair was not falling out. His excursions into *la dolce vita* had been few, brief, and strictly in the line of business. He shrugged.

"You sure you haven't got me mixed up with a few other guys?"

"Is possible," Lydia conceded. "Who can keep track? Me, I am still bohemian at heart but less so since having gainful employment in congenial company with perquisites of office."

"What company is this?" Max asked warily.

"The Resurrection Man."

"Burke or Hare?"

"Ha! You make a witty. Do not try to jive me, bozo, I am hep to Burke and Hare. The Resurrection Man is not grave robbers digging up bodies for medical students to cut up in spirit of scientific research, is resurrection of great art from trash bins. Also sometimes of not so great art, only sentimental value like letters tied with blue among my souvenirs, but who cares? So long as clients willing to pay, we happy to resurrect."

Being a highly intelligent man, Max was able to deduce what the self-styled countess was talking about. "What you mean is, you're doing restoration work?"

"*Jawohl, mein tovarich.* I fix. He fixes. They fix. We all fix. In atelier each has specialization. Mine is Byzantine icons, *figurez-vous*. Also I gild. In Byzantine icons is much gilding, I don't have to tell you, but also in frames, in bookbinding, in illuminated manuscripts, in etcetera is gilding. Is more etcetera than icons coming through the atelier, also in churches not removable from walls is halos and many etceteras to regild, so I make house calls on saints and martyrs, even. Is very elevating but I like better in atelier with comrades of the fix. This week I gild a cage for an old bird who would like to put me in, I think. But I do not kootchy-mootchy with clients, is not good for corporate image. Also Barto raise hell if he catch me."

"Barto being the Resurrection Man?"

"Of course."

"Runs a taut ship, does he? What's his real name?"

"Barto is Bartolo Arbalest. Is possible you do not know?"

"No, I've never heard of him. I thought I knew all the restorers around Boston. Where's the studio?"

"I cannot tell. Is top secret."

"You don't say? So how does Arbalest get his clients?"

"Through recommendations from galleries, auction rooms, antique dealers. Clients telephone for interview or write to box number. Is for their own protection, Barto explains. Thieves not know where clients' treasures are, not come to steal. Nobody minds if for tight security; Barto don't have to carry so heavy insurance, only that part he don't tell. He goes to client, makes appraisal of value, states fee for resurrection, take or leave. Almost always they take, Barto is very persuadable. Expert work, dependable service with written guarantee, no phone calls after business hours. Barto is first-rate operator."

"He sounds like one." To Max, Bartolo Arbalest also sounded like the answer to a swindler's prayer. "How come no phone calls after business hours?"

"Because from six to eight, Bartolo cooks. At eight we eat, is ritual solemn and uplifting. We are all wearing green velvet smocks and floppy berets with flowing silk tie in Rembrandt style. I am only one without beard, is pleasant contrast."

"Naturally it would be," Max agreed gallantly. "Why the smocks and berets?"

"Is more meaningful than soup and fish with silly little bow like cat's whiskers. We are of the new renaissance, we dress according."

"And after dinner you get to lick the dishes clean?"

"Bah, Bittersohn, you grow stupid with fatherhood. For dishes is serf in peasant costume with sleeves rolled up. Also to clean house and make beds in Hanseatic style with feathers inside. We are classy outfit, I can tell you."

"I can well believe it," Max replied somewhat abstractedly. "Are you saying you and the rest of the crew all live there with Arbalest?"

"Not crew. Is guild. Is time-honored custom for master and assistants to live together, though not much practiced since about maybe fifteenth century, except apprentices not getting paid and needing to be kept alive for purposes of exploitation. Great advantage of living together is everybody get to atelier on time not too hung over to do good day's work. Bartolo covers all bases, is no flies on him."

"No flies?" Max was outraged. "How the hell does Arbalest think he can run a medieval guild without any flies?"

Lydia Ouspenska shrugged and began adjusting her scarf. "Flies more authentic, I grant, but get stuck to paint and gilding size, disturb concentration by buzzing around. Voting by guild members is one hundred percent in favor of no flies, for reasons of not having wings and feet and mangled bodies providing more authenticity than clients care to live with. I must go. I am in quest of truffles for Barto to make pâté."

"Shouldn't you have brought a pig along with you to sniff them out?"

"You are amuse, Bittersohn, but not very. I will come to dine *chez vous* sometime when Barto take night off and send out for moo-goo-gai-pan with fortune cookies."

"That would be great, Lydia, we'd love to have you. I'll have Sarah give you a ring. What's your phone number?"

"Personal calls to members of guild is not acceptable to Barto, I will appear out of blue like tooth fairy and surprise you. *Au revoir, mon bon bourgeois.*"

"See you later, Mrs. Rembrandt."

Lydia and her scarf floated off, heading for Charles Street and Deluca's grocery store, Max surmised. Lydia probably wouldn't want to walk any great distance in those needle-toed shoes she was wearing; did that mean Bartolo Arbalest's medieval ménage was somewhere fairly close by? Or did it mean that Lydia had treated herself to a subway ride?

The self-styled countess must be old enough by now to qualify for a senior-citizen's pass. It wouldn't be like her to pass up a bargain, but would she have been willing to admit her real age? Maybe one of

Bartolo's artisans was doing a sideline in authentic subway tokens. Max took hold of the bench back with one hand, planted his cane tip firmly in the sand under his feet, and hoisted himself upright with only a twinge or two. It wasn't much farther to the office, he hoped Brooks hadn't had to go out on some urgent errand.

No, Brooks was in and delighted to see him. "Well, this is a pleasant surprise. All by yourself, eh? And no problems?"

"I'm not sure," Max said. "I ran into one of your old girl friends on the Common. Remember Lydia Ouspenska?"

"Of course. How could I not? But on the Common? Don't tell me she's down to panhandling?"

"Oh no, she was just passing through on her way to buy truffles. Lydia looks better than I can recall ever having seen her. She's eating regularly and high on the hog, or so she claims, and she's gainfully employed as a gilder in a guild. Ever heard of the Resurrection Man?"

"Why, yes, now that you mention it. I assume you're not referring to the ghouls who used to rob graveyards, ergo I deduce that you may be referring to a chap named Bartolo Arbalest who has a little shop on Third Avenue in New York where he does some restoring and odd jobs. Quite well, as I recall. He wears a smock and beret and trims his beard in the style of the late Rembrandt van Rijn."

"Right on the name, the beard, and the beret. Wrong on the address, unless Lydia's doing a hell of a commute. From what Lydia told me, I gather Arbalest's here in Boston and has either bought or rented a house big enough to accommodate not only himself and his studio—sorry, *atelier*—but also Lydia and an assortment of other people who work for him. It's an old Renaissance custom, she tells me. Each of them is a specialist in some aspect of restoration."

Brooks nodded. "A cozy arrangement. Are they—er—"

"Lydia says she's the only one without a beard, but that doesn't help much. They all get together around the wassail board every night wearing velvet smocks and berets, and Barto, as she calls him, cooks them a banquet. Unless he isn't in the mood, at which times they send out for fortune cookies."

"Do you know, Max, I think Lydia may have told you the exact truth, oddly enough. Bartolo offered me a job once. This was back in New York, of course; I'd no idea that he might have immigrated. Anyway, one of his conditions was that I'd have to dress as he did:

velveteen smock, great flopping beret, one of those silly bow ties getting into the turps or whatever every time I bent over. Naturally I explained that wasn't my style and that was the end of it."

"How long ago was this?"

"Oh, quite a while. As much as twenty years, I'd have to stop and think back to give you an exact date. I've been something of a rolling stone, you know. It was after I'd stopped my lecture tours, but before I started doing bird calls at children's parties and odd jobs at the Wilkins Museum. The parties were rather fun, actually. Perhaps you'd let me do one for Davy when he's about eight years old. Eight's a good age for bird calls."

"It's a deal. Davy's already imitating blue jays out at Ireson's Landing. He runs around flapping his arms and squawking." Max smiled, a trifle ruefully. "Lydia says I've turned into a *bon bourgeois*."

"Pah, how would she know? Max, this is extremely interesting information. Don't you think we ought to pay Bartolo a call sometime soon, just on general principles?"

2

ounds good to me," said Max, "but it may not be that easy. I asked Lydia for the address and she wouldn't give it to me. She says Bartolo doesn't want anybody to know, including his clients."

"Then how can he conduct business?"

"Contacts are made by telephone or by writing to a box number, then Bartolo pays a personal visit to the prospect, gives an estimate and a snow job, and takes the work away with him. When the piece is fully resurrected, he takes it back and collects his money. The rest of his money, that is; I'm sure he must extract a down payment when he takes on the job."

"He'd be crazy not to," said Brooks. "Does this rigmarole suggest to you what it does to me? How do the clients find him? Through the Mafia?"

"Yes, it does and no, they don't, according to Lydia. She claims they come through referrals from galleries and the auction houses. She may have wrong information or she may be lying, she's always been pretty good at both. On the other hand, supposing it's not stolen merchandise. Can you see anybody owning a piece important enough to warrant restoration at the kind of price Bartolo must charge being dumb enough to let him cart it off to an unknown address, unless they'd first got ironclad guarantees of his bona fides?"

"Certainly I can. What about Cousin Apollonia? Or Uncle Frederick, for that matter, though of course you never knew him. Old Fred prided himself on being an infallible judge of character, so naturally he got stung at an average of once a week. However, I do see your point, Max. Did Lydia give you any explanation for the secrecy?"

"She claims it's a matter of security. Bartolo's argument is that by concealing the whereabouts of his studio, he keeps thieves from coming and pinching the clients' treasures."

"I suppose that makes sense," Brooks conceded, "though not a great deal."

"Lydia did mention that it's also a way for Bartolo to keep from having to carry huge theft insurance," Max added.

"There is that angle to be considered."

"She also says Barto, as she calls him, is a very persuasive guy."

"And how right she is," Brooks agreed. "Talking to Bartolo Arbalest used to make me feel rather as if I were having an audience with the archbishop of Canterbury. Not that I've ever so much as laid eyes on the archbishop myself, but that's the general sort of feeling Bartolo evokes. Yes, I should say he could talk almost anybody into almost anything."

"He couldn't talk you into a velvet beret, though."

"Don't forget I'm a Kelling, my boy. I grew up in a tough school. You know, I'm finding it difficult to picture Bartolo as a fence's assistant, if that's what you have in mind. Disguising stolen paintings so they can be smuggled out of the country, that sort of thing?"

"It happens. What's your problem?"

"Well, I know that times change, and people with them, but back when I knew him, Bartolo Arbalest had a very strange reputation, considering the neighborhood he worked in. He was reputed to be absolutely, scrupulously, quite disgustingly sea-green incorruptible. But you know, Max, it does boggle the mind to think of Lydia Ouspenska's being linked up with anyone incorruptible. Oh dear, I hope she's not in trouble again."

"You and me both. Maybe I'd better call Sarah."

"Good idea. Sarah's fond of Lydia, you know. She does tend to like people; I can't think where she gets it from. Both her parents had about as much human feeling as a pair of frozen bluefish, though I always thought Elizabeth might have amounted to something as a human being if she hadn't married Walter and become so involved with Thoreau. But why involve Sarah? Why don't I toddle along and—"

"Lydia knows you too well, she'd spot you in a minute. Let's just see who's—hi, Kätzele, what's up? No, no problems. I'm with Brooks at the office. Listen, I bumped into Lydia Ouspenska on the way here. She's probably at Deluca's by now and I want her tailed. Is either Charles or Mariposa available? Lydia knows Charles, he'd have to disguise himself pretty well. I don't think she's ever seen Mariposa. Okay, either or both, only tell them to make it fast. She's wearing a black vintage outfit with white trimming and a black hat the size of a cartwheel, put on sideways. And carrying a parasol, she'd be hard to miss. No, no stakeout, I just want to know where she goes with the truffles. Over to you, kid. See you in a while."

Max hung up the phone. "Sarah's going to take Davy for a short walk. She'll try to intercept Lydia at the corner of Beacon and keep her talking till Charles gets his false whiskers on, then he and Mariposa will take over. Too bad Theonia's out on assignment, she could have done her bag-lady act. Have you heard from her?"

"An hour ago," said Brooks with quiet pride. "The miniatures were exactly where you thought they'd be. I'm to meet her and Mrs. DeMorgan at Back Bay, take them to lunch at the Copley, Theonia will hand over the goods, and I'll collect the fee. Can you manage the office till three or so? There's that chap coming in about his Degas ballerina."

"No problem. What else?"

The two occupied themselves agreeably for a while discussing various malefactions currently on the books and thinking up interesting ways to deal with them. Then Brooks went off to keep his appointment and Max began making phone calls, as was his wont. He'd completed a fair amount of business and rounded up one or two new jobs by the time Brooks got back from his luncheon with the ladies, having deposited the check on the way.

They were beginning to think seriously of shutting up shop, turning on the answering machine, and going home to see what their secret agents might have turned up on Lydia Ouspenska when a slight, dark figure slunk furtively through the door and closed it noiselessly behind him.

"Ah," said Max, "enter the little brown man with the blowpipe. Still looking for the eye of the idol, Bill?"

"Su-ure. Hi, Brooks. How's it going, Maxie?"

Bill Jones, as he preferred to be called, was wearing what he always wore: a cotton shirt that might or might not have been changed during the past week, a pair of chinos in somewhat worse condition, and shabby moccasins. No socks, Bill only wore socks during months that had an R in them. He also owned a dirty old raincoat, but this was hardly the weather for that. The summer sun had tanned him dark as a Bedouin, though some of it might have been dirt.

Seeing him thus, few would have guessed his guilty secret, that Bill Jones was in fact the younger brother of Boston's richest and most influential Greek importer and that he himself was a successful commercial artist whose idea of a wild night on the town was to attend a poetry reading with some attractive Radcliffe woman who'd either made or was about to make Phi Beta Kappa. That Bill had often gone from such highbrow revels to share Lydia Ouspenska's bed at the Fenway Studios, when she'd lived there, was no reflection on his morals. The relationship had been, in Lydia's own words, purely Plutonic; it was just that Lydia didn't own a spare mattress. Bill was just the man Max had been hoping to see.

Bill might in fact have come looking for Willkie Collins's *Moonstone*, he was generally looking for something. Usually it was information he sought, not for any special reason, Bill just liked to know.

Being scrupulously honest and the epitome of discretion, Bill got to know a great deal, of which he repeated very little. He was thus an invaluable friend and ally to Max, seeking no reward except an occasional invitation to dinner at Tulip Street so that he could sneak appreciative glances at Sarah and Theonia out of the corners of his soulful dark eyes. It probably wasn't by chance that he'd come here at so opportune a moment, he might well have been trailing Max across the Common to make sure he didn't get into any trouble walking alone. Doing good by stealth was Bill's forte.

Of course stealth was what Bill did everything by, even communicating. He didn't so much speak as breathe his words, and he didn't even breathe very often, at least not so that anybody could notice. While he could talk perfectly well when the mood was upon him, he frequently preferred to put his messages across by shrugs, glances, and drawing pictures in the air. His hands weren't much bigger than Sarah's. Right now they were fluttering like a pair of sparrows after the same crumb, eager to respond to what Max was about to tell. Max obliged.

"The leg's doing fine, Bill. I suppose you know Lydia Ouspenska's not at the Fenway Studios any longer. I met her on the way over here just a little while ago, looking like a million bucks' worth of two-dollar bills. Have you seen her lately?"

"No-o-o. She just—" Bill waved his old lady friend off and shrugged her into oblivion. "I thought she must have—" either died or gone off with some man. That Lydia might have gone with a woman wasn't even worth fluttering about, it could never have happened. "What's she—"

"She claims she's working for the Resurrection Man. Know him?"

Bill pantomimed a corpse laid out for burial. Max shook his head. "Not that kind. This guy has a business restoring antiques and paintings. His name's Bartolo Arbalest and Brooks says he used to work in New York."

Bill raised his eyebrows. "Are they—?"

"Oh sure, Lydia's living with him, though only in the Plutonic sense, as far as I know. Arbalest prefers to have his helpers staying in the house so he can get them to the studio on time in the mornings."

Bill smiled a wee smile. "Lydia does that? He must be some operator. Where's his—?"

"Good question," said Max. "We hope to have an answer in a while."

"Didn't Lydia—?"

"Her lips are sealed. She claims Arbalest has made all his elves take a vow of silence, for reasons of security."

"Hey-y-y."

Bill drew some rather alarming pictures. Brooks, who'd been quietly enjoying the pantomime, nodded.

"We've been wondering that ourselves, Bill. Not that it's any of our business what Arbalest is really securing himself against," Brooks added, for the code of the Kellings was a stern one, in spots. "Though I don't suppose that need stop us from trying to find out," he appended further after a moment's thought. The code of the Kellings had certainly never stopped his Cousin Mabel. "Lydia claims the idea is to keep thieves from knowing where the clients' priceless art treasures are being taken, so that Barto, as I gather she calls him, won't have to carry heavy insurance. She could be telling the truth, I suppose."

He, Max, and Bill shrugged in unison and enjoyed a merry chuckle together at this amusing fantasy. Then Bill started waving his hands again.

"So how does he—?"

"Make connections? House calls, according to Lydia. When I knew Bartolo in New York some years ago, he had a shop. People just strolled in with their Duccios under their arms and he touched up the bald spots. Now, it appears, he takes referrals by appointment from the more respected galleries and auction houses. It could be an upgrading of his image in the interest of higher fees, I suppose. Lydia didn't happen to mention, Max, whether Bartolo drives up to the client's door in a coffin brake?"

"Hell, I forgot to ask. It hardly seems likely he'd want to call attention to his comings and goings, if he's that secretive about where he lives. I'm surprised he's letting Lydia run around loose."

"He probably isn't," Brooks demurred, "except for occasional errands. The truffles may have counted as a desperate emergency, Max, you know what amateur chefs are like. You've been out of circulation, of course, but I'm back and forth pretty much every day, as are Theonia and Charles. If she were really on the loose, it does seem one of us would have run across her somewhere along the line."

"Unless the studio's out in the suburbs somewhere."

It wouldn't be. Max's guess was a regentrified former rooming house in the Back Bay. Lydia hadn't specified how many people were actually living in the house, but surely they'd each want a bedroom. Unless Arbalest carried his medieval-guild concept to its limit and made his artisans sleep rolled up in sheepskins under the workbenches. Lydia probably wouldn't mind, she'd slept in ruder places.

"As it is," Brooks went on, "I haven't heard so much as a whisper of her since Ernie Haire left Boston, much less of Bartolo Arbalest's having arrived. Bartolo never struck me as the sort to hide his light under a bushel. All this secrecy suggests to me, as I'm sure it does to you, that he's got himself into rather a bad fix in New York and is lying low till the dust settles. I just wish we knew what it's all about, one can't help worrying a bit on general principles. Lydia has about as much sense as a common coot."

"I've never found anything common about Lydia," Max objected. Except her love for the common man, he didn't have to mention that. "Well, let's not start tearing our hair till we see what the undercover agents have to report. What else is new, Bill?"

There was quite a lot, Bill told it graphically. More graphically

than verbally, anyway. Brooks made careful notes in his own secret
code, nodding from time to time as some piece of information fitted
snugly into one of the various webs he and Max were weaving. They
had all but wrapped up two of the cases on their docket, and were
interestedly dissecting a rumor that had filtered through to Bill by
way of Montenegro and Lima when a stage-caricature anarchist of
the old Bolshevik school breezed in.

"Hi, Dmitri," said Max. "Sit down and park your bomb."

"Oh, fudge, you rumbled me."

Charles C. Charles, for this could be none other, removed half a
pound or so of bushy black-crepe hair from pate and chin, detached
the matching eyebrows, and revealed himself in his Lord Peter Wim-
sey guise, except for the monocle he'd been too pressed for time to
remember.

Charles, a professional actor, had done a magnificent Mr. Hudson
for Sarah during her boardinghouse days, but had been forced to
depend for spending money on a job in a plastics factory. Since
Max's accident, he'd been doing much of the legwork for the agency
and was proving himself a man of more parts than he'd ever got to
perform on Boston theater stages. Even as he picked spirit gum off
his chin, he was turning into Sergeant Charles C. Charles, CID. First,
however, he did a brief aside.

"Mariposa went back to the house, she thought moddom might be
needing her in the kitchen. And now, sirs, to report. Pursuant to
orders received and understood, M and I liaised with Mrs. B and son
at the corner of Charles and Beacon. Finding her already in conversation with Countess O, we lurked until the latter party had kissed
both Mrs. B and son D several times and prepared to cross on the
walk light to the Public Gardens."

"You mean the PG?" Max asked.

"Yes, sir, if you prefer, sir. Countess O was carrying a little weeny
brown grocery bag, indicating to M and me that the truffle-procure-
ment operation had been successfully carried out. That the bag was
so small suggested to us that the countess hadn't had money enough
left to buy anything else. Otherwise she no doubt would have, she
being the way she is. Neither the size of her handbag nor the cut of
her costume was conducive to successful shoplifting and O has never
been much good at it anyway. She might conceivably have snuck

something into her parasol, but they were most likely keeping an eye on her in the store, knowing Countess O as they do."

"So, in short, you trailed her." Unless firmly taken in hand, Charles did tend to pad his roles. Max was eager to get at the nub.

"Yes, sir, we did, sir, my partner and I. M, I mean. We trailed Countess O to an address on—is it okay to say Marlborough Street? I've already used up the M."

"It's perfectly okay," Max reassured him. "Between Arlington and Berkeley?"

"No, Berkeley and Clarendon, on the Beacon side. It's the house with the fancy iron grilles on all the windows, both downstairs and up. New ones. Newish, anyway. The door's painted a sickly olive green and has a brass knocker with a face on it."

"Anybody's we know?"

"I hope not. It's more of a symbolic face, like a satyr or a dryad or maybe a gargoyle. I'm not too swift on dryads. Not shiny brass, the other kind."

"Is the knocker strictly germane to the report?" asked Brooks, trying not to sound waspish.

"Oh yes, sir, strictly germane, because Countess O used it to knock with. On the door," Charles added in the interests of perfect accuracy. "M and I walked on a short way, then paused for M to remove a hyperbolical pebble from her shoe while I employed my trusty see-back-o-scope in the hope of spotting the person who let her in. Unfortunately, the door was opened just far enough for Countess O to squeeze through. All I got to see was a hand with paint stains on it, and a little bit of a green velvet sleeve about the same shade as the door."

"Excellent, Charles, that's exactly what we wanted to know. You did get the house number, of course?"

"No, Mr. Brooks, because there wasn't one. Of course it was easy to deduce what the number ought to be by reading those on the adjoining houses, but the actual metal numbers, as I suppose they must have been, were gone. Being a trifle farsighted, I could even see the little nail holes where they'd been taken off."

"Well, that's interesting. Don't you think so, Max?"

"Could be. Jolly good show, Charlie. There's no other house like it on the block?"

"No, it's the only one with grilles all the way up and that olive-colored door and the face on the knocker. It's between the red door with the federal-style knocker and the purple one with the old-fashioned wind-up doorbell in the middle. You couldn't miss it. We walked down to Clarendon, then M split and I doubled back up through the alley with my Red Sox cap on to disguise me from above if anybody happened to look out. I wanted to see if there were grilles on all the back windows too, and there are. Every single one."

"And Lydia had gone straight back after she left Sarah, not making any detour or stopping to talk to anybody?"

"Like a homing pigeon, Mr. Max. That's not like her. You don't suppose she's had a brain operation or something? I had a walk-on once in a play where the mad scientist did a number on the beautiful heroine and she turned into a robot, obeying his every whim without question or hesitation. That was my big line: 'Great Scott, Chavender! Pauline, that wilful madcap of yesteryear, now obeys that unspeakable cad Dr. Testoob's every whim without question or hesitation.' The play didn't have much of a run."

3

"Too bad," said Max, "but you can't hit a home run every time. Did you see anybody else around the house?"

"There were people going by," Charles replied, "but nobody in particular, if that's what you mean. Nobody sitting on the steps across the street and watching the place, or anything like that. There was one man in the back alley whom I did wonder about a little. He was out in the alley behind the Arbalest house, doing exercises."

"What kind of exercises?"

"Jumping up and down, clapping his hands over his head, swinging his legs around, that aerobic stuff, you know. What hit me was that he had on a bright-red jogging suit. Long legs, long sleeves, the whole nine yards. It looked strange on a hot day, you'd have expected him to be wearing shorts and a T-shirt."

"Maybe he was trying to sweat off some weight," Brooks suggested.

"Could be, but as far as I could tell with that baggy sweat suit blocking the view, he didn't have a spare ounce on him. He was about Bill's size, only darker, and his hair was straighter. He wasn't black or Hispanic, more—oh, I don't know. Indian or Malaysian, maybe. I couldn't get a good look at his face; by the time I got close to him he was bent over double, swinging his head around upside down. I don't want to make something out of nothing. It could be just that he lives in a small place where there's no room to work out. Or that his wife collects Chinese porcelain and won't let him do it in the house for fear he'll break something."

"Why wife, and why Chinese?" asked Max.

Charles thought it over. "Wife because he wasn't a young kid," he said at last. "His hair was fairly long, when he was flapping his head around I noticed some streaks of gray among the black. Porcelain because—I don't know. Maybe it's just that Mrs. Sarah was washing the china out of the cabinet in the dining room this morning and I was lifting down the pieces off the higher shelves for her."

"Could be. Thanks, Charlie. Well, guys, I don't see much reason left for us to hang around here." Max glanced at his wristwatch. "My God, I didn't realize it was so late. We'd better get back to the house before Sarah sends an ambulance. Why don't you gallop ahead, Charlie, and tell her we're on the way? Bill, would you care to come back and eat with us?"

"Thanks, but I've—"

Bill's hands were less expressive this time, perhaps he simply didn't feel like having dinner at the Kelling house tonight. More likely, he was champing at the bit to get his espionage network perking on the subject of Bartolo Arbalest and his medieval-artisans' guild. Max could relate to that. If he'd had two sound pins under him he'd be hitting the trail himself. He picked up Great-Uncle Frederick's cane and pulled himself together for the homeward trek.

The walk back across the Common was uneventful except for the usual requests for largesse from assorted indigents, which neither Max nor Brooks could ever wholly ignore. As they turned into Tulip Street, Max caught Sarah peeking out from behind the library curtains. She was having a hard time trying not to be too protective, poor kid. His accident, which in fact had been no accident at all except for the fact that the persons trying to kill him had fallen short of their ultimate purpose, had taken as big a toll from her as from himself. He'd have to find some way to make it up to her. At the moment, a hug and a fairly resounding kiss were the best he could think of.

"Home is the hunter, home to the hill. So how's my *Fischele*?"

"Fine. I'm just so glad you were able to—"

Sarah had to break off and sniffle briefly into Max's shirt front to show how glad she was. Then young Davy rushed out in his pajamas, demanding equal hugs and permission to play horse with the silver-headed cane. Being an amiable child, he settled for the hugs and the promise of a bedtime story after daddy'd had a chance to rest his leg, and rushed off to help Charles put on his butler's coat and tie.

"Theonia will be down in a minute, she's changing," Sarah explained as she led the two men into the library. "Can I pour you some sherry, or would you rather have something else?"

"Sit down, Sarah, I'll do the drinks."

Brooks bounded off, brisk as a squirrel. He was back in a wink or two with liquid refreshments and a bowl of salted peanuts, to which latter he and Max were both addicted. They were just nicely settled when Theonia made a regal entrance in a sumptuous new tea gown she'd put together out of oddments picked up at various thrift shops. Theonia loved elegant gowns almost as much as Brooks loved peanuts, but she would never have been so extravagant as simply to go out and buy one. Besides, it was more fun to improvise. She accepted white wine and soda from the hand of her loving spouse, cooed an endearment by way of thanks, and raised her glass.

"Here's to our dear Max, long may he walk! We're so proud of you, Max darling. Sarah tells me you went out by yourself today."

"Just to the office," Max replied modestly. "Bill Jones dropped in to say hello. In sign language, of course. And I ran into Lydia Ouspenska on the way over."

"Really? That must have been a nice surprise for you. Is she well and happy?"

"Oddly enough, yes. How did you know?"

Theonia shrugged, she was always slightly embarrassed by her strange way of knowing things without being told. "I merely assumed she would be. Lydia's a survivor. What's she doing these days?"

"Guilding the lily."

Max passed on Lydia's description of the Arbalest setup. Theonia's large, dark eyes widened in surprise.

"And you say she actually lives there in that—*cloister* almost seems the appropriate word, doesn't it? How very interesting. One might have thought so effervescent a person as the dear countess would find such a life somewhat too confining."

"I suppose one might," Sarah replied, "but when one's down to the nubbins, there's a good deal to be said for a warm bed and three meals a day. Lydia certainly didn't show any reluctance about going back."

Sarah gave the others a brief rundown of her own part in the encounter, such as it had been. Conversation had progressed rapidly from how much Davy resembled his father to that marvelous outfit Lydia had been wearing, thence to vintage clothing in general. Sarah knew quite a lot about outmoded styles, partly because she'd inherited so many of her mother's. The Kellings and their circle had always believed in getting full value out of their garments; it took a long time to wear out a Mainbocher or a custom-tailored British tweed.

"Maybe Arbalest has her hypnotized." Brooks didn't mean it, he was merely offering the hypothesis as a mild joke.

Theonia, however, took him seriously. "I should think, dear, that Lydia Ouspenska would be awfully hard to hypnotize. Getting her to stop talking and concentrate would be the main problem. Unless of course the hypnotist was an unusually attractive man. You could manage her, Max."

"Why not me?" Brooks asked rather petulantly.

"Because, my darling, Lydia wouldn't dare let you try. She'd know she'd have me to contend with if she did." Theonia was the unlikely result of an encounter between an Ivy League anthropology student and a young Gypsy girl; the Romany did tend to work its way to the fore now and then, notwithstanding the Wasp half's penchant for fin-de-siècle tea gowns and the high standards of etiquette promulgated by the late Emily Post. "Sarah would find the situation mildly amusing."

"Only mildly," said Sarah. "Perhaps I'd better just slip up and see if Davy's all right."

"No, I'll go," said Max. "I promised him a bedtime story. Don't wait dinner for me."

"It's quite all right, take your time. Nobody's in a hurry tonight."

It wasn't every evening that the family had a chance to dawdle. The three in the library lingered over their drinks, talking shop until Max came back downstairs. Then Charles announced dinner, Theonia said "Shall we?" and they did.

They lingered over their meal, they lingered longer over dessert, they drifted back to the library still talking shop. As Sarah poured coffee into her first husband's great-grandmother's demitasse cups, it occurred to her that she and her loved ones were a guild too, though not always a commune. It was pleasant, in a way, being back in the old house she'd moved into as a bride not yet out of her teens and left ten years later as a widow about to marry again. Still, she'd be glad when she and Max and Davy could get back to the all-new house at Ireson's Landing.

It wouldn't be long, now that Max was walking so well. They might go home for the weekend and see how it worked. Max's nephew and his girl friend were house-sitting; they'd have to be warned in advance, though the place couldn't be in that much of a mess with Mr. Lomax taking care of the grounds, his niece coming in twice a week to clean as usual, and Max's sister Miriam just down the road a piece. Sarah was making mental lists of things to buy and do for their homecoming, when the doorbell rang.

Three quick, efficient rings; Brooks bounded off the sofa. "I'll get it. No sense in bothering Charles."

Answering the door late in the evening at the Tulip Street house was always a chancy business. This could be anybody from Sarah's Uncle Jem on his way back from a bibulous evening with some of his many cronies to a jewel thief just out of jail, craving revenge on the meddlers who'd put him there. They never locked the street door until bedtime, but the inner door was secure as a bank safe. Nor was it any idle whim that had caused Brooks Kelling to replace the purple windowpanes with bullet-proof glass.

The visitor must have passed inspection, Brooks was showing him in: a tallish, middle-aged man with suede-leather patches on the elbows of his shabby but well-cut tweed jacket. For the rest, he was wearing well-aged but likewise well-cut flannels, a pale-blue cotton shirt, and an apologetic little bow tie of no particular color or pattern. He was the sort who tended to remind everyone of someone else, possibly the late Leverett Saltonstall, more likely somebody's relative who taught something dull at one of Boston's many schools or colleges and showed up at funerals talking about other dead relatives whom nobody else among those present had ever met and wouldn't have cared to know. After a moment's thought, Sarah remembered who he really was. His name was Carnaby Goudge, his appearance was his stock-in-trade.

People who hire professional bodyguards often do not want them to look or act like bodyguards. A man who vaguely resembled a lot of other people, who spoke with the right accent when he spoke at all, who could pass as a valet, a brother-in-law, or some indispensable member of one's clerical staff, and still be quick enough on the draw to prevent anything unpleasant from happening to his current employer, seldom had to worry about his next assignment.

Carnaby Goudge was not an intimate of the Kelling-Bittersohn household, but they'd all run across him at various times in sundry places, usually posing as the most inconspicuous member of some tycoon's entourage. The omniscient Bill Jones had mentioned not long ago that the bodyguard was in the Boston area, though Bill had not as yet been able to find out what he was doing here. Affable greetings were exchanged. Sarah offered coffee, Theonia suggested brandy. Goudge opted for the latter.

"Just a spot, thank you. I suppose I ought to apologize for dropping in on you unannounced at so late an hour, but this is the first chance I've had and I thought you might like a piece of information. In view of this afternoon's little contre temps," he added with the slight twitch of the lips that was as close as he ever got to a smile. "I must say I was favorably impressed by your expeditious handling of the situation, even though the effort was quite unnecessary."

"You mean Lydia Ouspenska?" said Sarah. "You were tailing her? I never spotted you. But then I wouldn't, would I?"

"I should hope not, Mrs. Bittersohn. Madame Ouspenska's meeting with Mr. Bittersohn was no doubt serendipitous, but having his wife show up just as madame came out of the grocery store did give me pause to wonder. Once that other pair picked up her trail, I knew for sure. Not a bad job, I must say, for a couple of amateurs. Have you used them before?"

"Actually they're our maid and butler, at least they like to pretend they are. They live here and help out in various ways. Charles is a professional actor when he gets the chance, he's marvelous at disguises. Today's wasn't one of Charles's better efforts, but he only had a couple of minutes to work himself into the role. Are we to understand that you've become Lydia's official bodyguard?"

"Hers, among others. Mr. Arbalest takes great care of his artisans. And of himself, needless to say. They do have to get out of the house now and then, much as he'd rather they didn't. It's a full-time job looking out for them. I'm sure you realize that all this is highly confidential."

"And that your real purpose in coming is to warn us the hell off your territory," Max added with no rancor.

"It's merely that I see no sense in duplicating effort. And of course my job will be made more difficult if you come nosing around. Sorry, that did sound rude, but you surely realize the problems that could arise in maintaining clandestine surveillance if the Keystone Kops were to come chasing after one's clients. Oh dear, I'm being gauche again."

"Don't sweat it, Goudge, we can take a hint. But why the secret-agent act? Since when did Lydia Ouspenska pass up the chance of a male companion?"

Goudge cleared his throat, ever so delicately. "Such as the beautiful Max? The lady did mention at dinnertime that she'd run into a very dear friend whom she hadn't seen for quite some time. She hinted somewhat unsubtly that you and she, Bittersohn, had been—ah—but I've noticed before that Madame Ouspenska has a penchant for what one might call creative conversation. I quite understand your pausing to chat, and please feel quite free to do so again should the occasion arise. I do hope you weren't thinking of inviting her to visit, however; that could result in some awkward logistics. You see, I'm supposed to be nothing more than Mr. Arbalest's personal chauffeur and errand boy. He doesn't want the artisans to know I'm guarding them also."

"But why, Mr. Goudge?" said Theonia. "Doesn't he trust his employees?"

"Oh, it's not that at all, Mrs. Brooks, it's purely for their own safety. Mr. Arbalest worries, you know. As well he might, all things considered."

"What sort of things were these?" asked Brooks. "I might mention that Arbalest once asked me to work for him, when he had his shop in New York. I knew he'd had problems getting help, but I couldn't think why he wanted me. Antique-restoring is really not my field."

"Mr. Arbalest may have been getting desperate by then. He'd lost one assistant to some strange variety of food poisoning. Another apparently jumped off the Brooklyn Bridge. A third made some dreadful mistake in the chemicals he was working with and got a noseful of cyanide. The word got around that Bartolo Arbalest was an unhealthy man to work for. He finally had to shut up shop and relocate."

"Where did he go?"

"First Los Angeles, which didn't work out, then that place in Texas, where they have all the pink and blue skyscrapers. Houston, I believe it's called. For quite some time, Mr. Arbalest was doing quite well out of the oil barons, but he hated the climate, then things began happening again. One poor lady illuminator's car went out of control for no apparent reason and slammed into an abutment, killing her instantly. Another was strangled with a rope of Spanish moss during an apparent mugging. Finally the rest of his artisans got wind somehow of what had happened in New York and L.A., saw the handwriting on the wall, and quit in a body while they still had bodies left to quit in."

"So the sensible course for Arbalest then was to come back east," said Max, "but not to New York. This time I gather he's playing it smart."

"Yes, indeed. Very smart, considering. Mr. Arbalest got the really clever idea of keeping his artisans in what actually amounts to protective custody. So far, the arrangement seems to be working quite well. He's contrived a sort of Knights of the Grail atmosphere, with them all wearing green plush smocks and black velvet berets and floppy great ties. He presides over meaningful discussions on the mystical inner significance of sticking things back together after they've fallen apart. Too bad their tricks don't work on humans. And he cooks them—us, I should say, since he's got me living there too—sumptuous meals, with decorous allowances of the finest aperitifs and table wines, which we're also expected to discuss at incredible length. It's all very elevating."

"One can see where it might be," Brooks sympathized. "Do you have to wear a smock and beret like the rest?"

"Heavens to Betsy, no. I'm only the chauffeur. I do have a natty livery in shades of brown and russet to harmonize with the colors of Mr. Arbalest's third-hand Rolls-Royce. Jodhpurs and boots are included, presumably in case Mr. Arbalest decides to trade in the Rolls against a coach and pair. Around the house I dress quite simply in a sack coat, black waistcoat, and striped trousers, and answer the telephone in a manner neatly combining hauteur with affability. If the caller's a particularly lucrative client, I'm allowed to inject an extra smidgin or two of affability. I assume you know how Mr. Arbalest is handling his contacts."

Max nodded. "According to Lydia, he accepts only referrals from the better galleries and auction houses and won't even tell prospects where his studio is, much less let them into it. He makes appointments by phone or mail, then visits the clients with fanfare of trumpets and beating of drums. And you standing by in your jodhpurs, I suppose?"

"Oh yes," said Goudge. "I enter a respectful three paces behind the master, wearing white gloves and carrying a briefcase, a portfolio, or a leather carrying case, depending upon the size, shape, and condition of the article to be resurrected. Should the client be gauche enough to offer me a seat, I respond only with a pitying glance and remain standing vigilantly at attention behind the chair Mr. Arbalest is by then occupying."

"What if the chair's up against a wall or something?"

"Then I do the best I can. Aside from the security factor, Mr. Arbalest feels that seeing me standing there tends to put a psychological brake on the prospective client's loquacity. He prefers to do the lion's share of the talking himself. Once the interview is completed and the contract signed as it invariably is, for Mr. Arbalest is a most persuasive man with a sales pitch, I open the receptacle I've been guarding and continue to maintain vigilance while he, with his own hands now encased in white gloves which I have produced from the receptacle and assisted him to put on, places the ailing object inside. I then get to zip, snap, or strap, as the case may be, and pick up the briefcase, portfolio, or carrying case. After the ceremony of leave-taking, which generally goes on a shade too long for my taste, I precede Mr. Arbalest back to the car so that I can hold the door for him with my free hand. I place the object reverently on the front passenger seat, take my place behind the wheel, and drive off. We are, if I may say so without braggadocio, a class act."

4

"Maybe you should make a movie," said Max. "How many birds does Arbalest keep in his gilded cage?"

"Counting myself and the maid, eight."

"Eight? That's quite a household. Mind telling me who they all are?"

"Is it important that you know?"

"Probably not. I'm just asking."

"All right, Bittersohn, I suppose I owe you one. Madame Ouspenska, of course, you already know about her. More than I do, I expect. She's the only woman, except Katya."

"Katya's the maid?"

"Oh yes. Elderly, ill-favored, unsound in her English, and not very bright, but good-natured and a willing worker. Chosen as much for her lack of sex appeal as for her cleaning skills, I suspect. Faced with the choice between her and a harem, one supposes Arbalest decided Katya would be cheaper to feed and easier to manage."

Max smiled. "That brings up some interesting questions."

"I know," said Goudge, "and I could give you some interesting answers, but I'm not going to. To get on with the inventory, there's Marcus Nie, about forty-five, lean, balding, taciturn, totally dedicated to his craft, which consists mostly of swabbing or chipping old varnish off large paintings of cows and sheep, as far as I can make out. Rosa Bonheur, you know, and that lot."

Goudge dismissed the first woman to have been awarded the Grand Cross of the French Legion of Honor with a flick of his fingers. "In short, Nie handles the dog work. The other restorer is Art Queppin: fat, hairy, chatty, flamboyant, getting on for sixty. Sings bawdy songs while he works, to the disgust of Nie, who has to be stabled in a separate stall so that he can concentrate on his eternal chipping and swabbing. Queppin's far the more skillful of the two; he does the more important parts, such as relining old canvases and repainting missing bits of great-grandpa's sideburns. Mr. Arbalest also takes a hand at the paintings when he's not out drumming up business. He's the best of the three, but gets the fidgets if he has to sit too long at the same job."

Brooks chuckled. "I remember that. In New York, Bartolo was always popping over to the coffee shop. He'd sit where he could see his own shop door and go bouncing back if he spotted a customer wanting to get in. With a half-eaten doughnut in his hand, like as not. Of course he couldn't operate like that now, situated as he is."

"Poor man," said Theonia. "The jailer always becomes the prisoner. How remarkable that Mr. Arbalest has chosen to do so."

"What's remarkable to me," observed Sarah, "is that so many ghastly things have happened to his workers. Such a string of calamities could hardly be coincidental. It almost makes one wonder whether he's a victim or a villain."

"Victim," Brooks answered without hesitation. "Though I must say," he added more slowly, "it would take a very special kind of madman to victimize somebody by slaughtering the people who worked for him."

"It certainly would. On the other hand, if Arbalest was, say, running some kind of fix-it shop for stolen art works that had got damaged during robberies, the murdered employees could have been the ones who asked the wrong questions, or tried to blackmail the boss for bigger pay when they found out what was really going on. Doesn't that make more sense than mass murder for purposes of annoyance?"

"Sarah, I did mention that Bartolo always had a reputation for scrupulous honesty."

"Well, naturally, Brooks dear. He'd need one, wouldn't he? It's not so difficult to be honest up front, what counts most is what's happening out back. If Mr. Arbalest is as expert a salesman as Mr. Goudge says he is, wouldn't you think he might also be a fairly convincing actor? I'm sorry, Mr. Goudge, I didn't mean to interrupt.

You've mentioned four artisans, counting Lydia. What about the other two?"

"First, Mrs. Bittersohn, I'd just like to say that thus far I've seen no evidence that Mr. Arbalest is engaged in anything clandestine. That, of course, doesn't necessarily mean he wouldn't like to be. Please bear in mind that I'm either with him or near him almost every hour of every day, and that I am, to say the least of it, a trained observer."

Carnaby Goudge took another careful sip of his brandy. "I'll grant you the hypothesis that Mr. Arbalest could conceivably be marking time running a legitimate operation, ruthlessly spurning any approach from the lesser fry among the art underworld, while waiting for a really juicy plum to fall his way. One does realize that crimes of historic importance don't happen very often. One must only hope that nothing of the sort turns up while I'm in Mr. Arbalest's employ, because I should then become an awkward person to keep around and a most unsafe one to let go."

He gazed affably around at his hearers. "That is, of course, assuming Mr. Arbalest was in fact running a secret Augean stable and had imaginative ways of cleaning house. If I'd thus far discovered any reason to think he was, I should not be sitting here now pouring out my soul to you; I'd be legging it for Paraguay as fast as I could go. To get back to your question, Mrs. Bittersohn, the remaining two artisans are Peter Laer and Jacques Dubrec. Laer is a woodcarver, Dubrec is a Jacques of all trades and a master of several. He gets the jobs nobody else is equipped to handle, such as repairing old porcelain and objets d'art; particularly the smaller, more delicate pieces that are the most easily broken."

"I should think those would make up a large proportion of your business," said Theonia.

"You're quite right, Mrs. Kelling, they do. They're the atelier's next-biggest source of revenue, after paintings and prints. Last on the list, but by no means inconsiderable, is antique woodwork. Most of these jobs come through antique dealers and auction houses. The atelier doesn't actually take in large pieces and refinish them, this would be quite outside the scope of Mr. Arbalest's operation as it's presently conducted. Laer does things like carving a new wing for an early German angel, matching a broken chair leg, or creating a new pediment for a vandalized highboy."

"But doesn't restoring an antique lessen its value?" asked Theonia.

"That depends on the condition. Some pieces arrive literally in fragments. Putting what's left back together and recreating the missing parts makes the piece usable; a restoration is at least more desirable than a blatant copy. If it's a damaged altar, a carved balustrade, or something of that sort, Laer occasionally goes out to see what needs to be done. He makes sketches, takes photographs, perhaps pulls out the damaged section either to repair or to replicate, then returns to the studio and gets to work. Finally he goes back out to remove any broken parts that remain and fit in the replacements."

"And you go along to guard him."

"Always. I hold the ladder and hand up the glue pot or chisel in a properly subservient manner, thus impressing on the client what a privilege it is to have so preeminent an artisan plugging up his wormholes. It's always taken as an act of faith that our client will in turn point out the restored portions to his own clients, assuming he plans to resell."

"But it's not included in the contract that you stick around to make sure he does?" said Max. "What are Laer and Dubrec like?"

"I'd say they're the most normal members, relatively speaking, of our latter-day *Schildersbent*. Neither is a young man. Laer's a widower with a grown son and daughter, both of whom fortunately live abroad. There's no estrangement, they write back and forth every month or so and telephone on major holidays, but they don't show any urge to visit, which I don't suppose Mr. Arbalest would let them do anyway. I believe Dubrec was married at one time, but he doesn't talk about it."

"Another silent type?"

"Oh dear, no. I'd rank him third in loquacity to Mr. Arbalest and Madame Ouspenska when the group are having one of their round-robin fireside chats, which of course don't happen by the fireside at this time of year. Anyway, it's only a gas log. Sorry, I'm digressing. And I do apologize for having taken up so much of your time, but I don't often get a chance to chat with colleagues, if I may be so bold as to call you so."

"Sure, go right ahead." Max stood up and reached for his cane. "Drop in again when you're over this way, Goudge, there's usually somebody around. By the way, our secret operative mentioned hav-

ing seen a vaguely Asian-looking guy doing aerobic exercises out in
the alley behind Arbalest's house. He wouldn't have been one of
your Schilders, by any chance? Longish black hair showing a little
gray? Dressed in a bright-red winter-weight jogging suit?"

Goudge let his lip curl just ever so. "You did mention that your
chap's an actor, as I recall. I suspect what he actually saw was somebody's wash twisting in the breeze. We're near the river, you know.
There's a woman in the basement apartment on the other side of the
alley who has a habit of putting strangely assorted garments out to
dry on one of those folding clothes racks, trusting soul that she is.
Either she has amazingly eccentric taste in clothes, or else she's some
kind of costume designer."

He shrugged off the woman in the basement apartment. "As I
mentioned, I spotted your tail and his vivacious lady friend as soon
as they arrived on the scene. After the three of us had escorted
Madame Ouspenska safely home, your two went on down to Berkeley Street, where they parted company. She walked on ahead in the
direction of Newbury, he nipped into the alley to check out whether
Mr. Arbalest had installed grilles on all the back windows as well as
the front. That rather impressed me, your chap could be quite good
with a little more experience. However, if you plan to use him often
on surveillance, you'd do well to have his eyes tested. Well, I expect
I'd better get back before Mr. Arbalest throws a fit. Thanks for your
hospitality, ladies, it's been a pleasure."

"Ain't that the truth," said Max after he'd seen their unexpected
guest safely off and limped back to the library. "Anyone care to
venture an opinion as to why Goudge was in such a loquacious mood
tonight?"

"Elementary, my dear boy," said Brooks. "He knew Bartolo and I
were old acquaintances, he assumed I either already knew or could
easily find out about Bartolo's bizarre series of calamities. He'd
watched Lydia hailing you and Sarah as old friends; he hadn't been
close enough to hear what she was saying to you, but he thought she
must have given you an earful about the atelier. By running on about
things he assumed we might already know, he created an atmosphere
of confidence and comradeship, or thought he did. Bridge building, I
believe it's called."

"Then why did he blow up the bridge by telling us that asinine lie
about the man in the alley?"

"Because his own eyes need to be examined?" Sarah offered. "Because the man was one of the artisans who'd sneaked out of the atelier when he should have been working, and Goudge was covering up for him?"

"Why?"

"So that Brooks wouldn't tell Mr. Arbalest? No, that doesn't make sense. If the man wasn't supposed to be there, why would he have made himself so conspicuous hopping around and clapping his hands? I give up."

"Whoever it was, he doesn't appear to fit any of the descriptions Goudge gave us," said Brooks.

"Mr. Goudge didn't actually describe the last two," Theonia pointed out.

"But he did say Laer and Dubrec were the most normal of the lot. I don't see anything all that normal about this chap's cavorting around in public in a heavy suit under a broiling sun."

"If it was a chap, darling. It could have been a woman. One might have a hard time telling, if she was upside down in a baggy sweat suit. In that case, of course, she wouldn't have been a member of Mr. Arbalest's guild."

"We mustn't rule her out," said Sarah. "I suppose, like me, you've been picturing Katya the maid as blondish, heavyset, and Slavic because of the Russian-sounding name. But people do give their children odd names. From Mr. Goudge's description, though, Katya doesn't sound like the sort of woman anybody would bother to lie about. You don't suppose Mr. Arbalest is keeping a clandestine mistress in a secret room behind the boiler or somewhere? He's the one who made those rather odd security arrangements, therefore he'd know how to get around them. How hard would Mr. Goudge be to fool, Max? Is he really as good as he seems to think he is? What do we know about him?"

"Not a lot. The word around is that he comes from a wealthy Connecticut family and went to Yale or Brown or somewhere suitably Ivy League."

"I can believe that." A loyal Bostonian, Sarah was unimpressed by Yale and Brown. "What did he study?"

"Nothing, apparently. The way I heard it, he had two hobbies, target shooting and stalking wild animals. He didn't shoot the animals, apparently, he just liked to sneak up on them and watch what they did. After he flunked out of college, he tried being a nature photographer, but that didn't work out so he got the bright idea of becoming a professional stalker. He worked for a detective agency for a while, then branched out on his own as a bodyguard. He appears to be hardworking, competent, and conscientious. He must be at least reasonably trustworthy or he'd have been rubbed out by now. Goudge doesn't seem to have any trouble finding work, evidently his customers come to him by word-of-mouth recommendations. He doesn't advertise or even have an office, as far as I know. Any thoughts on the subject, Brooks?"

"Just one. Goudge may not need an office, but he must have some kind of hideaway where he can at least keep an answering machine, his extra sneakers, and a few changes of clothing to fit his various roles. I visualize a small flat in a mildly tacky building right here in Boston, or maybe over around Central Square."

"And I visualize my wandering husband going to bed," said Sarah. "Not to be a nagger, Max, but I don't want you waking up tomorrow stiff as a new boot. Shall I draw you a bath?"

Hot baths were part of Max's therapy, but he shook his head. "Not tonight, thanks, I'll just take a quick shower. Too much soaking makes me itchy. So does that setup of Arbalest's. Why do you suppose we're all so interested?"

"Lydia's involved," said Brooks, "so we naturally expect there's something insane and probably illicit about it. And because Charles, of all people, would certainly have been able to tell a costume on a clotheshorse from an Asian in a sweat suit. Theonia, would you like me to brew us a pot of tea?"

His wife shook her well-tressed head. "No, dear, no tea-leaf reading tonight. I'm not feeling the least bit oracular, just rather weary and glad to be home. I think I'll go to bed now too. Don't be long, Brooks my love. I've missed you."

5

It is a well-known fact of life: Once a statement, a name, or a circumstance has been brought vividly to one's attention, one starts picking up further references to that same subject everywhere one turns. Not more than two days after they'd first become aware of Bartolo Arbalest and his secret studio, the people at Tulip Street found this happening to them.

Actually, it happened to Max. Not the earliest of risers, he was lingering over an extra cup of coffee, Brooks having bounded off to the office at what Max considered the crack of dawn and the rest of the household busy at their various chores. His sister had given him a cordless telephone as a get-well present, he'd got into the habit of carrying it wherever he went to help compensate for his awkwardness in getting around. The phone rang now, and he answered. Of all people in the world, Cousin Percy Kelling was on the line.

Whether Percy was more Sarah's cousin or Brooks's was irrelevant to the matter at hand. Percy was the son of Theodore Kelling. Long before Sarah had come into Max Bittersohn's life, her Uncle Theodore, who was probably not an uncle at all but was surely some kind of complicated connection, Kelling relationships being what they were, had hired Max to get him back his Corots.

It is alleged that there are a great many more Corots extant than Corot ever got around to painting; it has never been said of a Kelling that he didn't make perfectly sure of what he was buying before he forked over his money. Theodore's gentle maidens and tranquil birch groves were the real McCoy, the guaranteed A-1, simon-pure article, bought in Paris by Theodore's own grandfather back when Corots were still going fairly cheap. Theodore would have treasured the paintings out of filial piety even if they hadn't turned out to have been sound investments. Furthermore, he liked them, and there weren't a great many things that Theodore did like. He'd been almost pathetically grateful to Max for getting them back, even going so far as to pay the bill without taking his usual two percent discount for cash on the barrelhead. It was not surprising, then, that Percy had followed his sire's example and turned to Max when confronted by a similar emergency.

His emergency wasn't all that similar, actually; this time it wasn't the value of the object, it was the principle. Nobody enjoys being robbed, but certified public accountants, especially high-class ones with large staffs and many fat-cat clients, are particularly sensitive to the clandestine removal of portable assets; even more particularly when the assets are their own and the removal has taken place from their own house while they were asleep upstairs. To say that Percy was wroth would have been to understate his condition by a considerable margin. Percy was mad as hell.

He was not blaming his wife. Percy made that point more than once, leading Sarah, who'd come to see whether Max wanted more coffee and remained to eavesdrop, to suspect that Mrs. Percy was at her husband's elbow hissing in his ear.

And why shouldn't she hiss? It was Anne, not Percy, who'd inherited from an aged aunt an ancestral portrait supposedly dating from the late eighteenth century. The portrait had presumably been done by an itinerant painter, it depicted a rosy-cheeked tot of perhaps five or six years, holding a battledore and shuttlecock in her left hand and balancing a green parrot about half her own size on the extended right forefinger. Precisely how so small a child could have sustained the weight of so large a bird on one diminutive digit was something Percy left Max to explain, Max was supposed to know about this sort of nonsense.

Anyway, the painting was assuredly a true American primitive. At least Percy's wife, Anne, was sure, and it was her painting and her money behind it. All Kelling wives had money in greater or lesser amounts. Percy would not have been attracted to a lesser, not that he was consciously mercenary but because that was the way his hor-

mones worked. Even Max understood that it was just as easy to fall
in love with a rich girl, although he himself had not done so.

This did not come out in his conversation with Percy, of course.
What did come out was that the painting, when handed over to Mrs.
Percy Alexander Kelling by the executors, had been in sad shape.
Confident that it was worth restoring, Mrs. Percy had asked advice
from a friend who'd recently had her own great-grandfather cleaned
and revarnished. The friend had recommended Bartolo Arbalest,
and given Mrs. Percy his telephone number.

Bartolo had come, seen, and conquered even Percy's skepticism.
He'd shaken his head sadly over the condition Mrs. Percy's aunt had
let such a fine painting get into. He'd confirmed its age within a few
years of Mrs. Percy's own estimate, he'd explained what needed to be
done and how the work should be gone about. He'd named a fairly
staggering fee that would include a hand-carved frame created ex-
pressly for the painting. This would put Mrs. Percy one-up on her
friend, who'd settled for having the old one regilded. Mrs. Percy had
signed his contract without a wince.

The work had been done, not in haste but within a reasonable
period. The child and the parrot had come through the operation far
better than might have been hoped. The frame was not too fancy,
not too blatantly gilded, it was exactly right for the painting. The
entire effect had been so harmonious, so gracious, so well worth the
expense that Percy himself had suggested demoting a competent but
unexciting portrait of his father-in-law to the dining room and giving
Anne's ancestress the place of honor over the drawing-room mantel.

But last night, regardless of locks, bolts, and bars, the house had
been entered; the painting had been stolen. Nothing else had been
taken, only the child and her parrot. Not the silver, not Mrs. Percy's
pearls, not even the Corot that had been Theodore's wedding present to his son and the bride. This was very strange. It was almost
insulting. It was downright infuriating, and what was Max Bittersohn
going to do about it?

"Get paid, for one thing."

That was Sarah hissing. Max had already been dragged into doing
far too many thank-you jobs for his wife's relatives. If Mrs. Percy had
been willing to invest that kind of money in having her parrot resurrected, she could also pay for getting the picture back. Surely Percy
could find some reasonably legal way to take the expense off his

income tax. That was no skin off the Bittersohns' noses one way or the other.

"I suppose there's no use in my asking how long this business might take." Percy sounded as if he'd been eating sour grapes.

"None whatever," Max told him cheerily. "We'll get on the job right away. May we have the name and address of the woman who steered you to Arbalest?"

Mrs. Percy came on the line. She couldn't see why Max wanted Topsy Hughes's number, but she supposed he had to start somewhere. Max wrote down what she told him. When he'd got off the phone, he showed his notes to Sarah.

"You may be interested to know that Bill Jones mentioned the Hugheses to Brooks and me yesterday. He thought they might be going to call on us. It seems great-grandpop disappeared one night last week. They're rather antsy about whether the police will be able to get him back, not so much on account of the old man himself as because of the amount they'd paid Arbalest to fix him up. It was the same story: the house entered without apparent difficulty in spite of an expensive alarm system, other and more valuable things sitting around, but only the portrait taken."

"This must be one drop of comfort for Percy," Sarah remarked. "At least he didn't waste money putting in an alarm system that didn't work when it was needed. Did Bill have any ideas about what may have happened to the Hugheses' painting?"

"I don't think so. He just thought we might be interested."

"So we are, aren't we? Nothing taken in either case except the piece that had just come back from Mr. Arbalest. I wonder if the old man was the only painting of the Hugheses' that his people worked on. Should I call up Topsy Hughes and ask her?"

Max raised an eyebrow. "Do you know her?"

"Well enough. I've met the Hugheses once or twice at Anora Protheroe's, back when she used to have big parties."

Back when Alexander was alive, Sarah meant, but she still tended to avoid mentioning her first husband's name to Max.

The Protheroes must both be in their eighties by now. Sarah had known them all her life, as had her parents and grandparents and most of the other Kellings. George was the dullest man alive, but Anora liked company and gossip. Maybe it would be wiser to call Anora instead. She'd either know everything that mattered and a lot that didn't about Topsy's robbery or else she'd be delighted to find out.

Sarah didn't have to look up the number, she'd dialed it often enough. Phyllis, the ancient maid, answered: "Protheroe residence." Her voice sounded oddly stuffed-up.

"Hello, Phyllis, this is Sarah Bittersohn. I hope you don't have a cold?"

"Oh, Sarah! Sarah, thank God you've called. I don't know what to do, she's just sitting there. She won't even speak to me. She just sits."

The elderly maid's voice had risen to hysteria pitch. Sarah had to be sharp with her. "Phyllis, stop that. Who's sitting? Mrs. Protheroe?"

"Y-yes." At least Phyllis was down to sobbing now instead of screaming. "Just sitting. I don't know what to do."

"Where is she sitting?"

"On the floor."

"Which floor."

"At the foot of the stairs."

"Good God! Did she fall? Is she hurt?"

"I don't know. She won't tell me."

"Where's Cook?"

"In the kitchen. Having palpitations. I had to get her a pill. Sarah, can you come? Please! I don't know what to do. She won't tell me. Please, Sarah!"

"All right, Phyllis, I'll come as fast as I can. Wrap a blanket around Mrs. Protheroe and try to get her to drink some hot tea. Can't Mr. Protheroe do something?"

"He's gone."

"Gone where?"

No answer came, the line was dead. Sarah put down the handset, none too steadily. "Max, something's terribly wrong at the Protheroes'. It sounds as if Anora may have had a stroke and George is either dead or disappeared. I can't not go."

"Hasn't the maid called the police?"

"Phyllis could never do that on her own. She only does what Anora tells her."

"Want me to call them?"

"It's no use. Phyllis wouldn't let them in. She's scared of her own shadow. And Cook's having palpitations."

"Damn! All right, then, let's go."

"You don't have to, I can manage." Sarah sniffed hard and reached for her crumpled breakfast napkin. Max put his arms around her and kept them there until she'd had her weep and wiped her eyes.

"Better now, Kätzele? I know you don't need me, I just want to come. Okay?"

Sarah gave him a kiss. "I always need you. You'd better phone Brooks while I fix my face. Tell him about Cousin Anne's parrot, he may have some ideas."

"No doubt he will, he always does. Where's Davy?"

"With Theonia. They've gone over to the Public Gardens to ride the swan boats and feed the ducks, they'll be out half the morning. I'll tell Mariposa where we're going, she can see to his lunch and his nap if we're not back in time. Shall I bring the car around?"

"No, I'll walk with you." Max pushed the button that connected the office phone; Sarah went to alert Mariposa and change into a more suitable outfit. They were out of the house in seven minutes.

Parking was impossible on Beacon Hill. The Bittersohns' two cars had their own reserved parking spaces close to the corner of Beacon and Charles in the vast underground garage beneath historic Boston Common, only a hop, skip, and jump from Tulip Street, not that Max was up to any one of the three. He made it in excellent time, though; they were soon in the car, past Kenmore Square, headed for Chestnut Hill.

Once they'd got more or less clear of traffic, Max asked, "Phyllis didn't say anything about George except that he's gone?"

"That's all." Sarah was holding tight to the steering wheel, keeping her eyes fixed on the road. "George hasn't left the house once in the past five years, as far as I know. I think Phyllis must have been trying to tell me that he's had a heart attack or something and Anora's gone into shock. George is well into his eighties, you know. He eats too much and drinks too much, and the only exercise he ever gets is walking back and forth from the table to his easy chair."

Sarah fell silent for a minute, Max left her alone till she felt like going on. "I know he's a dreadful bore, but he's sweet in his way. They've both been kind to me over the years. They never had any children of their own, and, as you know, my parents weren't all that deeply interested in parenting, so the Protheroes rather took up the slack sometimes. It was mostly Anora, of course; George always reminded me more of a fubsy old teddy bear. He'd never do much but he'd be there, you know, telling long, silly stories and getting them all mixed up and dozing off in the midst. Nobody's ever heard the end of one of George's stories. Perhaps they never had any endings."

Max gave his wife a wry little smile. "There's an end to every story sooner or later, kid. If something's happened to George, I just hope for both their sakes it was quick and easy. It's worse when things drag on too long. How do you suppose Anora would manage without him?"

"Who knows? Phyllis and Cook are neither of them in any great shape, I suppose she might pension them off. George did that with Dennis a few years ago, after their Pierce-Arrow finally disintegrated into a little heap of fine gray powder. Dennis used to drive the car and do odd jobs: mow the lawn, weed the flower beds, wash the windows, that sort of thing. Since he retired they've been hiring people to come in by the hour and using the local taxi service when they've wanted to go anywhere, which they mostly don't."

"It's a big place to keep up. She might consider going into one of those new retirement complexes."

"I don't know, Max. I can't picture Anora's ever leaving that house until she's carried out feet first. If something's happened to George, I expect she'll wind up playing nursemaid to Cook and Phyllis. If she's able. Oh, I do hope she hasn't had a stroke! What she really ought to do is find a nice couple to live in, though I can't imagine who'd be willing to take on a job that size."

"She'd find somebody."

Max couldn't think who'd want the job either, but he was of a sanguine disposition. He deliberately switched the talk to his mother's latest clash of wills with the gas company. Sarah was laughing by the time they pulled up in front of the Protheroe house.

This was a neighborhood of big old wooden houses with good-sized yards around them. Their architecture varied from the sublime to the near-ridiculous; the Protheroes' was in the beporched and beturreted style of the late Gothic revival, with a dash of Anglo-Indian bungalow and just a touch of the Taj Mahal. Unity had been attempted by painting all its ins, outs, ups, and downs in the same rich chocolate brown, and all the trimmings in white. To some, the house suggested a giant devil's-food cake iced by a mad *condittore*; it had always made Sarah think of a Bailey's hot-fudge sundae with whipped cream, marshmallow, and walnuts. But no cherry on top. Even today she felt a momentary twinge of regret at not being able to spy something shiny, round, and red perched atop the front gable.

Everybody who came to the house, or even walked past, got the feeling that it had been set a little too close to the road. In fact, the road had been brought a little too close to the house after the horse had been totally eclipsed by the small, high-riding horseless carriage; and these in turn by the Packard, the Peerless, the Marmon—great boxes on wheels that needed more room to pass each other going and coming. As a result, the graveled turnaround was not quite so spacious as it ought to be. Sarah decided she'd better leave the driveway free for a possible ambulance, and parked at the curb.

Phyllis must have been waiting with her nose pressed to the window, she'd got the front door open before Sarah and Max were halfway up the front steps. Sarah was about to give the tearful servitor a comforting hug when she caught sight of Anora, huddled on the parquet floor next to the newel post, swathed in a shocking-pink down comforter, immobile as Plymouth Rock. She couldn't see Anora's face, it was turned toward a dark-red mound a little bit farther into the hallway.

The mound was George. He was lying face up in a welter of clotted blood, his maroon bathrobe decently pulled down over his fat legs. A pole about the size and length of a garden rake was sticking straight up out of his chest. Max yelped "Police!" and glared around for a telephone.

"Right over there," said Sarah. "In the corner behind the stairs. Be careful, don't—"

Step in the blood. She couldn't say it. She knelt beside Anora, trying not to look at what was beside her, and unwrapped enough of the comforter so that she could get her fingers on the dazed woman's wrist. Sarah wasn't much good at pulses, but she could at least tell that Anora's was beating, not racing, not lagging too far behind where it probably ought to be. The beats were strong enough to count, for whatever good that might have done. Sarah didn't try, it was enough to know the heart was still on the job. If only her old friend wouldn't just keep sitting there, staring at that appalling shaft going straight down into her dead husband's chest.

"Anora," she pleaded. "Anora, it's Sarah. Can you hear me? Are you all right? Please say something. Anything."

"What?"

She had spoken. Thank God.

"Anora, do you know who I am?"

"Sarah. You said Sarah. Sarah, what's happened to George? I can't get him up."

"I know, Anora, you mustn't try. Max is calling an ambu lance. They'll be along very soon."

"Call Jim."

"Jim who?"

"Harnett, of course. Call him. Quick."

"Oh, Dr. Harnett. Yes, of course. Max, look for Dr. James Harnett. He's local. The number's probably in that little book beside the telephone. Ask him to come as fast as he can."

Max was already dialing the number, Sarah went on talking to keep Anora from drifting off again. "How long have you been sitting here, Anora?"

"I don't know. I can't remember. Phyllis, quit that disgusting snuffling. Get me some tea. What did you put this stupid blanket around me for? I'm stifling. Don't just stand there, take it away."

"Get the tea, Phyllis," said Sarah. "I'll tend to her. There you are, Anora, you must be stiff from sitting so long. Can you stand up, do you think?"

"I don't know. Stop flustering me. You can't help, I'd fall on you and squash you flat. Max, come here. Help me up. When's Jim coming?"

"Sure, Anora. The ambulance is on its way."

"I don't want the ambulance, I want Jim Harnett."

"You'll get him. His wife's calling the hospital now, he's on his rounds."

"Humph! Just like a man, always where you don't want them to be. Oh, my God, George! George, what's to become of me now?"

That was when she really fell apart.

6

No doubt about it, the Old Guard were tough. Anora's breakdown lasted all of three minutes, then she was on her feet, letting Max and Sarah lead her away from the dreadful scene. Once in the morning room, with the sun streaming in through the southeast-facing bay, Sarah noticed for the first time how appallingly stained and dabbled her old friend's robe and nightgown were. She sent Phyllis for hot water and fresh garments and told Max to go out to the kitchen, check on Cook, and not come back till he got the word.

Together, she and Phyllis got Anora cleaned up and decently garbed. By the time Phyllis was sent to make fresh tea and tell Max he was free to return, Anora was respectably settled on the button-tufted red-plush Biedermeier chaise with her feet up, a knitted afghan screening her nether limbs, and four sofa cushions stuffed behind her back.

"Shouldn't she be lying down?" was Max's first reaction.

Anora took umbrage. "I've never yet taken anything lying down, I'm not about to start now. And if you don't like watching me cry, you can go peddle your papers. I've got a right to do as I please in my own house, even if I am a damned fool for doing it. What's all that hullabaloo outside?"

"I expect it's the ambulance I sent for," Max told her. "And the police."

"The police? Are you out of your mind? What did you do that for?"

"I had to, Anora. You do realize that George has been murdered?"

"Oh yes, I know he has. I don't believe it, but I know it. Who did it, Max?"

"That's what we need the police for, it's their job to find out. Do you feel up to letting them ask you some questions?"

"No, but I suppose they'll ask me anyway. For heaven's sake, Phyllis, quit bleating like a lost sheep and go let them in. And bring me that tea I asked you for half an hour ago. I don't know what's got into everybody this morning. Max, maybe you'd better let them in yourself, they were your idea. Just don't bring them in this room until I've had time to drink my tea, assuming I ever get any."

Anora had plenty of time to drink her tea, the police were stopped cold by what they found in the hall. Sarah had no desire to go out and watch what they were doing, it was bad enough listening to their voices and the sounds of their feet. They'd have to take out the spear, most likely, in order to fit George into the ambulance. Was that what all the scuffling was about?

Perhaps Anora had slipped partially back into her earlier fugue state; she drank a second cup of tea under Phyllis's pleading that she had to keep up her strength and even managed a bite or two of toast. That small victory attained, Anora allowed herself the grace of a short nap with two of the sofa cushions temporarily laid aside. Once she was settled, Sarah decided this was a good time to slide out to the kitchen and see for herself whether Cook was in any real trouble.

She found her old friend relatively free of palpitations and in a quandary about the luncheon menu. It was a relief to stand there debating whether the consommé ought to be served heated or jellied. The weather forecast was on the jellied side but it could not be gainsaid that, no matter what the temperature, hot foods were more comforting in time of trouble. Unless the trouble happened to be tonsillitis or fever, in which cases Cook pinned her faith to lemon sherbet. Mrs. Protheroe didn't have fever on top of everything else, did she?

Sarah was able to assure Cook that she didn't. Anyway, it was too late now to freeze lemon sherbet for lunch; what about a nice baked custard? Foods that slipped down easily stood the best chance of getting past the lump in a new-made widow's throat, Sarah knew that from past experience. She'd better go back to the morning room and see whether Anora was awake yet.

"Wouldn't you like to sit down and have a cup of tea first?" It was plain to see that Phyllis, having served her mistress, was now ready for one herself. "Oh, there's the doorbell. I have to go."

"I'll get it," said Sarah. "Sit down, Phyllis, you've earned a rest. That's either more police or Dr. Harnett."

It was the doctor. George was having his picture taken now, preparatory to being taken away. The spear was still in his chest, they must be leaving it for the pathologist to cope with. Dr. Harnett was too much a professional not to stop and take a look.

"God! Right through the heart. That thing must be sharp as—it's a wonder Anora didn't drop dead too instead of just going into shock. Where is she—ah—Sarah Kelling, isn't it?"

"Sarah Bittersohn, actually. I've remarried."

Five years ago, but the doctor wouldn't remember. Dr. Harnett's wife came to Anora's parties but he hardly ever did, he always had patients to see. They lived nearby and raised tropical fish, as a child Sarah had been taken to see their aquarium. There'd been one huge gourami who'd had a tank all to himself, Mrs. Harnett had said his name was George. She hadn't explained whom they'd called him after, but Sarah had noticed a resemblance. Her eyes stung with sudden tears. She hustled Dr. Harnett into the morning room.

"Anora, Dr. Harnett's here."

Anora already had a man with her, standing next to the chaise, looking as if he could use a good night's sleep, wearing a summer-weight tan suit that could have done with a pressing. A plainclothes policeman, Sarah assumed. He scowled as she and the doctor approached.

"Sorry, miss. I'll have to ask you—"

"Oh, shush." Sarah wasn't a bit afraid of policeman; she'd had too many dealings with them, one way and another. "This is Dr. Harnett, he'll tell you when she's ready to talk. I'm Max Bittersohn's wife, Sarah."

"Oh. Okay, Mrs. Bittersohn. Levitan, Homicide."

Anora ignored the policeman but managed to raise the ghost of a smile for the doctor. "Hello, Jim. Sarah, you're getting to be more like your Granny Kay every day of your life."

"Save it, Anora, I want to take your temperature." Dr. Harnett stuck a thermometer under her tongue, fitted a blood-pressure cuff around her flaccid, flabby upper arm, took her wrist in one hand and his stethoscope in the other, and listened. He took out the thermometer and shrugged.

"You'll live."

"I'd prefer not to."

"Humbug. So this is Kay's granddaughter? The little girl who came to see our fish? I thought that was Walter's daughter."

"This is Walter's daughter, Jim. They grow up, you know. Don't you think she favors Kay?"

"Very much, now that you mention it. Kay was a lovely woman. I never could understand why she married that brother of Theodore's. Albert, was it?"

"No, Howard, the handsome one. Howard wasn't such a bad fellow. At least he wasn't always off chasing after some skirt, like Albert."

"But he wrote poetry."

"You can't hang a man for that, Jim. Though I will say Howard carried it too far. I don't see why people who insist on reading their own verses out loud every chance they get always have to put on those dying-duck voices. That was the one thing in the world George dreaded, Howard Kelling coming at him with a piece of paper in his hand."

Anora was talking fast and loud now, working off some of her shock in the way most natural to her. "George wasn't afraid of anything living or dead, except having to listen to Howard's poems. Most people didn't realize that, you know, they thought George was just a dim old stick. But I swear to you, George Protheroe was as brave as any man who ever lived. He'd have outfaced a charging lion. Who did this man say he was?"

The man in the tan suit stepped closer. "Lieutenant Levitan, Mrs. Protheroe. I'm in charge of homicide. So you're saying your husband wouldn't have been afraid of somebody coming at him with a spear?"

"Lord, no. Spear or cannon, it wouldn't have made a particle of difference to George. He'd have walked straight up to that murdering devil and laughed in his face. And I suppose that's exactly what he did."

"Who found him, Mrs. Protheroe?"

"I—" Anora choked up. Sarah took her hand.

"It's all right, Anora. Don't talk if it hurts."

"Huh. Do you think anything could hurt worse than I'm hurting already? I found him myself."

"When was this?" asked Levitan.

"I don't know. Half-past seven, maybe. Eight o'clock. We're not an early-rising household. We're all old, we nap a lot."

"Pretty bad, wasn't it?"

"Yes. It wasn't so much that George was dead, you know. I was prepared for that, as much as one can ever be. I knew something was bound to happen fairly soon. It was the spear I couldn't stand. And the blood. So horribly much blood."

Levitan wasn't letting her drift off again. "What about that spear, Mrs. Protheroe? Where did it come from?"

"I don't know. There's so much stuff in this house. I don't remember any spear, but I'm old. I forget. Anyway, there it was sticking up out of him like a bean pole. From his heart. He had an enlarged heart, didn't he, Jim?"

"Yes, Anora. George had a big heart in every way, God rest him."

"I couldn't have stopped him, Jim. Nobody could. I just wish I'd gone with him."

"You can't go yet, Anora," Sarah protested. "We need you here."

"Fiddlesticks! George needed me, nobody needs me now. And don't you go trying to cheer me up, Sarah Kelling. If I want cheering, I'll hire a band."

Yet Anora was sounding a shade less desolate. Phyllis came in with tea and a basket of tiny cornmeal gems, hot from the oven. Cook's palpitations must have subsided. Sarah poured, Anora took a cup, Phyllis pressed her to try the gems.

"Please take one, Mrs. Protheroe. Cook's feelings will be hurt if you don't."

"Huh. And I'm not supposed to have any feelings, is that it?" But Anora picked up one of the steaming morsels, eyed it resentfully for a second, bit off a nibble, and washed it down with a mouthful of tea. Levitan, who'd been sipping gingerly from the all-but-transparent china, put down his empty cup with a faint sigh of relief and got back to business.

"How come your husband was the first one up, Mrs. Protheroe? Were you aware that he'd gone downstairs?"

"I was aware that he hadn't gone up. George had been sleeping down here in his study for quite a while, the stairs had got to be too much for him. It was either this or install an elevator up to his bedroom, we didn't want all that mess and bother."

"You don't have one of those chair-lift things?"

"Don't be ridiculous. You've seen my husband, or what's left of him, poor soul. George could never have fit on one of those things, and I'd never have let him try. He was too fat, like me. But he did still enjoy his food, God bless him. We'd had a nice little roast of pork for dinner, with applesauce and sweet potatoes and a strawberry parfait to follow. Last thing on earth we should have been eating in this hot weather, but that was what George said he wanted and I'm glad we gave it to him, though I don't suppose I'll ever be able to face a roast of pork again."

Anora groped vainly in her dressing-gown pocket. "Blast! Hand me one of those tissues, Sarah. I must look like the devil, sitting here snuffling like a pig after truffles, but I can't help it so you'll just have to put up with me."

"We don't mind, for goodness' sake. What did you do after dinner?"

"Sat for a while and watched some idiotic television program. Then George started nodding off, you know how he always did. I shook him a little by the shoulder and told him he'd better go to bed or he'd be spending the night in his chair and wind up with a crick in his back. Once he'd got to sleep, I'd never have been able to handle him alone. Phyllis is about as much use as a butterfly. Anyway, I helped him into the study and got him settled. By that time I was ready to call it a day myself."

"Are you still sleeping upstairs?" Sarah asked her.

"Oh yes. You know me, I like my creature comforts. I read till about midnight, then dropped off to sleep and didn't wake up till about seven o'clock, which is pretty good for me these days. I don't know whether George got up more than that once during the night. He generally did, his kidneys were in awful shape. Weren't they, Jim?"

"Pretty bad," the doctor agreed. "How could they have been anything else, considering the way he ate and drank? I told him he was eating himself into the—well, I was wrong, wasn't I? You know, Anora, what's happened here is a dreadful thing for us, but a quick death isn't the worst that could have happened to a man who'd been abusing his body for eighty-five years. Sorry, I suppose that was tactless."

The doctor's apology actually drew a hint of a smile from Anora. "Since when have you ever bothered yourself about tact? Just tell me one thing, Jim. Did it hurt him much?"

"I should say very little. I haven't examined him myself, you know, but the spearhead appeared to have stabbed straight into the heart, which would have caused almost instant death. George's reflexes were so sluggish that it was very likely all over before he'd begun to feel pain. I don't know whether there'd be any point in doing an autopsy, that will be for the medical examiner to decide. Strange as it may seem, considering the length of time I've been in practice, I've never been involved in a case like this. I don't see how it could have been misadventure, unless George had been trying to act out one of his yarns about spearing an elephant or something."

"Don't be such a mealymouth, Jim Harnett. Of course it's not misadventure. My George was murdered, you know that as well as I do. Somebody deliberately broke into this house with a spear in his hand and skewered poor George like a joint on a spit."

"But why would anybody do such a ghastly thing?"

"Don't ask me, unless it was a crazy Eskimo who took George for a walrus. Anything's possible these days, the whole world's gone crazy. A fine way for my mother's daughter to wind up a widow, thank God mother's not around to see this day. Sarah, you tell Max I want him to find that brute and bring him to me. After I get through with him, this fellow here can come and gather up the pieces. What did you say your name was?"

"Lieutenant Levitan, ma'am. It's not Mr. Bittersohn's job to find the perp—er, the criminal. It's up to the police, that's what people like you are paying us for."

"Bah. Then what are you standing around here for? Why aren't you out perping?"

"Because I'm still hoping to get some help from you, Mrs. Protheroe. You say you woke up at seven o'clock this morning. Did something wake you?"

"Yes, a full bladder. Write that down so you won't forget. Do you want the full details, or will you take my word for it that I went to the bathroom, did what I'd gone for, then came back to get my robe and slippers? I know, you're about to ask why I didn't put on the robe and slippers before I went. The answer is that I was in too much of a hurry. The reason I put them on when I did is that it looked like a pleasant morning. Instead of going back to bed, I decided to make myself some tea and toast and take it out to the back veranda. It's cool then, and I like to watch the early birds catching their worms. My cook and maid can testify that this is something I often do in the summertime. We don't normally have breakfast till nine, and I like a little something while I'm waiting. Their feelings are always hurt because I don't wake Cook to make the tea and Phyllis to carry it out to me. Why should I? They need their rest, and I find it far less bother to wait on myself. Less bother to me, anyway. I always leave the kitchen in a mess and they have the fun of cleaning up."

"So that's what you did this morning?"

"No, that's what I meant to do. What I did was stumble over my husband's body at the foot of the stairs. Don't ask me what I did after that, because I can't remember. I think I sat down beside him. I must have stayed like that quite some time; I was still there when Sarah came, whenever that was. I do remember thinking I ought to take the spear out. It looked so dreadfully uncomfortable, sticking up out of him. George hated being uncomfortable."

"Did you touch the spear at all, Mrs. Protheroe?"

"No, I just couldn't. I was afraid something vital might come with it. This was a new experience for me, you see. I'm afraid I'm not handling it very well. I'd always thought of myself as a fairly commonsensical person but one never knows, does one? Do you think I've got hardening of the arteries, George? I'm sorry, Jim. My grandmother used to say that if you accidentally spoke the name of an absent person, it meant that he was thinking about you. Poor George, maybe he's thinking of me now, wherever he is. I'm going to miss him horribly, you know."

Sarah hugged the bereft old woman a little harder. "Of course you are. But you couldn't miss George unless you'd had him, Anora. Not everyone's lucky enough to have someone to miss. There's nothing the matter with her, is there, Dr. Harnett? Don't you think what happened is that Anora went into shock? That's a perfectly normal reaction. Wouldn't you say so?"

"Certainly I would. No doubt you do have some hardening of the arteries, Anora, as anyone your age naturally would; but I can't see any sign that it's affecting your mind. Do you remember anything else about when you were sitting there with George?"

"Well, I do recall thinking that I must do something about George before Cook and Phyllis came down and went into fits. I'd managed to convince myself by then that he really was dead. He was so cold, and he hadn't moved, and his eyes were so still. So terribly still. He seemed to be looking at me, but I could tell he wasn't seeing me. I believe I had some thought of getting up, but I'm none too nimble at the best of times, and I felt so weak, and there was nothing handy to haul myself up by. Except the spear, and I couldn't touch that. I felt —oh, frozen, like in one of those nightmares where something awful's chasing you and you can't move."

Levitan intervened. "You're quite sure you never touched the spear at all, Mrs. Protheroe?"

"Yes, quite sure, even if I was in a fog. It was such an alien thing, you know. I believe I was actually afraid of it. But George wouldn't have been. He must have walked straight out when he heard whoever it was in the hall and—oh, God! How could a thing like this have happened right here in his own house?"

"That's a good question, Mrs. Protheroe. Did your husband have any known enemies?"

"Enemies? George? Sarah, tell him."

"I'll try." Sarah drew a deep breath and tried to put words together. "I was telling my husband on our way here that George was like a big old teddy bear. He just sat in his corner and you looked at him and felt comforted. George couldn't have made enemies, he— well, he wasn't exciting enough. He didn't do much. Though he'd exert himself to help someone in time of need. For instance, when I was a widow without any money trying to run a boardinghouse, George persuaded an old college chum of his to be my tenant. He and Anora came and helped me get the room ready, that's the only time he ever came to my house. Do you see what I mean? Did George ever work, Anora? I mean, have a steady job?"

"Oh yes, when he was young. His people were importers, they'd started in the China trade ages ago, like the Kellings. George was back and forth to the Orient a number of times after he'd got out of college, and for several years while we were first married. The last time he went to India, he caught some dreadful fever. The doctors couldn't say what ailed him, but whatever it was, George was terribly sick for a long time and never really got well."

"I didn't know that, Anora."

"Not many did. He didn't like to talk about it and he didn't want me to. George was not a lazy man by nature. This disease, whatever it was, just sapped all his strength. He'd fall asleep in the middle of a meal. You know how he was, Sarah, you've seen him do it. George couldn't possibly have kept up the business by himself. We sold out after his father died and just lived on our income. Fortunately there was enough to get by on, it hasn't been a bad life. I ought to be thankful I've had him so long. That's your doing, Jim."

"Oh, come now, Anora. George never took his medicine and he wouldn't stick to a diet. I'd say the credit goes to you, and to the basic fact that George had the constitution of an ox. I'm afraid I'll have to leave you now, I was due at the hospital an hour ago. Are you quite sure you don't want something to help you sleep?"

"Thank you, Jim, but I might as well get used to being alone. What I've got to do is rouse myself and start making the funeral arrangements, assuming this policeman here will let me."

"We'll help you in every way we can, Mrs. Protheroe," said Levitan. "If you'll have your undertaker get in touch with us, we can handle the details with them."

"Have you taken him away?"

"Yes, the ambulance has gone, and so have the homicide crew, while we've been talking. They've finished the photography, fingerprints, the whole bit; we won't bother you again unless something comes up. I'm afraid there wasn't much we could do about that hall carpet. We had to cut out a piece for evidence, you may want to call in somebody to clean and repair it. Or take it up and get rid of it. Is there anyone you could get hold of right away?"

"I have some people who do odd jobs for me, they'll cope."

"Good. Now, about that spear, Mrs. Protheroe. I don't want to keep nagging you, but are you quite sure you didn't have one kicking around anywhere? This is a big house, and you do seem to have a lot of, uh, knicknacks and stuff."

"I've told you before, Lieutenant Levitan, that to the best of my recollection, there is not nor ever was a spear in this house. I'm quite aware there's a lot of stuff around. Much of it came from the Orient, and I'm willing to concede that a member of the family might at some time have brought back a spear as a souvenir. If so, it would have been tucked away in the attic along with a great many other things that were here when I moved in as a bride and have never got around to throwing out. George and I used to talk about cleaning the attic, but we never did, it was just too daunting. I haven't been up there in ages, I'm too old and fat to climb the stairs."

"What about your maid, or the cook?"

"Phyllis wouldn't go up there on a bet. She's scared to death of mice and spiders, not to mention ghosts. Cook's domain is the kitchen, and there she stays. I further doubt that any little brown man who'd entered the house for the purpose of murdering my husband would have been content to spend much time rummaging through that mess up there for a spear to stab George with when he could perfectly well have bashed him over the head with that big poker from the drawing-room fireplace. That's what I'd have done if I'd ever felt an overwhelming urge to kill. Which I never have, so you might as well cross me off as a possible murderess. If I think of anything that might be helpful, I'll let you know. Sarah, it was Wasserman's you used for Walter and Caroline, wasn't it? And you found them satisfactory?"

"Oh yes, they've been burying Kellings for generations. Would you like me to call them for you?"

"If you don't mind. Lieutenant Levitan, thank you for coming. Phyllis will show you to the door."

"Never mind, I can find my way out. You're a great lady, Mrs. Protheroe, if you don't mind me saying so."

"Of course I don't, why should I? Good perping."

"I suppose he does think I'm the culprit," she remarked before the policeman was fairly out of earshot. "He went on and on about that spear. I suppose that's understandable enough, he can't have run into them often. It's usually guns or clubs or kitchen knives, isn't it, Max?"

"Or whatever comes handy. Levitan can't seriously think you speared your husband. A thrust like that would have taken plenty of force. You're just not strong enough."

"Certainly I am. All I'd have had to do would have been to push him down on the floor, plant the spear point over his heart, and lean on the shaft. My weight would have done the rest. George would have been too stunned to stop me, or else he'd have thought I was joking. He'd never in God's world have believed I could do him any harm. And I couldn't have, Max, believe me."

Anora had to take another tissue. "George used to say to me sometimes, 'Why do you put up with a crock like me?' and I'd tell him, 'Because I love you, you foolish old goat.' And I did, you know. I'd get awfully exasperated with him sometimes, but I never stopped loving him. What's to become of me now?"

"You'll be all right, Anora. Just do the best you can from day to day and sooner or later things will work themselves out."

"And it won't be for long, there's some comfort in that. Oh, Sarah, did you get hold of the undertakers?"

"Yes, they're sending someone out right away to talk to you about the arrangements."

"Then I'd better go put some clothes on. Now that the police have cleared out, neighbors will be calling to find out what's going on. What do you think I should tell them?"

"There's no sense in trying to keep this quiet. I'm sure it will be in the news by noontime, if not before. I think the sensible thing would be to call one or two friends yourself, or have Phyllis do it. Then shut off the phone and don't let Phyllis open the door except to the undertaker or people you know. Those media reporters can be awful pests."

"Oh, Lord, I hadn't thought of that. All right, Sarah. Just don't breathe a word to your Aunt Appie, she'd be out here sympathizing all over the place. I couldn't stand that. Jim Harnett's gone to tell his wife, I expect. Marianne's a good soul, she'll come if she knows I want her. And Ellie Pratch. I'll ask them to lunch, that will give Phyllis and Cook something to do so they won't be out there having the horrors. You and Max are welcome to stay, but I'm sure you have other things to do."

"Well, we did run off and leave Theonia stuck with Davy," Sarah admitted, "and Max has to go to the office. Don't you, dear?"

"Yes, I do, but could I ask Anora one more question before we go?"

The old woman sighed. "Go ahead. I've answered so many already, one more can't hurt. What is it, Max?"

"When you were talking to Levitan about the spear, you mentioned a little brown man. Was there any special reason?"

"Did I say that? I wonder why. Sounds as if I'd been reading

Willkie Collins. Oh, I remember. It was yesterday afternoon, George
and I were sitting on the east veranda. It was shady there then.
That's one of the nice things about this house, we have a veranda for
every time of day. George was reading the paper, or pretending to,
and I was working on my needlepoint. You don't care about that, the
thing of it is that I'd forgotten to bring my little scissors out with me.
So I went in to get them, then it struck me that lemonade and cookies might be enjoyable, so I stopped to ask Cook to send some out
when she got them ready. All in all, I suppose I was in the house for
ten or fifteen minutes. When I went back out, George was up out of
his chair, leaning over the railing."

7

$\mathbf{M}$ax was still waiting for the punch line, but Sarah had caught on immediately. "George did that? How unusual. What do you suppose impelled him to get up?"

"He told me a little brown man in a bright-red jogging suit had just run across the front lawn and back into the garden. George was curious to see what he was up to. George thought the man looked like a Tamil."

"A Tamil? Aren't they Sri Lankans or something?"

"If that's what they're calling themselves now. George thought perhaps the man might have come from Ceylon or down around Madras. He'd been in both places himself; back when he used to travel, he'd even picked up a smattering of the language. I think George was hoping the fellow would come back and talk to him."

"Did you see the man yourself?" Max asked her.

"Oh no. I'd hardly expected to. I was quite willing to grant that George would know a Tamil when he saw one, but that red jogging suit was a bit too much to swallow. I expect George must have nodded off, the way he did, you know, and had a dream about the old days. That happened quite often. Sometimes the dreams were so vivid that he'd be absolutely convinced they'd really happened."

"Do you suppose that's where some of his stories came from?" Max asked.

"Very likely. That would explain why he could never remember the endings. You know how it is with dreams, you always wake up too soon. Anyway, Phyllis came out with the lemonade and I forgot about the little brown man. Or thought I did, but apparently I didn't. Why, Max? Surely you don't think he means anything?"

"It's curious, that's all. One last question, Anora; have you ever done any business with a man named Bartolo Arbalest? He calls himself the Resurrection Man."

"Yes, certainly we have. As a matter of fact, Bartolo was here not long ago. George's niece's daughter, Jane, has finally decided to make an honest man of the chap she's been living with for the past two years or so, and they're having a formal wedding, of all things. So George and I decided we might as well give her the elephant candlesticks. You remember them, Sarah."

"Yes, of course. They're Indian, aren't they? Silver gilt, with filigree howdahs on their backs and fancy gold and silver blankets with rows of miniature bells on the edges. You used to let me brush my fingers along the bells and make them tinkle. It was the tiniest, sweetest sound."

"That's right." Anora was almost smiling. "Children always loved the elephants, Jane was crazy over them. Once when the family was visiting, she and her brother got into a tug-of-war over whose turn it was to ring the bells. In the melee, one of the howdahs got broken and the other elephant's trunk got twisted out of shape. Jane cried and cried. But anyway, I put the elephants away, meaning to have them repaired sometime. You know what that means. That filigree is so delicate, I didn't even know where to take them. So the upshot was that they just sat for years in the butler's pantry. Then this wedding came up and I didn't feel it was right just to go out and buy something, so I thought of the elephant candlesticks."

"How did you get on to Arbalest?" asked Max.

"Serendipity. Ellie Pratch mentioned that a cousin of hers had had some gewgaw repaired—I forget what—by this new man who'd just come to Boston from the West Coast and started a shop doing restorations, and that he'd done a wonderful job. The best part of all was that you didn't have to take the work to him, you just called up and he came to your house. So I called Bartolo and out he came. We had a lovely visit, he and George got to talking about Oriental antiques. It was one of the most interesting evenings we'd spent in a long time, I hadn't seen George so animated since I don't know when."

"Have you got your elephants back yet?"

"Yes, Bartolo was quite prompt, and I must say he did a beautiful job, or somebody did. Of course we could have bought Jane a real elephant for what he charged, but he'd told us in advance how much it was going to cost and explained all about his atelier, as he called it. He has various other artisans working for him, all of them experts at one thing or another. Bartolo's conversation gets a bit high-flown at times, and he's certainly not overburdened with false modesty, but evidently he's as good as he claims to be."

"I've heard that Mr. Arbalest is quite the showman," said Sarah.

"Oh, lordy me, yes. He swooshed up to the door in a Rolls with a chauffeur in livery. I haven't seen such elegance since that time Mary Roberts Rinehart came to tea at my aunt's house in Bar Harbor before it burned down. The chauffeur came in right behind Bartolo carrying what looked to be a suitcase, and stood next to his chair the whole time we talked, not moving a muscle. I didn't know whether to offer the man a seat and a drink or send him out to the kitchen with Cook, so I kept my mouth shut for once and let George handle the conversation. George really enjoyed himself, it was quite like old times. When they got ready to leave, I did ask the man—Gould or something, his name was—no, Goudge—if he'd like a velvet pillow to carry the elephants out to the car on."

"Didn't that crack him up?"

"I thought his lips twitched a bit, but I couldn't be sure."

Talking was doing Anora good, she had a little color in her face by now. "That suitcase thing he'd brought with him was all padded on the inside, as it turned out. Goudge spent about twenty minutes getting the elephants stowed inside, with Bartolo eagle-eyeing him every second. That did give one a feeling of reassurance, as I presume it was meant to do. And when the elephants came back, you couldn't see any sign of where they'd been mended. They were all cleaned up too. Nothing so vulgar as being highly polished of course, but they looked absolutely magnificent. I rather hated to part with them, but seeing Jane so pleased was worth the sacrifice. She even wrote us a thank-you note, which was quite something for Jane. Now if only she doesn't get robbed again!"

"When was she robbed, Anora?" Max asked rather sharply. "Was it since you gave her the elephants?"

"Yes, it was just last week. Fortunately all the wedding presents are over at her parents' house, since she's to be married from there. She and Carl have only a small apartment in the Fenway. There's supposed to be a security system in the building and they have all sorts of locks and chains on their door, but you know there's no way to keep out a really determined thief. Though why anyone would go to all that effort and then not even steal the television set is beyond me. Anyway, Jane's going to look for another place so she can show off the elephants. But I mustn't keep running on like this, no doubt you have things to do. I can't tell you how much I appreciate your coming."

They were going through the usual parting rituals when Phyllis came looking for Anora. "Mrs. Harnett's on the phone, Mrs. Protheroe. She wants to come over. Shall I tell her you're resting?"

"No, say I'll expect her for luncheon in about an hour. Ask if she'd mind inviting Mrs. Pratch to come with her. Otherwise I don't want to see anybody except the undertaker's man. And be sure you make him show you his card before you let him in. Turn down the telephone as soon as you've finished talking with Mrs. Harnett. I don't want to take any more calls. Then draw me a bath and tell Cook to fix something light."

"What would you like, Mrs. Protheroe?"

"I don't care what, a soufflé or an omelet, perhaps. Set the table in the breakfast room. Get the Persian runner out of the upstairs back bedroom and spread it over that ghastly mess on the hall carpet. We'll have to get someone to take it up but I can't handle that today. Lay newspapers under the runner so you won't get its back all stained."

Anora was back in charge, Phyllis exuded relief as she held the door for the Bittersohns to go out. "She'll be all right now that we've got company coming," she whispered. "I'm just so thankful you called when you did."

"Don't hesitate to phone us if anything else happens," Sarah urged. "And take care of yourself, Phyllis. Don't get overtired. Let me know if things are too much for you, I'll see that you get help."

"Will you bring the little boy next time? Mrs. Protheroe loves children, just so they don't start breaking things."

They said a final good-bye, Sarah got back behind the wheel and waited for Max to get his leg comfortably stowed.

"Okay, kid, let 'er roll. Sarah, did you believe that story Anora told about George seeing a little brown man in a red jogging suit?"

"Well, I can't imagine Anora making it up, and I never saw any

sign of George's having psychic powers. If it was a dream, as she
seems to think, it must have been an awfully strange coincidence.
Unless Mr. Arbalest got to telling them about the quaint little chap
who does calisthenics in his alley during that chummy talk they must
have had. Did you notice that Anora called him Bartolo?"

"I imagine getting on first-name terms with his richer clients is
part of Arbalest's sales technique."

"Yes, I suppose it would be," Sarah agreed. "Still, I do think
brown men in red jogging suits would have been an odd subject to
come up during a highbrow conversation on Oriental antiquities."

"Maybe the jogger's old enough to qualify as an Oriental antiquity
himself."

"Very clever, dear. If the man were that old, he'd hardly have been
doing calisthenics. Besides, Charles said his hair was black."

"He could have restored the natural color with that glop they
advertise on television."

"Bah, humbug," said Sarah. "Charles also said there were gray
hairs showing."

"Then he only restored some of the color. Typical ruse of your
ageing red-suited Tamil jogger. Setting said jogger aside for the
nonce, have we any bibelot that needs restoring?"

"Something along the lines of an opening wedge, you mean? Max
dear, can't you think of a cheaper way to get in touch with Bartolo
Arbalest? How about sending Brooks over to apply for a job?"

"I thought of that, but it wouldn't work. Brooks is adamant about
the velvet beret."

"Then why don't we just walk up and thump the knocker? You
don't actually suppose Mr. Arbalest emits an evil aura that causes
little brown men to go around spearing people, do you? And if by
any chance he does, wouldn't it be a job for the police or a witch
doctor instead of us? Darling, I just don't want you to get hurt
again."

"I don't want me to get hurt again either," Max assured his wife
with unequivocal sincerity. "I just want to find out what the hell kind
of racket Arbalest's running. Or who's running one against him, as
the case may be. You didn't happen to notice anything missing from
Anora's house that would have been valuable enough to kill poor old
George for?"

"No, but I didn't look; I was too concerned about Anora. Maybe

she and Phyllis will turn up something once they've pulled themselves together and begun checking around. There is an awful lot of
stuff in that house, of course, and some of it must be good. The
Protheroes are old money, and there's all that Oriental art and what-
not."

"Would an inventory have been made at any time?"

"I'd be inclined to doubt it. The insurance would have been far
more than they'd have wanted to pay, and I can't think why else
they'd have bothered. George was too indolent and I don't believe
Anora cares all that much. She's interested in people, not things.
Still, I suppose she wouldn't want not to find out what the killer's
motive was. One can't just sit idle and let awful things happen. Are
you going to tell Lieutenant Levitan what we know?"

"What do we know? That a man who suffered from narcolepsy
might or might not have seen an Asian in a red jogging suit run
through his yard? Let's save it till we have something worth telling. I
think the logical place for us to start is with your Cousin Percy's
parrot. Being assigned to track down a piece Arbalest has recently
worked on should give us a legitimate reason to approach Arbalest."

"So it should," Sarah agreed. "Shall we go together, or draw
straws?"

"I think I'd better tackle Arbalest alone, or else take Brooks with
me, since he's the one who knows the guy."

"Then I'll pop out to Percy's house. He'll be at the office by now,
of course, but Anne will be home. Weeding, no doubt, she lives for
her garden. I'll ask for a photograph of the painting. If not, I can
make an Identikit drawing from her description so we'll know what
we're looking for. Anne has a pretty good eye for detail and color,
I'll take my paints with me."

Sarah had done some book illustrating during her earlier life,
these days her talent often came in handy for other purposes. She
was also adept at extracting possibly useful facts that the victim
might not have thought important enough to tell the policemen investigating the crime. Too bad she couldn't take Davy along, but
Anne would have a stroke if he did any of the things very young boys
are all too prone to do. She mustn't stick Theonia with him much
longer, she'd have to work something out with Mariposa.

It was a great relief to have Max out and about, or would be,
provided he didn't try to take on too much too fast. Sarah toyed with

the notion of getting Charles a chauffeur's livery and letting him do for Max what Carnaby Goudge was doing for Bartolo Arbalest. She failed to persuade herself that Charles would be any good as a body-guard, but at least he could drive the car and look impressive. Only then they'd be short a houseman. She really must do something about additional help. First things first.

"I'm sorry I shan't be around to drive you to Arbalest's. Charles could do it, couldn't he?"

"Who needs him? If I don't feel like walking, I can always take a cab."

"How's the leg now?"

"Still attached to the rest of me. I might lie down for a while with Davy before I tackle Arbalest."

"That's a good idea. He'll be much happier about his nap if you're taking one with him. I was just wondering how to cope. I couldn't possibly take him to Anne's, and Theonia's patience must be stretched fairly thin by now. I'm going to drop you off at the house and take a chance on finding a place to park."

Luck, for once, was with her. There was an open space on Tulip Street, Sarah tucked the car into it neat as a button with almost a foot of space to spare. In the dining room, they found Theonia, Mariposa, and Davy eating toasted-cheese and tomato sandwiches while Charles did a semi-hilarious singing-waiter routine. Nobody appeared to have missed them much, though everyone was glad to see them back.

"Davy and I made extra sandwiches in case you showed up," said Mariposa. "I'll go stick 'em under the broiler."

"Sit still," Sarah told her. "I'll do it. Do you want iced tea, Max?"

Max said he did and inquired how many ducks Davy had fed while Theonia gave Sarah a progress report on the morning's events. She and Davy had carried out their scheduled program with regard to walks, ducks, and swan boats. Brooks had left a telephone message for Max, to the effect that Bill Jones had dropped in with some interesting news. Brooks would be happy to pass it on if Max would come to the office sometime after two o'clock.

"Brooks also said that Cousin Percy had kept him on the phone for fifteen minutes demanding to know what progress has been made in getting his—or rather Anne's—painting back," Theonia went on.

"I gather Percy was less than satisfied by Brooks's report. Just as a matter of curiosity, who does that man think we are?"

"I know, Percy can be an awful stuffed shirt when there's money involved," said Sarah. "Also when there isn't, I must admit. I thought I'd take a run out there this afternoon and see what I can find out from Anne. She's fairly sensible most of the time. Unfortunately young children make her nervous, which isn't surprising considering what hellions her own grandchildren are. But it does mean someone will have to keep an eye on Davy for a couple of hours after he and his father have their nap. Do I have any volunteers?"

"Sure," said Mariposa, "How about it, Chico? We get out the maracas an' have us a fiesta, then maybe we go out in the yard an' you play on the swing while I rest my feet. Olé!"

"Olé!" yelled Davy.

So that little problem was taken care of. Before Brooks and Theonia had moved in, the tiny back area between the basement door and the alley behind Tulip Street had been a depressing waste of rocks, weeds, and trash cans. Brooks had cleaned up the mess, built a functional bin to hide the trash cans and a new board fence for privacy, as well as a sturdy door to replace an old one that had been badly damaged and crudely mended. He'd bricked over the center to accommodate outdoor furniture and lugged in sacks of loam and peat moss to make flower beds. He'd planted cooking herbs and the more rugged sorts of low-growing shrubs and flowers. He was in the process of espaliering a dwarf pear tree. Now the garden held comfortable chairs for grown-ups to sit in, plus a custom-built, spill-proof swing for a little boy to play on. A safe, pleasant place for a child and his minder to spend a summer afternoon. That minor domestic problem solved, Sarah finished her sandwich, got her menfolk comfortably settled, and went to collect her sketching gear.

8

O f course hemerocallis doesn't offer much of a challenge."

Sarah was quite ready to agree with Cousin Anne, she herself could not recall ever having felt challenged by a hemerocallis. It was no earthly use trying to get on with the job she'd come for until she'd been given the complete guided tour and delivered what Anne would consider a sufficient amount of approbation, gratification, and laudation.

That was all right, Sarah was enjoying the stroll. Anne's garden was a welcome change from that depressing morning visit with poor old Anora Protheroe. While not quite on the level of Sissinghurst or Winterthur, it was beautifully planned and impeccably maintained. She did most of the work herself, with only a young fellow once or twice a week to spade, mow, or rake as season and occasion demanded.

Even the compost heap was a work of art in its way. Anne held strong views on the subject of compost. She listened quite spellbound as Sarah explained how Mr. Lomax, the caretaker out at Ireson's Landing, had tilled new life into worn-out soil by judicious applications of codfish heads and guts obtained from a nearby fish-packing plant. It was in a spirit of amity and contentment that the two finished their stroll and sat down to rest under a spreading horse-chestnut tree.

Anne's iced tea wasn't much compared to Theonia's and her offered cookies had come out of a package, but the mint was fresh picked, the lemon fresh sliced, and the surroundings lovely enough to make up for the slight staleness of the gingersnaps. Now they could talk.

"About your painting that was stolen," Sarah began, "you wouldn't happen to have a photograph of it, by any chance?"

Sarah might as well have asked for a stuffed anteater, Anne was completely taken aback. "A photograph? Of the painting? Why, no, it never occurred to me. I do keep a detailed photographic record of the garden each year, naturally, but as for a painting—well, we hadn't had our little girl with the parrot all that long, and Percy had tended to regard her as a rather poor joke. As much as Percy ever takes anything as a joke, anyway. That was before Mr. Arbalest told us what she was worth, needless to say. Since he found out her market value, Percy has been quite pleased with her. Percy has a great sense of justice, you know; he was as distressed as I when we found her gone. Of course she's a portable asset, and you know how Percy is about assets; but it's more than that, we've both grown quite fond of her. You do understand how anxious we are to get her back?"

"Oh yes," Sarah assured her. "I quite understand."

"Then how do you propose to go about finding her? I assume I'm entitled to ask, now that I'm a client."

Anne was not being sarcastic, she wouldn't have known how to be. Sarah groped for an explanation that might satisfy a person whose heart belonged to her compost heap.

"I suppose we work more or less the same way you might if you were setting out to develop a new hybrid hemerocallis. We start with what we know, the way you'd start with a familiar plant, then we think what might be a logical next step and try that. If it doesn't work, we try something else. All sorts of unexpected things might come up, but we just persist, as you would till you'd finally got the plant you were after."

"Ah, now I understand. You make it so beautifully clear."

Sarah was relieved to hear Anne say so, though she couldn't imagine why Anne thought so. Probably her cousin's wife had interpreted Sarah's words in a way she could comfortably handle. Clearly the important thing was to stay within a context where a gardener would feel at home. Having got the range, Sarah carried the conversation a step further.

"Suppose there's an exotic plant you've seen somewhere that

you'd like for your garden, but you don't know where to find it and you can't ask because you've forgotten the name. So you hunt through gardening books and seed catalogs until you spot a picture of it. You might still have to search for your plant at a lot of different nurseries, but at least you know now what you're looking for, and that makes it easier."

"I know exactly what you mean! There was this—"

Anne was all set to launch into a story about just such a horticultural quest, but time was running on. "So what I'm here for," Sarah told her in the downright Kelling style that was often confused with arrogant rudeness, "is to get a picture of your painting, so that however many agents we wind up having to use will all know exactly what they're looking for. Since no photograph is available, I want to make what you might call an Identikit sketch from your description."

"Oh dear, I'm not much good at describing things."

"That's all right, Anne, I'll worm it out of you. Percy said it's a painting in the American Primitive style of a little girl holding a very large green parrot on one of her fingers."

"Yes, that's quite right. Percy is much better than I at this sort of thing."

"I'm sure he isn't. You have the gardener's eye, that's what we need here."

"We do?"

"Absolutely," Sarah insisted. "Now, I expect you know about the itinerant painters who used to go from village to village doing portraits of anybody who had the money to pay for them. You may not have heard that they often spent their winters painting figures without any heads on them, always dressed in nice clothes and often with some pretty touch, like a pet or a child's toy or a bunch of flowers thrown in at no extra charge. Or a parrot."

"How nice of them," Anne said politely, "but why no heads?"

"The idea was that the client could pick out the figure he liked best, then the artist would get the subject to pose so that he could paint in the appropriate head. The artist would frequently make several copies of the same figure, which of course would all wind up looking different because they'd have different heads. Like a bed of mixed dahlias," Sarah amplified. "The foliage looks pretty much the same on all of them, but the heads will vary."

It would not do to let Anne get started on dahlias, she hurried on.

"So I've brought along a book on folk art and I'm hoping there may be something in here that may remind you of your own painting. Let me know if you see even a minor detail that jogs your memory."

Because paintings of the genre are so stylized, it didn't take Anne long to begin spotting resemblances. "Our girl was standing sideways with one foot in front of the other like this, and she had those same tiny little feet and heelless black slippers. Only her face is chubbier, like this other one here, and her hair is lighter brown."

Anne was even able to select a dress, only it needed certain alterations and was the wrong shade of blue. "It was more, oh, how can you describe a color?"

"You compare it to something else," said Sarah. "Can you show me a flower of the right shade?"

"Oh yes, easily. What a splendid suggestion. And I can find you a leaf to match the parrot."

Once they'd got that far, the rest was a breeze. Combining bits and pieces from the various plates with snippets from the flower beds, Sarah managed a sufficiently accurate watercolor sketch in less than an hour. Anne was charmed.

"How terribly clever! I don't suppose there's any chance of my having it, in case you can't get back the other one?"

"I can do you an oil painting that would be more like the original if it comes to that," Sarah promised, "but we do have a fairly high rate of success at getting back the originals. Can you show me exactly where the painting hung, and how you think the thief may have entered the house?"

"Oh yes, though it's a shame to go inside on a day like this."

Anne gave a last yearning glance toward a bed of geraniums red and delphiniums blue and led Sarah into the drawing room. The space above the mantel was now occupied by the likeness of a grim-faced elderly man in a banker's gray business suit, clutching a sheaf of papers in a stern and purposeful manner. Mortgages he was about to foreclose on, Sarah surmised.

"We put father back because the room looked so bleak with that big bare space over the fireplace," Anne explained, "but he doesn't really go at all well with the new slipcovers. Our little girl was exactly right; the parrot picked up on the green of the foliage, there was even that same yellow in his beak as in the centers of the roses. Even

Percy noticed how badly father clashes. I do so hope you get her back!"

Anne stroked the gaily flowered chintz as she might have comforted a stricken child, assuming she'd been as devoted to children as she was to her garden. What could Sarah do but murmur words of cheer and comfort and ask whether any of the locks had been forced.

"The police couldn't find any sign of forcing," Anne replied. "But they must have got in somehow."

"*They* being the robbers?"

"Or robber. One person could have managed the painting easily enough; it's not that big, although that lovely frame Mr. Arbalest put on makes it look—oh, important. The smaller size was an advantage, to my way of thinking. Father takes up too much room to have a tall flower arrangement on the mantel, and I'd had something rather special planned for my garden-club tea in September. Nicotiana for fragrance, bergamot for old times' sake and to pick up the pinks in the painting, and Harry Lauder's Walking Stick for laughs."

"It sounds charming." Sarah was ready to believe that of any arrangement Anne might do, even though she couldn't imagine what her cousin-in-law meant by Harry Lauder's Walking Stick.

"It would have been rather nice," Anne agreed wistfully. "Now I don't know what I'll do. So many of the summer flowers will be gone by then, and the chrysanthemums barely getting started. Of course petunias are always with us, but one can't get really creative with a petunia. At least I can't, and goodness knows I've tried."

Sarah let Anne run on while she made an occasional polite rejoinder and went on checking locks. It was in the lean-to greenhouse off the dining room that she struck pay dirt, by poking a bamboo stick up into a ventilator.

"Look at this, Anne, the entire vent's rising right up. They took the screws out. Piece of cake."

"But it's such a small hole," Anne objected.

"Not all that small," Sarah insisted. "I could wiggle my way through, not that I'm about to try in this dress."

"But you couldn't have got the painting through."

"I wouldn't have had to. Once the thief was inside, he or she could have unlocked any door or window, set the painting outside, then locked up again from the inside and crawled back out the ventilator hole, sticking the fan back in to plug up the hole and collecting the painting from wherever he'd stashed it. Nobody would have been the wiser as to how he came and went if he hadn't forgotten to screw the fan down after him. I'd make sure that's done as soon as possible, Anne, in case the person takes a notion to come back. So now we know the burglar was smallish, slim, agile, and a bit careless. That's a step in the right direction, at least. I must say I'm surprised that the police overlooked this vent."

Anne shrugged. "Frankly, I don't think they were all that much interested. Once they found out nothing else had been taken, no money or jewelry or even the silverware, they more or less shrugged off the painting. That's why Percy decided to call your husband. How is Max's leg progressing?"

"Quite well, thank you. He still can't drive the car, but he's walking with just a cane instead of a crutch. Max would have liked to come with me today," Sarah lied politely, "but he had to see another client in Boston."

Not that Bartolo Arbalest had been a client when she'd left Tulip Street, but Sarah wouldn't be at all surprised to find he was one by the time she got back. Word-of-mouth advertising worked beautifully so long as it meant one satisfied customer telling another prospect. However, once those same customers started broadcasting the word that a connection with Bartolo Arbalest might also lead to an encounter with robbery, arson, or murder, he and his artisans would have to pick up and move again. If anyone ever needed help, it was Bartolo Arbalest.

As Sarah stood looking up at the deceptive little vent, a mad thought seized her.

"Anne, you haven't by any chance seen a strange man around here during the last day or so? Someone small and either deeply tanned or else naturally brown-skinned, like an East Indian?"

"Why, yes," Anne replied quite matter-of-factly. "He was over behind the Russian olives. I keep them low and clipped, you know, to provide background for the azaleas."

Sarah felt she'd got more than she'd bargained for. "When was this?"

"About half-past five this morning. I always get up early during the summer, that's the nicest time for weeding."

"Was he running?"

Anne shook her head. "I'd say he was more what you might call lurking."

"Really?" said Sarah. "And was he by any chance wearing a red jogging suit?"

Mrs. Percy Kelling was not given to levity, Sarah was very much surprised when Anne burst out in a rush of giggles. "Hardly! He was wearing a rhubarb leaf."

"Anne!"

"Well, perhaps I shouldn't say wearing. Actually just—er—holding it. Where it would do the most good."

"Do you mean to tell me he was naked?"

"Well, yes, though one hardly likes to come straight out and say so. It was quite a large rhubarb leaf." Anne clearly didn't want Sarah to think she'd been associated with any really gross impropriety. "They are, you know. I always let my rhubarb bolt once the hot weather sets in, the blossoms are rather striking and the leaves grow quite enormous. I mean, the poor man was doing the best he could in the circumstances, one has to give him credit for that."

Sarah was willing enough to do so, but she couldn't help asking, "What did Percy think?"

"Heavens, you don't think I'd ever tell Percy?"

"Why not? He is your husband."

"That's precisely why. Percy would not understand. Percy is an admirable man in many ways, Sarah. On the whole our marriage is as happy as one can reasonably expect, but there are certain things that Percy does not accept and never will. He doesn't ask me to help with his bookkeeping, and I—"

Anne paused to consider just where this declaration might be taking her. Knowing Anne, Sarah decided she'd better help out. "And you don't tell him about naked men in the garden. That's quite understandable. But didn't it occur to you that this might have been the person who'd stolen your painting?"

"Of course not, why should I have thought anything of the sort? Remember, Sarah, I didn't know then that the painting had been stolen."

"Right, I beg your pardon, Anne. So what did you do, just go in the house?"

"Yes and no. You see, I was dressed in my weeding clothes, a pair of dungarees and an old T-shirt. Percy thinks they're disgusting but one does have to be comfortable for weeding. I'd slipped down the back stairs and out the kitchen door, meaning to work for a couple of hours so I'd feel I'd really earned my breakfast."

"Noble of you."

"Oh no, that's what I usually do. I keep an attractive housecoat hanging in the plant closet where I do my flower arrangements, so that when I go inside all I have to do is scrub up and change into the housecoat to be presentable when Percy comes down. He doesn't mind a housecoat, he thinks they're rather sweet and feminine. We have breakfast together, then he goes off to work and I either go back to the garden or get dressed and do errands or whatever. Anyway, there was that scrawny little fellow squatting behind his rhubarb leaf, thinking I didn't see him."

"Awkward for you," Sarah prompted. "Then what happened?"

"Well, I didn't think it quite the thing to walk over and ask what he was doing there. I assume the man was either a nudist who'd been for a stroll and lost his way or else he'd been mugged and robbed of his clothes and dumped out of a car. One hears such awful things on the news these days. Anyway, I finally decided the tactful thing would be to go in and change into my housecoat, bring the dungarees and T-shirt back out, and just drop them on the ground close to where he was hiding. Then I could stroll back to the house as if I didn't realize he was there, and he could put them on and go away. I left my old sneakers, too, I couldn't tell whether he was barefoot. I just didn't want him darting out and grabbing me."

"Naturally you didn't," Sarah reassured her. "In the circumstances I think you acted very sensibly and humanely."

"Well, I don't usually go strolling around the grounds in my housecoat, but at least I was decently covered. And the clothes were gone when I looked out the window, so the man must have understood. Anyway, that's what I did. Then Percy came down and we had breakfast."

"And that was when you discovered the painting was gone?"

"That's right. As Percy was getting ready to leave for the office, he went into the drawing room to get a file he'd brought home, meaning to work on it after dinner, which of course he hadn't done, as I'd known he wouldn't. He saw at once that our little girl was missing, then we had this great hullabaloo with the police. Percy was dreadfully late getting to the office and I simply couldn't settle down to weeding without my old dungarees, though of course I could have worn something else. Absurd, isn't it?"

"Not really. These things are always a dreadful shock, one does feel disoriented for a while. You'll be all right tomorrow, Anne."

"I certainly hope so, I hate to let the garden get ahead of me. It was so good of you to come out, Sarah, at least one feels we've accomplished something constructive. Do you think I should call the police back and tell them about that loose vent in the greenhouse?"

"It wouldn't hurt, they might find some useful fingerprints. None of them will be mine, I didn't touch the metal. And don't you touch it, either, until after they've been and gone."

"Should I offer them tea? One doesn't know the protocol," Anne half apologized. "In British mysteries, the bobbies are always being treated to beer, but I can't see Percy standing for that."

"Oh no," Sarah reassured her. "What you do is just thank them for coming. And now I must be going. I'll have Brooks take some colored photographs of my sketch so that we can begin circulating them where they might do some good. Thanks, Anne, you've been extremely helpful. And you can tell Percy Kelling I said so."

9

Refreshed from his nap, Max Bittersohn gave his son a good-bye hug and picked up the silver-headed cane. Setting up this appointment hadn't been the easiest task he'd ever tackled; Bartolo Arbalest was a cagy man, as he had every reason to be.

What had turned the trick were Brooks Kelling's name, the news about Percy Kelling's wife's parrot, and the real clincher, George Protheroe's appalling death. Brooks was going along to testify that Max was really who he claimed to be. Strategy called for the two to meet at the Washington statue near the Arlington Street entrance to the Public Gardens and walk the rest of the short way together. They were scheduled to arrive on the Resurrection Man's doorstep at half-past two on the dot; Mr. Bittersohn must understand that Mr. Arbalest had to be extremely careful about who got let into his atelier.

Mr. Bittersohn understood perfectly, he was rather surprised that Arbalest hadn't put up more of a struggle. Maybe it was the way old George had been killed that tipped the scales, there was something awfully persuasive about a spear through the heart. It was also possible that Carnaby Goudge had put in a good word for Max. The bodyguard might be getting bored with the jodhpurs, the high thinking, and the confinement. He might also be getting a bit edgy, Goudge didn't like violence. Anyway, he usually seemed to prefer working on a short-term basis. Bodyguarding seemed an odd life for a Yale man, but Max supposed Goudge could have done worse. At least he'd stayed out of politics.

So Max made a beeline for the Washington statue. As he'd expected, Brooks was already at their rendezvous, sitting on a bench surrounded by a flock of hopeful pigeons and explaining patiently that he had nothing to give them. He was suggesting that they fly over toward the popcorn peddler but they weren't listening, pigeons never did. When he saw Max coming, he stood up and brushed off his pant legs; Brooks was neat as a cat in all his ways.

"Ah, there, old comrade in arms," he called out. "How goes the battle?"

"I have not yet begun to fight," replied Max. "Shall we dance?"

They crossed over to the Back Bay, meandered along to Marlborough Street timing their steps neatly, found the house, climbed the stairs, and examined the gargoyle on the knocker with professional interest.

"Shows a certain resemblance to Cousin Dolph, don't you think?" said Brooks. "Do you care to thump, or shall I?"

"Go ahead." said Max. "I'll just stand here looking solid and dependable. Better wait for the countdown, we still have three seconds to go. Okay? One—two—three—knock!"

Brooks barely had time to get in the first thump before the door opened just enough to reveal a wary eye, a wisp of beard, and a small slice of velvet beret. "Hello, Bartolo," he chirped. "You can come out from behind the barricades. This is my Cousin Sarah's husband Max, guaranteed genuine and in fairly good repair. May we come in?"

"Oh yes, yes, please do. Just a moment while I unfasten these chains. They're a beastly nuisance, but we do have to be so careful. Mind your step, Mr. Bittersohn, I'm afraid the tiles may be a trifle slippery."

"Very handsome," said Max. "Moorish inspiration, made in Portugal, I expect, circa 1926."

"Er—probably." Arbalest appeared a trifle chagrined. He would no doubt have preferred that Max assume they'd been painted and glazed by Saracens around the time of the Second Crusade.

The house, at least the entrance hall, did have a general flavor of the Alhambra. The light fixtures were in the shape of flambeaux, a stagy-looking battle-axe with a scalloped blade hung on one wall, there was a fair amount of wrought iron and carved Spanish oak around. This could have been one of the richer monasteries or one of the glitzier Ramada Inns. In such a setting, Bartolo Arbalest's green velveteen smock, sienna-brown velvet beret, and flowing burnt-umber silk tie were obviously the garb to wear.

Max checked surreptitiously to see whether Arbalest was wearing corduroy or velveteen trousers. He was betting on corduroy, and corduroy they were. Arbalest was as tall as Max, maybe an inch taller, dark-eyed and ruddy-skinned. He carried himself well, though there could be no doubt that his loose smock had been adopted not only for its aesthetic appeal but also to conceal the *embonpoint* that self-styled gourmets who send their artisans out for truffles tend to collect. His dark beard was artistically flecked with gray, as was his abundant, wavy hair, at least the half that was visible, the beret being worn very much on one side of Arbalest's majestic head. Maybe the other half was bald, Max speculated rather hopefully.

Still, Max knew a work of art when he saw one. Bartolo Arbalest was all that and then some. He was ushering his callers past the elegant, now-empty drawing room into a smaller room, lined with books and furnished with a carved, leather-topped desk that held some leather-bound portfolios, a Tiffany lamp, and a French telephone in shiny brass and mother-of-pearl. There were an easy chair and a not-so-easy chair, both covered in dark brown leather. A brass orrery sat on a mahogany pedestal.

Another mahogany pedestal bore a marble carving of a hand in the manner of Rodin, only the hand was making an obscene gesture. On the walls hung a Delacroix of two gazelles fighting over a dead lion, a decidedly overweight Correggio madonna with a glowering child clinging desperately to her knee, and a small Uccello profile of a noble lady with a towering head dress and no chin whatsoever. Max smiled. Arbalest smiled back.

"All my own work, it's a way of keeping sane. Assuming, of course, that I ever was. Do sit down, I thought we'd be cozier here. What can I offer you? Tea? Chilled wine? I've a rather pleasant blanc de blancs."

"Nothing, thanks," said Max. "We don't want to take up too much of your time. Bringers of ill tidings aren't apt to be welcome visitors."

"My dear sir, don't let that trouble you. I've become quite adept at receiving bad news, I suppose Brooks has told you something of my history. Though I have to admit I quite lost my aplomb when you told me about George Protheroe's horrible death. You say he was actually murdered? And with a spear? How can such horrible things happen? And why him, of all people? Robbery, I suppose, but I can't imagine a more inconvenient house to rob. The mere logistics of trying to sort out what's worth stealing from what isn't would daunt even Mercury, god of thieves and pickpockets. What did get taken, by the way? Not the elephant candlesticks, I hope?"

"No," said Max. "Fortunately Mrs. Protheroe had already sent them along to the bride. As of this morning, she wasn't able to tell us anything helpful. Neither was her maid."

"What about Sarah?" asked Brooks. "She has a sharp eye, didn't she notice any empty spaces on the whatnots?"

"She was pretty well taken up with Anora. The poor woman was in a bad way, as God knows she had reason to be. Sarah's my wife," Max explained to Arbalest. "Her family have been friends of the Protheroes more or less forever. I understand you and old George hit it off pretty well. Did he strike you as the sort of man to make enemies?"

"*Au* very much *contraire*. Not to speak with disrespect of the recently defunct, but one thought of him more as a dear old overgrown dormouse looking for a teapot to curl up in. George was quite the most restful person I've ever had dealings with. A likeable man, you know, but hardly one to scintillate. He did know a fair amount about Oriental silver; we had a couple of really pleasant discussions, for which I'm grateful. It's a pity he didn't stick with his importing business. Or rather his family's. That's the problem with being born to wealth, it saps the will to go on. Who holds the money bags, if I'm not being too inquisitive? Is it his wife?"

"It's both," said Brooks with some asperity. "Or was. George went into the family business directly from college and was doing quite well, I believe, until he caught some devastating fever that left him permanently impaired. Did you know that, Max?"

"Anora told us just this morning. Sarah hadn't known, either."

"That doesn't surprise me, it happened so long ago. I was only a youngster myself at the time, but I can remember my parents wondering whether George Protheroe would ever leave the hospital. They'd never have believed he'd outlive them both by many years. Entirely thanks to Anora, of course. A good woman really is above rubies."

Only trained observers such as Max and Brooks would have noticed Arbalest's wince. What good woman had he lost? Wife?

Mother? Girl friend? That artisan in his Houston atelier who'd
racked up her car on an abutment? Tough for him, no doubt, but
surely not germane to the issue at hand. Max wasn't much for small
talk on the job, he decided it was time they got down to business.

"Mr. Arbalest, you've set up quite a security system here. You
keep your workers under your own roof, you provide them and yourself with a trained bodyguard, you have grilles on all your windows
and enough locks on the doors to start your own jail. This leads me
to deduce that the string of calamities that has hit your previous
employees, and now seems to be spreading to your clients, adds up
to a deliberate terrorist effort aimed at yourself. Do you know why
this is so and who's behind it?"

This was a bit much for Arbalest to handle, he reacted with asperity. "Not to be rude, Mr. Bittersohn, but isn't that rather a personal
question for you to be asking on such short acquaintance?"

"I can be even ruder, Mr. Arbalest. Have the police in New York,
Los Angeles, or Houston ever investigated you as a possible murderer?"

"What?" The Resurrection Man's face had turned an even sicklier
green than his smock. "See here, Mr. Bittersohn, when you telephoned me a while ago, you led me to understand that you wanted to
discuss certain problems relating to clients we have had in common.
Now you come barging into my house and—"

"A simple yes would have been sufficient, Mr. Arbalest. You could
hardly have expected not to be an object of interest to the cops,
considering your profession and your track record on calamities. I'm
sorry if I've upset you, but I think we should all know where we're
coming from. Any art restorer, especially one with your abilities and
connections, must have had a few offers. You know what goes on in
the art underworld, you couldn't possibly not know. Right, Brooks?"

"Oh yes. I was even approached a few times myself, back when I
was odd-job man at the Wilkins Museum."

"Right, and I've been propositioned more times than I can remember, mostly with regard to insurance fraud," said Max. "Theo-
retically, it's possible any of us might have accepted, if the price was
right and we were that sort of people. Having refused the offers,
we've all taken a certain amount of grief from people we've disappointed. Neither Brooks nor I has been set up for a murder charge,
thank God, but you've been far more vulnerable, Arbalest, because

you offer a wide scope of opportunities and you're not accustomed to dealing with crooks. Any cop worth his salt would have had to ask himself whether your employees' deaths had been in fact legitimate accidents, whether they'd been rubbed out as a result of their own criminal activities, or whether you'd either killed them or had them killed because they'd found out things about your operation you didn't want them to know. The possibility that your employees were being killed simply to get back at you would have had to be a poor fourth on anybody's list. Except maybe your own. Right, Mr. Arbalest?"

"I'm afraid so. I'm sorry I was short with you, Mr. Bittersohn, naturally the subject is a tender one with me. It's unfortunately true that I've had illicit propositions made to me from time to time. It's equally true that I've turned them all down. I've always tried to be tactful about refusing, so as not to create ill feeling, but I suppose I have to grant the hypothesis that some disappointed client may have chosen to revenge himself—or herself, I should add, since not all women are above rubies, sad to say—in this dreadfully circumlocutious way."

Arbalest picked up a niello-ornamented silver paper knife, scowled at its sharpness, and put it down. "I've never felt personally threatened, oddly enough. Not that I'm trying to make myself out a hero, actually I'm a terrible coward. It's the work that's under attack, Mr. Bittersohn. That's why my artisans and now my clients have been subjected to these outrages; there is some malignant agency that wants to prevent me from doing what I was set on this earth to do. I quite realize this sounds fanciful and high-flown, but my work is my life. To rescue from neglect and decay some once-beautiful work of art, to give it back to the world as a joy instead of a sad reminder of loveliness that once had been, that is my mission. Now you know why I call myself the Resurrection Man. You did say you wanted the truth."

"Yes, I did."

Max was by no means sure he'd got it. A man who was his own best salesman mightn't have too hard a time talking himself into being his own malignant force. Arbalest's admitting them into the guild hall, or whatever he called it, didn't necessarily constitute a proof of injured innocence. He could just as well have come to the office or offered to meet Max and Brooks somewhere on neutral ground. Having them here could be construed almost as a "see, I have nothing to hide" ploy. He'd no doubt had plenty of chances to practice on the cops.

It was time for a reciprocal gesture, Max shoved out a pawn. "I suppose Goudge told you he called on us at the house night before last to explain why we should quit tailing Lydia Ouspenska."

A vigorous nod set the velvet beret flopping. "Yes, indeed. Madame Ouspenska is a very gifted lady. Mr. Goudge tells me she's also an old friend of yours."

"She got poisoned at my wife's dinner table once. Those things establish a bond, you know. We were all relieved to find out Lydia's being so well taken care of here. I'd never seen her looking so healthy."

"How very kind of you to say so, Mr. Bittersohn. She'll be sorry to have missed your visit, she's out on assignment just now. A matter of a flaking halo."

Max obliged his host with the smile that Arbalest was clearly expecting. "Lydia told me she makes house calls on saints."

He thought Arbalest relaxed just a bit. "Oh, Madame Ouspenska —she's asked us to drop the title—is a lady of many parts. She's marvelous at church work, of which we get a good deal, heaven be praised. She's also a positively inspired miniaturist, as you perhaps know."

"Byzantine icons?"

"Oh yes, definitely. There's simply nobody to touch Ouspenska on icons, though unfortunately we don't have many of those coming through the atelier. But we do get an occasional illuminated manuscript, she's a grand illuminator. In more ways than one, I may say, she positively lights up our lives with her never-failing joie de vivre. Really, it's a privilege to have Madame Ouspenska in the guild."

"I'm glad you feel that way." Arbalest must have been pretty hard up for joie de vivre, Max thought. Much as he himself liked Lydia, he'd have been driven to howling frenzy in a matter of hours if he'd ever been stuck with her at close quarters. "Tell her we're sorry to have missed her. I suppose she's got Goudge waiting at the church now? He mentioned last night that he generally goes along when she's on an outside job."

"Indeed he does, they have a most agreeable relationship. He's inclined to be somewhat taciturn, you know, and she's so charmingly effervescent. *Entre nous*, I suspect our Carnaby's a trifle smitten."

Brooks chuckled. "From what I know of your Carnaby, not much will come of it."

"Oh, I do so hope you're right. Such attachments never work, you know. Sooner or later the bloom rubs off the rose, then the sniping begins. Eventually there's a major dustup and one of the pair storms off in a huff. Sometimes they both do. I couldn't handle that. Not now, when I've struggled so hard to organize the guild and get everything working so well. At least I thought I had, until I got Mr. Bittersohn's phone call."

Arbalest picked up the silver paper cutter again. For a second it looked as though the man might be going to stab its sharp point into his well-oiled leather desk top, but his nobler nature prevailed. "Well, gentlemen, do you have further questions or would you like to see the atelier? You'll be our very first outside visitors, you know; I'm not quite sure how to introduce you."

"You'd better not be too obvious about who we are," said Max. "How about if he's Mr. Brooks and I'm Mr. Tickle? Brooks can be an artisan applying for a job and I'll be the plumber looking for a leak."

In a sense Max was just that, but Arbalest shook his head. "Couldn't you both be prospective members of the guild? You could even move in with us if you feel it's necessary, though where we'd put you I'm sure I don't know. All the bedrooms are in use and I can hardly ask any of the present occupants to double up. We really could use more space, but I don't know where we'd get it."

"Then there's your answer," said Max. "Brooks can pose as an architect trying to figure out how to enlarge the house and I'll be the building inspector telling him he can't do it."

"Couldn't you both be architects?" Arbalest was a little out of his depth with Max, as people often were.

"Sure, why not? Come on, Brooks. Grab yourself a pencil and let's tear the place apart."

10

Fashions in cities change. Boston's Back Bay, created prosaically enough during the nineteenth century by dumping a great deal of soil on top of a great expanse of mudflats, had had its day of glory. In 1883, King's *Handbook of Boston* said of "the grand Back Bay section," that "these broad and handsome streets are lined with imposing and stately edifices, the architectural designs of which, in many cases, are most ambitious and elaborate."

Alas for stateliness, many of these ambitious and elaborate edifices have been chopped up into apartments and rooming houses or adapted to various other purposes, some of which the illustrious architects of Grover Cleveland's administration would have held in horror. Somehow or other, Bartolo Arbalest had got hold of a property that had remained pretty much as it had been built. Either he'd bought the house outright, though God only knew what it must have cost him, considering real-estate prices in the area, or else he'd found a landlord desperate enough for a paying tenant to let him do as he pleased.

Perhaps Arbalest saw his atelier through the eyes of love, or maybe he thought smocks and berets made up for the overall air of bleakness and the unavoidable clutter on the long tables at which the artisans were working. Brooks, a man of many parts, all of them in excellent working order, saw at once what was wrong and how to fix it. The basement level, once the cozy domain of the cook and the servant's hall, had been converted into a brightly lighted space about as cheery and inviting as a sardine cannery.

"I think your problem here is less of space than of efficiency, Mr. Arbalest," he said briskly. "These long tables and backless benches are no doubt picturesquely reminiscent of the Middle Ages, but they must be hellishly inconvenient and uncomfortable to work at. Furthermore, keeping all the supplies jumbled together on those big shelves at the back of the room means that everyone must have to keep hopping up and down to get what he needs. I'd strongly recommend dividing the room up into separate cubicles, each with sufficient work space, shelves, and cabinets to meet the artisan's specific needs, not to mention a comfortable swivel chair on casters to keep him from breaking his back. You also ought to have individually arranged lighting instead of just those overhead fluorescents."

Brooks warmed to his new role. "This gentleman here on the end, for instance, obviously needs a sturdy turntable that could be raised and lowered with a foot pedal, leaving his hands free for his work. He also needs a rack for his chisels with an attached holder for his oilstone, a shaded drop light, and no doubt a few other things which I'd be glad to discuss with you, Mr.—"

Arbalest picked up his cue. "Oh, I beg your pardon. Mr. Brooks, this is Mr. Laer, our specialist in wood carving. Mr. Brooks and his assistant, Mr.—ah—Tickle, are here to see what we can do about improving conditions in the atelier for your greater convenience. Please, everyone, express your feelings and ideas to these gentlemen freely, you know I'm always ready to go along with whatever is in your best interests. Mr. Brooks, why don't I just introduce you and Mr. Tickle to our artisans and leave you to poke around all you like? I have some work to do upstairs, we can discuss your recommendations later on. Might we persuade you both to join us for dinner and one of our round-table discussions?"

Brooks and Max exchanged glances. They hadn't bargained for such an open-arms reception. All they'd need now would be Lydia bouncing back from the church, flinging herself with Slavic enthusiasm upon Max the beautiful detective and expressing loud hopes that he'd come for the purpose of investigating her personally and in detail.

"Thank you," said the beautiful detective, "but I have a previous commitment. I believe Mr. Brooks does also. Would it bother you, Mr. Laer, if I took a few measurements?"

Mr. Laer said he didn't care what they did so long as they didn't mess around with his chisels. He went on with his work; Max and Brooks began doing what they'd ostensibly come for. Upstairs they'd hastily fitted themselves out with what architects' props Arbalest could provide: a steel tape, a charming though anachronistic ivory slide rule, and a couple of yellow writing pads. They'd brought pencils of their own and plied them busily. Brooks, being Brooks, threw himself wholeheartedly into the job, jotting down notes and drawing precise little sketches. Max flapped around zipping the steel tape in and out and fiddling with the slide rule, covering his pad with figures that didn't mean anything, trying not to look too knowledgeable about what was happening at the worktables.

Max's real interest was not in the studio but in the men working there. Goudge hadn't said much about Laer except that he seemed to be one of the more normal members of the guild. Max wondered how Goudge defined *normal*. He himself would not have cared to be alone for long with the wood-carver and his chisels; there was a shade too much fury in the way that Laer attacked his work, too little genuine affability in his laconic replies to Brooks's questions and suggestions. Max could see why the offspring of a man like this might prefer to conduct their paternal relationship by long-distance telephone.

Max wondered whether Arbalest had picked his artisans for their appearance as well as their skills, Laer fitted his role so aptly. He was stockily built, of medium height, five foot eight in his thick-soled boots, as Max determined by adroit use of the steel tape. Probably he was a few years younger than his grizzled beard would suggest. When he pushed back his beret to scratch his head Max saw that he was bald, perhaps that was why he didn't object to wearing the beret. His complexion was ruddy and weathered. Either Laer had worked outside a lot in his previous jobs or else he was the sort who went in for mountain climbing and camping outdoors in the wintertime. It seemed odd that a man of this type would choose to be cloistered with an overfed sybarite like Arbalest and spend his days in this stuffy basement where visitors were never allowed.

Laer must be a strong man, it showed just in the way his stubby fingers grasped his chisels. He'd rolled up the sleeves of his smock to the elbows, his bare arms showed muscles and sinews more genuinely impressive than any professional weight lifter's. His short, heavy-thighed legs supported a barrel-shaped torso that had no flabby bulges, his shoulders were massive from years of heavy lifting, his bull neck showed no sign of excess fat. A formidable man, Max decided.

An expert craftsman, Max had no doubt about that. At the moment, Laer was working on a small carved-mahogany cabinet that had been damaged in a fire, creating a new door to replicate the charred and battered remains that lay on the table beside him. There was just barely enough left of the old door to show what the pattern must have been; Laer was working along without hesitation or slip, not using any sort of guidelines that Max could see, checking his work by an occasional glance at the blackened fragments that had survived the fire. Max thought he'd like to know more about Peter Laer but this wasn't the time to get too personal. He added a few more bogus figures to the incoherencies on his pad and followed Brooks over to the next table.

There was nothing of the outdoorsman over here. Jacques Dubrec, the odd-job man, was tall, pale, fiftyish, and slight, though a certain puffiness around the jawline led Max to suspect a modest potbelly under the loose-hanging smock. His beard was no more than a modest, carefully trimmed goatee, coal black on the edges, pure white down the middle like a bobolink's back, or a baby skunk's. His hands were long-fingered and deft, his scholarly stoop went well with his thick-lensed glasses. Nearsightedness must be an advantage in his profession.

Max wondered whether Dubrec had been trained at a museum. The project he was working on would have daunted many experts, from the looks of the many fragments that had been carefully sorted out and prepared for resurrection. Before it got dropped or smashed, the piece had evidently been a porcelain ornament in the shape of a bird cage, bedizened with more flora and fauna than an Edwardian lady's Sunday hat. Bavarian, Max judged, designed for and possibly by Mad King Ludwig. Just picking up the pieces would have been a major undertaking. Put together, the thing must stand almost two feet high.

"I'll bet you're a whiz at jigsaw puzzles."

That was the kind of dumb remark the restorer was no doubt used to hearing from laymen. Dubrec didn't answer but flashed Max a smile that would have been pleasanter if his teeth had been in better condition, and went on studying the shard he was holding and the

assemblage he was about to stick it to. He had to be absolutely
certain that he knew precisely where and how the two must fit together, but not let them touch for fear he might cause some infinites-
imal speck of further damage to the fractured edges. Once Dubrec's
mind was firmly made up, he applied the thinnest possible line of
epoxy glue, the colorless kind, to just the middle of the break. This
would flow out toward the edges when the pieces were fitted together, making a perfect bond and adding no thickness that could
cause problems as more bits were attached.

Some of the ornamentation would be missing: petals gone from
the roses, chips out of the birds' beaks and feathers, nicks at joints
where a perfect fit had not been possible. Dubrec would mix chalk
with his epoxy, fill in the breaks, tint the filler to match perfectly with
its surroundings.

Arbalest must be charging a bundle for this job, but the effect
would be worth the trouble and expense. By the time Dubrec got
through, there wouldn't be a crack or a chip visible to the eye of
anyone except another Dubrec.

The artisan hadn't seemed to be minding the colleague who'd
been bawling out what was probably a dirty ballad in Gaelic, Swahili,
or possibly just heavily accented English ever since the visitors had
arrived; but he did obviously find the strangers themselves dis-
turbing. Brooks himself was too good a craftsman and Max too much
an admirer of fine craftsmanship not to respect Dubrec's need for
concentration. They got out of his way and went over to placate the
man who'd been so loudly courting their attention ever since they'd
entered the atelier.

Art Queppin was as fat, hairy, and red-faced as Carnaby Goudge
had described him, maybe even more so. His beard was a great
tangle of reddish fuzz. His beret was shoved to the back of his head,
his smock open halfway down his hairy sweaty chest. At close range,
his ballad turned out to be in an atrocious imitation of Scottish
dialect and was about a bonnie wee lassie who never said no. Queppin appeared to be running something like an assembly line, his table
was covered with paintings in various stages of being restored. One
canvas was being relined, a wood panel was in the far more drastic
process of having its painted surface completely detached from the
rotted and worm-eaten wood and transferred to a sound new back-
ing.

The painting could not be seen at this stage, it was being stabilized by a sort of cardboard made by pasting first a layer of cotton, then layers of newspaper over its surface. Each layer had to dry overnight, then another would be pasted over it until a thickness of about a quarter of an inch had been achieved. Eventually Art Queppin, or more likely his as-yet-invisible assistant the dauber and chipper, working from the back, would scrape away the old wood down to the gesso ground on which the actual painting had been done. Then the new canvas would be applied and Bartolo Arbalest would collect another fee.

At the moment, Queppin was engaged in the less heroic process of mixing tiny puddles of paint and applying them with finicky dabs to the freshly cleaned surface of what must have been a sadly flaked floral painting by one of the less distinguished members of the Dutch School. He didn't mind a bit having company while he worked, he couldn't have been more cordial. The problem was that he didn't want to talk about improvements to his work space, he wanted to sing Max and Brooks all the verses of "Roll Me Over in the Clover."

It was no use. Try as they might, they could not shut their scatological serenader up long enough to get any sense out of him. The self-styled architects made play with their tapes and their pads until Queppin got to number eight and was knocking at the gate, then they thanked him for his splendid cooperation and went to find Marcus Nie.

Nie did have a room to himself, as Goudge had mentioned, but it wasn't much of one, just a walled-off slice of the laundry room. Despite the fact that the entire atelier was air-conditioned, no doubt as much for the artworks' protection as for the artisans' comfort, and that an exhaust fan was turned on in the one narrow, grated window, the air in here was flavored with fumes of turpentine, mineral spirits, denatured alcohol, and a few more exotic scents that Max didn't even want to think about. Thymol, he deduced, and ether, and maybe even a dash of cyanide; chemicals to be used rarely and with utmost discretion.

There was a long, shallow sink on the wall under the window that had the fan in it. This would be where the trickier processes were carried out. The restorations they were doing here might not be precisely museum quality, but then most of the pieces Arbalest's elves were working on wouldn't be up to museum standards, either.

Not that there wasn't a lot of stuff in museums that Max Bittersohn himself wouldn't have given house room to; and furthermore, much of the restoring that had been done by alleged experts over the centuries ought better to have been classed as vandalism. As far as Max could see, Bartolo's artisans were turning out work that was as good as most and a damned sight better than some he'd run into. He turned his attention away from technique and toward the technician.

Marcus Nie would never be hanged for his beauty. His head was shaped much like an old-time cheese box, long and angular, covered with yellowish skin that sagged down in folds like an elderly bloodhound's. The hair on top was fair, sparse, and fine, plastered down with some kind of goo to let the yellow scalp shine through, meandering down along the sides of his face in the shape that Sarah's grandfather would have called Dundreary weepers, stopping short of the chin as if Nie hadn't felt it worthwhile to play out the farce to its end.

Nie was probably as tall as Dubrec. It was hard to tell, the way he was hunched over a large drafting table with that voluminous smock hanging around him, but his arms were long and so were his badly stained hands. He had on a black-rubber photographer's apron, transparent plastic cuffs were pulled up over his sleeves. He paid no attention to the two visitors but went on soaking bits of cotton in whatever solvent he was using—most likely a standard mixture of denatured alcohol and turpentine—and dabbing at the dirty, darkened shellac on the canvas before him.

Sure enough, this was an animal painting: a head-on portrait of two remarkably stupid-looking sheep and a handsome goat with longish tawny golden fleece, great curly horns, and a disconcertingly knowing expression. If this was supposed to be one of those Victorian moral allegories, then Max Bittersohn's money was on the goat.

11

Getting Marcus Nie to take an interest in the possible refurbishment of his workroom was a lost cause from the start. Even Brooks, who could coax a friendly tweet out of a hermit thrush, wasn't able to raise anything more than a curt, "It's okay the way it is."

He and Max poked around a while, dodging piles of stretchers and plywood sandwiches that lay on the concrete floor, held down by concrete blocks and concealing bulged canvases that were being flattened out by this simple process for cleaning and restretching. Sure at last that Nie wasn't going to open up, they called it quits and went looking for the one member of the household on whom they hadn't yet laid eyes.

They found her in the kitchen with a half-peeled onion in her hand and tears on her cheek. The mound on the chopping board gave out a pretty strong hint about the evening's menu.

"Onion soup tonight, eh?" chirped Brooks. "You must be Katya. Our friend Lydia Ouspenska told us about you."

Katya was obviously pleased to be noticed, but disturbed by two strange men roaming loose in the house. "Mr. Arbalest not like—"

"Mr. Arbalest knows we're here, don't worry about that. He wants us to make plans for remodeling the kitchen. How would you like some nice cabinets where you can store things out of the way and not be having to dust them all the time?"

This room had surely not been the original kitchen. It must have been installed sometime in the 1930s when the original huge basement kitchen and scullery, geared to a way of life that had depended largely on cheap immigrant servants, had become impractical and been phased out of the household's operations. The one in which Katya was peeling her onions was also long overdue for an updating; if Arbalest was such an ardent amateur chef, why hadn't he already done something about it?

Money, most likely. Having to change his base of operations couldn't have been cheap. Cross-country moving would have been hellishly expensive even if he'd driven himself in a rented truck. Setting up housekeeping in Boston, along with providing board, room, and salaries for his strangely assorted household, must be making a big dent every month in however much income the Resurrection Man was able to generate and collect.

Furbishing up the house might have called for more flair than cash. Some of the furniture had probably come with the place. Arbalest would have known how to collect more at bargain prices, his artisans could have spruced it up for him. They could even have helped with painting and papering, though that would be like using racehorses to pull a plow. Maybe he'd just decided to stick with what was already here and screw in weaker light bulbs; that entrance hall had been pretty crepuscular and the shades in the drawing room had been most of the way down. His wood-paneled office with its wall of bookshelves would have needed nothing more than a rub-up with butcher's wax to look opulent, no wonder Arbalest had chosen to conduct his interview there.

But kitchen remodeling would have required a good deal more than flair. Cabinets, stoves, sinks, refrigerators, and dishwashers didn't come cheap, and what would have been the point in spending cold cash on a room that nobody but himself and a none-too-bright maid of all work would be spending any time in? Much cheaper for Arbalest to extol his kitchen's period charm and proclaim in loud and plummy tones what a crime against aesthetics it would be to change one priceless inch of this deliciously camp survival from the Art Deco period.

He might even be right. Sarah had taken on in a similar vein when Max had tried to get her to swap the ancestral potato masher for a food processor; although her arguments had been more along the lines of Yankee skepticism as to whether newer was in fact better and, if it wasn't broke, why fix it?

Time was beginning to press, they still had to talk to Arbalest again and it behooved them to be out of there before Lydia got back. Nevertheless, Max wasn't quite ready to leave Katya alone with her onions. One of the kitchen's few amenities was a large window that let in plenty of light and commanded a wide view of the alley, not that there was much to see except back fences, trash bins, and cars squeezed into straight and narrow parking places.

"Nice view," he said. "You like looking out, Katya?"

"Yiss."

"Do you ever see a man in a red suit doing his exercises out there?"

"Yiss. Funny. Jump."

Max had envisioned Katya as short and chunky, and he'd been right. Her once-blonde hair was pulled back into a skimpy knot with straggling ends, she had on a green wash-and-wear uniform and white nurses' shoes. It was a trifle startling to watch her lay aside a partially denuded onion and start bouncing up and down, clapping her hands over her head even though she was still holding the paring knife, laughing like a child.

After a few bounces, she stopped short, wiped the grin off her face, and looked around for her onion. Max presented it to her with a courtly bow.

"Very nice, Katya. Do you see the man often?"

"No. Only sometimes. Too bad."

"Mr. Arbalest comes in here and helps you with the cooking, doesn't he?"

"He cooks. I only good for peel and boil water."

"Then Mr. Arbalest must be in the kitchen a good deal of the time. Does he ever watch the man in the red suit do his exercises?"

"Yiss. Not like."

"Why not?"

Katya's only answer was a spreading of the hands and a hunching of the shoulders. She turned back to her chopping board and picked up yet another onion, it was time to leave her to complete her aromatic chore.

As they went looking for Arbalest's office, Max remarked, "I suppose you noticed the grille on the window?"

"Yes," Brooks replied, "very interesting. The one in Bartolo's office also unlatches from the inside. Want me to nip into the drawing room and check it out too?"

"Why don't we just ask Arbalest?"

"By all means ask me anything you like."

The man of the house must have overheard, he came out through an open door just ahead of them. They looked in and saw a dining room glorious with damask, china, silver, and crystal; Arbalest had evidently been setting the table. It was hard to picture Nie or Laer at ease in so resplendent an ambience, Max wondered if they changed into fresh smocks for dinner. Of course it would be more medieval to come to the table dirty. Max was as well pleased he and Brooks wouldn't be staying to share the meal.

"I suppose you want to talk to me," Arbalest was saying a bit fretfully. "Shall we go into my office?"

"Just for a minute, if you can spare the time," said Max. "I think your maid's got the onions all chopped."

"You've been talking to Katya, then?"

"We've been talking to everybody, but they weren't talking back much. Did you pick your artisans for their lack of conversation?"

"Oh, they chat freely enough when they're not working. Most of them, anyway. I suppose Queppin sang for you?"

"If that's what it was. Tell us something, Mr. Arbalest. We notice you have grilles on all your windows. Do they come open from the inside?"

"Yes, certainly, I'd be terrified if they didn't. What if there was a fire? It's too appalling to think of anyone's being locked in. I'm not running a jail here, you know, I'm just trying to protect my clients' valuable possessions."

"And your artisans?"

"Naturally. They're fully aware of our need to take proper precautions; I made sure they understood the security rules before they moved in, and would be willing to cooperate. Anybody who wasn't willing didn't get hired, it's that simple."

"Then in fact everybody's free to come and go as they please?"

"Within reason. Naturally I expect my artisans to work during business hours and to return at a reasonable hour if they go out in the evenings, simply because nobody wants to get up in the middle of the night to let them in."

"They don't have door keys?"

"What would be the good? There'd still be the chains to release, and there's no way to do that from outside unless one's remembered to take along a hacksaw. These are simply the normal precautions any householder living in a big city has to take nowadays, Mr. Bittersohn, as you surely realize."

"You don't have an alarm system?"

"No. They cost too much to install and there's always the chance of setting them off when you don't mean to. I believe our present security system to be quite adequate, and so does Mr. Goudge."

"He ought to know. You say he always trails any member of your guild who leaves the house."

"Only for their own protection, Mr. Bittersohn."

"I understand that. But what if two of them go in opposite directions at the same time, or Goudge has to drive you out on a call?"

"I drove myself for a good many years, I expect I could do it again if I had to. But that's a good question. So far, the problem hasn't come up. Our people are so comfortable here that they just don't want to go anywhere, it seems. Of course we haven't been together all that long; they may start to get a bit restless after a while. Madame Ouspenska did yesterday, as you saw, but that was no problem. I simply invented a little errand for her to do, she had her outing and was back in good time. I suppose if everyone did start rushing off in all directions, we'd just have to find Mr. Goudge some assistance. I don't suppose you and Brooks—"

"Not in our line, I'm afraid. Goudge must know somebody."

"I suppose so." Arbalest grimaced. "More money going out, my overhead is frightful. But our artisans are all people of mature years, as you've seen for yourself. Maturity was one of the things I looked for. Along with superior skills, of course. I sometimes think I must be an obtuse man in some respects, but I do try to learn from experience. I'm confident that this arrangement will work."

The mask of calm urbanity was slipping. "It has to work. I can't fail again. Brooks, you're my friend. For God's sake, help me!"

The telephone on Arbalest's desk emitted a genteel buzz. He swallowed once, composed his features, and picked up the handset. "Hello? Yes, Goudge. No, just the heavy cream. Thank you. Then we'll see you shortly."

He turned back to his visitors, his expression bland, his voice steady. "Goudge was phoning from the car. He's about to do a small errand, then he and Madame Ouspenska will be coming back to the house. Unless they get stuck in traffic, they should be here in ten minutes or so. Perhaps you gentlemen would prefer—"

"We would," Brooks assured him. "Nice to see you again, Bartolo, we'll be in touch."

Max picked up his cane and started to get up. "One quick question, Mr. Arbalest. Why don't you like that man in the red suit?"

Arbalest was taken aback. "What man?"

"Your neighbor who does exercises in the alley. Katya says you don't like him."

"Katya. I'm sorry, I ought to have explained about Katya. She's a dear, sweet soul and a capable worker within her sphere of comprehension. Like myself, however, she has her limitations. Her mental age, as far as I've been able to figure out, is about six and a half; her life is one long fairy tale. Or else she needs glasses, I hadn't thought of that. Perhaps I ought to have Goudge take her to get her eyes tested. I do thank you most profoundly for coming, gentlemen. Please let me know if Mrs. Percy Kelling gets her girl with parrot back, it's really quite a nice little primitive."

Polite as he was, Arbalest couldn't get rid of his visitors fast enough. They'd barely got through the door before they heard him locking it behind them.

"Well," said Brooks as they reached the sidewalk, "that was an interesting visit. What did you make of it?"

"For one thing, that Arbalest must be every bit as obtuse as he thinks he is if he honestly believes his workmen don't come and go as they please," Max answered. "Those first-floor windows can't be more than eight feet from the ground; Nie and Dubrec are both tall and Laer's powerful. Queppin might have a little trouble getting in and out if he's as fat and flabby as he looks in that goofy smock. Unless he keeps a collapsible ladder under his bed."

"As well he might," Brooks agreed. "It further occurs to me that a craftsman as good as Dubrec ought to be a handy fellow with a picklock. I don't say he's made keys to fit all the locks and fixed the door chains so that they can easily be slipped apart from outside, but I do suggest that he probably could if he put his mind to it. I could, myself, though perhaps not so artistically."

Brooks was no braggart, he was merely stating a fact, and Max believed him. "I know you could, and so could Dubrec. If not for money, then just for fun, like Wouter Tolbathy."

The late Wouter Tolbathy had been a man of uncanny technical abilities, and even uncannier notions of how best to use them. He'd been a great friend of Sarah's Uncle Jem. Max had never met Wouter alive but had been forced on two occasions to cope with the horrible consequences of his merry pranks. Max wished he hadn't thought of Wouter Tolbathy. Despite the heat that had been building up in the pavement all day, he could feel his blood running cold.

"For God's sake, Brooks, tell me I'm wrong."

"We can but hope, Max. The world's a frightening enough place these days without another Wouter Tolbathy running loose in it. You mentioned Queppin; is he the jovial Falstaffian egoist he lets on to be, or was it just that he knew who you were and was afraid to talk?"

"I wondered that, myself. It could have been you he recognized. It could also be that Queppin's mother taught him not to talk to strangers, or else that he's just an arrogant bastard."

"Oh, he's certainly an arrogant bastard." Brooks paused to scrutinize a foraging sparrow, shrugged, and walked on. "The question is whether he's something more than that."

"Since you're asking, I'd say probably. I can't see anybody as avid to show off in front of an audience as Queppin appears to be committing himself to a setup like Arbalest's, unless he's in fairly desperate need of cover."

"The thought did cross my mind that Bartolo might be running a hostel for talented knaves. What did you think of Laer?"

"I thought I wouldn't want him standing behind me with a chisel in his hand. The guy could just have been steamed at us for barging in and interrupting his work; he was certainly mad as hell about something. It could have been paranoia, I suppose, though I rather favor Nie for staff fruitcake. What do you think?"

"Well, Nie does seem to breathe in fumes day in and day out. They might have pickled his intellect, though the room's adequately ventilated and I shouldn't think he'd be working with them all day long. He evidently helps Queppin with the dog work; from the number of canvases they had sitting around, there's obviously plenty to do. I shouldn't be surprised to learn that Nie's on drugs. You don't by any chance suppose one of the others is his supplier?"

"Arbalest, for instance? It's a thought. That would be one way to keep up the insurance on his Rolls-Royce."

12

A rhubarb leaf?" yelped Max. "What the hell for?"

Sarah laughed. "For obvious reasons, I should think. If the man entered through the greenhouse vent, and I honestly couldn't see how else he got in, then he'd never have made it in a baggy sweat suit. I didn't measure the opening, but it can't be more than a foot and a half square. Anne described him as a skinny little fellow. I assumed he'd peeled down to get through the hole and, while he was inside stealing the painting, some animal came along and swiped his clothes."

"What animal?"

"A dog, maybe. More likely a raccoon, if there was any food in the pockets. They'll eat anything and they're very skillful thieves. Isn't that right, Brooks?"

"On the button, Sarah. That's why raccoons have been so successful in adapting themselves to city and suburban environments. They're clever, strong, and they don't wear those black burglar masks for nothing. If there was any food in the pocket, a dog would simply have ripped up the clothes to get at it. A raccoon would have carried them well away from the house, then rifled the pockets. They have hands, you know, not just paws. They grow as big as dogs and they're nasty fighters. If I were buck naked in a stranger's garden and some raccoon had got hold of my clothes, I don't think I'd care to risk a tug of war to get them back."

"Okay," said Max, "I'll grant you the raccoon, but what happened to the painting?"

"Maybe the man had it hidden away in the garden and took it with him when he went off in Anne's clothes. More likely he'd handed it out to an accomplice, who'd driven off with it not realizing that the thief himself had been robbed."

"But Sarah dear," said Theonia, "why couldn't the two of them have gone off together? What would have been the sense in leaving the man in the red suit—or rather the man not in the red suit, assuming he did in fact have one to take off—to find his own way back to wherever he'd come from?"

"Perhaps because he wanted to be seen?"

"Not as an exhibitionist, surely, or why would he have bothered with the rhubarb leaf?"

"No, I think it would have been the red suit that Anne, or at least somebody, was intended to notice. That would have been such an odd thing to have on at this time of year. Charles mentioned yesterday how out-of-place the man in Arbalest's alley looked in his red jogging suit on such a hot day. And that one was jumping around, apparently doing all he could to attract Charles's attention short of grabbing his arm and shouting in his ear. Katya gave you to understand he puts on the same performance whenever he sees her or Mr. Arbalest watching out the kitchen window. But what really convinced me the red suit means something was when Anora told us about poor old George getting out of his chair to watch a Tamil in a red jogging suit run across their lawn the afternoon before he was killed."

"You take that as proof positive?" said Brooks.

"Absolutely. Maybe you don't realize what an earth-shattering event it was for George Protheroe to stir his stumps just because somebody ran through his yard, but I do. That sort of thing just isn't done in Chestnut Hill, at least not in broad daylight right under the residents' noses unless one has a pretty sound reason, like chasing a runaway child or at least a family pet. And in that case, the runner would have stopped to ask George if he'd seen a stray Sealyham or whatever. You know that. Naturally he'd want the neighbors to know he wasn't galloping through their pachysandra just for the fun of it. Anyway, that's my theory. Does anybody have a better one?"

Nobody had, they gave Sarah the benefit of the doubt and decided to take their coffee out in the garden. After Anne Kelling's magnificently landscaped acres, Brooks's staid little beds of marigold and alyssum didn't do much for Sarah.

"I was hoping we might get out to Ireson's Landing for the week-end," she remarked wistfully, "but with Anora in such a pickle and so much else happening, I don't suppose—oh, hello, Charles. What's the matter? Is Davy awake?"

"It's Mr. Goudge, moddom. He's cometh."

"Like the iceman. I wish they still had them, I'd have liked a ride in his wagon. All right, Charles, show him out here and bring the brandy. Max, you don't think Mr. Arbalest's sent him to bodyguard us?"

Max didn't think so at all. He thought Mr. Goudge wanted a first-hand report on the visit to the atelier, and he couldn't have been more right.

"Good evening," said Goudge. "Kind of you to see me. Mr. Brooks and Mr. Twister, was it?"

"No," said Max, "but what difference does it make? That's quite a setup you've moved into, Goudge. Would it be tactless to inquire where Nie gets hold of whatever he's on, and who's using the windows as a means of egress and ingress?"

"Quite tactless and fairly useless," Goudge replied readily. "Nie never goes out, he receives no mail or packages. I can only assume he gets his jollies from sniffing that hell brew he uses to clean the paintings. As for the windows, you no doubt refer to the inside latches which your eagle eye would of course have discerned in a trice."

"Two trices," said Max. "One trice for Brooks and one for me. He triced first."

"How nice for him. The object of the latches, as Mr. Arbalest may perhaps have explained, is to keep the inmates from being fried should any of those combustible fluids in the atelier decide to combust. As one of the inmates, I find my employer's precaution wholly commendable. As to the egress and ingress, what you would not have been able to notice, though I do think you might have surmised, is that I have all the latches electronically bugged. Should a latch be opened, the occurrence will register on a board in my bedroom by means of a buzz and a flashing light. Being a light sleeper and a fast dresser, I will then leap from my bed and be downstairs in time to find out who's up to what, and possibly even why."

"Do you catch many?"

"Business has been disappointingly slow. So far the only one I've caught was Queppin. He got stuck in the window and I had to help him get unplugged. He explained his purpose, I got the car and drove him to his appointment. He invited me to accompany him inside and be introduced to one of the lady's business associates. I demurred on the grounds that it would not be safe to leave the Rolls unattended in that neighborhood, this being the response I deemed least likely either to wound his sensibilities or to arouse his derision."

"Tactful of you."

"I am always tactful. I suggested that I go back and pick him up in an hour's time, he agreed that an hour would suffice. I parked in a convenient spot where I could maintain surveillance, met him as arranged, and drove him back to the house. Since then I have taken him on similar errands at less inconvenient hours, with the stipulation that he refrain from singing in the car." Goudge offered his small apology for a smile. "Queppin's quite a lavish tipper."

"Couldn't somebody else have sneaked out of the house while you were off on some such errand?" Brooks asked.

"Oh yes, but I'd know the latch had been opened because the light on my board would have remained on. I'd then take a surreptitious nose count to ascertain who was missing and be on hand to assist at the reentry. The inmates all know I'm a chronic insomniac, or think they do; they wouldn't make anything of my happening to be up and about at odd hours."

"Even when you were peeking into their bedrooms?"

"They wouldn't know I was peeking. One of my small domestic tasks is to keep all the door hinges well oiled."

"A thoroughly admirable Crichton," murmured Theonia.

"Thank you, Mrs. Kelling. I modestly admit to being all that and then some. Would it be impertinent of me to ask your husband whether my name came up during the conversation with Mr. Arbalest?"

"I don't suppose so. Would it be impertinent, Brooks dear?"

"Not at all. The answer is yes, but not in any adversely critical sense. Bartolo mentioned, for instance, that you agreed with him as to the tightness of your house security system."

"Which must have surprised you."

"Yes, but we hadn't been shown up to your bedroom. Bartolo also said something about having you take Katya to have her eyes tested."

"Did he, indeed? Whatever for, I wonder?"

"While we were chatting with her in the kitchen, it developed that she, like our man Charles, claims to have seen a man in a red jogging suit doing exercises in the alley. By an interesting coincidence, your late client George Protheroe, who as you no doubt recall was found murdered yesterday morning, told his wife the afternoon before that he'd seen a man in a red jogging suit cutting through their yard. He thought the man might have been a Tamil."

Goudge raised his eyebrows a trifle. "What a strange thing for Mr. Protheroe to have thought. Why a Tamil?"

"Why not?" Sarah broke in. She was rather annoyed by Goudge's air of gentle derision. "George had traveled extensively in the Orient, he'd known lots of Tamils and could even speak the language. His wife was inclined to think he knew what he was talking about. Furthermore, my Cousin Percy Kelling's wife, the one who was robbed of that American Primitive painting you'd just taken back to her, had what may have been a related experience this morning. Would you like to hear about it?"

"If you'd like to tell me."

Goudge's voice was courteous and colorless as usual, but a flicker of perturbation had crossed his face. As Sarah told, the perturbation grew to anger.

"Damn! Oh, I do apologize, Mrs. Bittersohn, that was quite unpardonable of me. But all this talk about little brown men in red jogging suits does tend to get under one's skin."

"We couldn't agree with you more," said Brooks. "Would you care to tell us why you tried so hard last night to convince us that the man was only a clothes rack, why Katya claims that Bartolo doesn't like him, and why Bartolo lied to us this afternoon when we'd told him what Katya had said about seeing him in the alley?"

"That's rather a staggering question, don't you think? And a somewhat cheeky one, if I may say so."

Brooks Kelling refused to be insulted. "Cheek for cheek, Goudge. On the contrary, I'd say the question's about as pertinent as it can get. This is twice you've come to us fishing for information. It's not that we don't enjoy playing games with you, but we're not going to get far if you insist on trying to keep all the aces up your sleeve. Now would you care to answer my question, or would you prefer to cash in your chips and go home?"

"You do believe in laying it on the line, don't you? Naturally I'd rather stay in the game, Mr. Kelling, but the embarrassing fact is that I simply cannot answer your question, at least not the way you want me to. All right, I lied about the acrobat in the alley. I did so because Mr. Arbalest had let me know quite emphatically, though not in so many words, that the subject was not one he cared to have discussed. Being a loyal employee, by and large, I conceived it my duty to cover for him. I don't suppose he cautioned Katya. She wouldn't have grasped what he was talking about and it wouldn't have accomplished anything if she did. Katya seldom gets to see anyone but himself, except when she's helping me serve the meals, and she does know enough not to chatter in the dining room."

"What if somebody's sick in bed? Wouldn't she have to wait on them?"

"Perish the thought. That's the butler's job."

"Doesn't she ever go out of the house?"

"Never. She'd only get lost unless someone went with her, and so far nobody's offered. Katya's really quite dim, you know."

"Then who does the grocery shopping?"

"Mr. Arbalest himself, with his faithful dogsbody tagging along to push the cart and carry the bundles. Occasionally I'm given the privilege of performing some small commission on my own. Only this afternoon I negotiated the purchase of a pint of cream without supervision. And, as you know, Madame Ouspenska was recently allowed the even rarer privilege of buying a teaspoonful of truffles. That required some rather fancy footwork on my part, I may add. Once I'd seen her safely to the house, Mr. Arbalest himself opened the door for her as previously arranged and engaged her in conversation, giving me time enough to whip around to the back door, let myself in, meet her in the front hall with my little silver tray at the ready, and carry the truffles back to the kitchen with due reverence and circumspection."

"The inmates, as you call them, aren't allowed in the kitchen?"

"Let's say they're not encouraged. If they want anything, they have but to ask and it shall be given unto them, usually by your humble servant, sometimes by Mr. Arbalest himself. If he and I are going to

be out in the evening, I prepare a tray of drinks and snacks and make
sure the candy dishes are filled so that our birds won't have to go
prowling for extra goodies. If any of them did go to the kitchen, they
wouldn't find her there. Once dinner is cleared away, Katya retires to
her own room and watches television. As to whatever she told you
this afternoon, it was probably the truth or a reasonable approxima-
tion. Katya hasn't wits enough to think up a lie."

"Bartolo seems to think she has, though he called it a fairy tale."

"He would. That's Mr. Arbalest's métier, after all, fixing things up
to look pretty. Lies are ugly, fairy tales are cute. In fact, of course,
they tend to be fairly bloodcurdling, only we kiddies aren't supposed
to notice the grue. So anyway, there you have it."

"Have what?" said Max. "Tell us about the man in the red suit. I
assume you've seen him yourself."

"Oh yes, but I haven't much to tell. I can't see anything remarkable about him. He might be a Tamil, or a Frenchman, or a
Prooshian for all I know; he's quite dark, short, and probably slight,
though it's hard to tell. That red jogging suit that you've mentioned
so often is on the voluminous side. Unlike your wife's cousin, I've
never had the chance to see him in his rhubarb leaf; assuming he is
in fact the same chap, which seems, with all respect to Mrs. Percy
Kelling, most unlikely."

"Does he always wear the suit?"

"I have no way of knowing. He's worn it on the occasions when
I've seen him, or else I may have seen him at other times in other
garb and not recognized him. If you were about to ask me why I
suppose he wears such a heavy garment in August, I would venture
to suggest (a) that he may be fresh from the jungles of Malaysia and
feel the cold here even though we find it hot, (b) that he has nothing
else to wear, (c) that he likes his red suit, or (d) that he wants to look
noticeable when he's doing his exercises so that he won't get clob-
bered by a sanitation truck bombing through the alley to pick up the
garbage. Further than that, I'm afraid I can't go. My powers of imagination are very limited."

"What about Arbalest's?"

"That's another delicate question. I can only say that Mr. Arbalest, since he does most of the cooking, is in the kitchen far more
than I; ergo, he has many more opportunities to observe our enigmatic neighbor. Katya's there with him often as not, keeling pots,

bashing spuds, or whatever she does. The culinary arts are quite beyond me. Anyway, I assume she's noticed Mr. Arbalest watching the little brown man with distaste and sensed his air of revulsion. Katya does have that same primitive way dogs have of picking up people's feelings. You might be able to get more out of her than you have out of me, though I doubt very much that you'll be given another opportunity. Not to hurt your feelings, but I don't think Mr. Arbalest wants to see you again."

Goudge shot out his wrist and glanced at his remarkable watch. "Oh dear, I must get along, it's almost time to take Mr. Queppin for his weekly outing. Shall I say au revoir, or must it be adieu?"

"Oh, let's make it au revoir," said Max. "You fascinate us, Goudge. Have a nice trip. The butler will see you out."

The basement door had been left ajar, he raised his voice. "Hey, Charlie, put your pants back on, Mr. Goudge is leaving."

"Yes, sir. At once, sir. This way please, Mr. Goudge."

"Good thing one of us has some class," Max remarked when the departing guest had been properly sped. "I hope you all enjoyed that little bedtime story. Too bad Davy had to miss it."

"It does seem a pity, when Mr. Goudge tried so hard," Sarah agreed. "Does he really underestimate his own powers of invention, or did Mr. Arbalest have second thoughts about needing our help and send him here to warn us off?"

"I expect we shall know when the time comes." Theonia indicated the decanter with a stately nod. "Would anyone care for a spot more brandy?"

Nobody would. They sat watching the bats snapping up bugs under the gaslight in the alley until Sarah noticed Max trying to get more comfortable in his lawn chair and not succeeding. She picked up his cane for him, Brooks picked up the brandy snifters, Theonia picked up the decanter, they all picked up their heels and went in to bed.

13

Disgusting!" Sarah was much too properly brought up to hurl the morning paper across the room, she folded it back together with a petulant swipe of her hand and handed it to Mariposa. "Here, use it to line the garbage pail. Why can't those ghouls let up on poor old Anora? Has she phoned yet?"

"Nope, I'd tell you, wouldn't I? Dave, you quit playin' with that egg an' get down to business, or I don't give you no tortilla to take with you on the swan boat. No sense holdin' out your cup, Señor Max, you already drunk up all the coffee an' I ain't makin' any more."

The alleged man of the house snorted. "Well, you're in a gorgeous mood this morning. What's the matter, Mariposa? Charles giving you a hard time?"

"He wouldn't dare. Some fool kid climbed over the back fence an' started poundin' on the back door about two o'clock. Woke me up an' I couldn't get back to sleep. You know me if I don't get my sleep."

"What did the kid want?"

"You think I'm dumb enough to open the door an' ask? I come up to kitchen an' hollered out the window. I says what do you want? He just up an' over the fence like a monkey, I never seen nobody move so fast. Might have been my cousin Tito, he's goin' to get an earful next time I see him."

"You didn't get a good look at his face?" said Sarah.

"Nope. All I saw was a skinny backside in red joggin' pants whizzin' up over the fence. Tito wears red joggin' pants, that's how come I thought of him."

"But surely Tito wouldn't have run away from you, Mariposa."

"Hey, right on, now that you mention it. Tito'd have hung around and tried to hit me up for a loan. Sarah, I don't like this."

"Neither do I. Maybe Brooks had better string some barbed wire above that fence."

Sarah didn't feel like elaborating. Charles must have told Mariposa about the man in the alley behind Marlborough Street, but as far as Sarah knew, nobody had told either of them about the red-garbed runner George Protheroe had seen the day before he died, nor about Anne's nudist with the rhubarb leaf. Could it possibly have been the same man each time?

Anyway, it was reasonable enough to surmise that Mariposa's late-night visitor had been the man from Marlborough Street; or rather from Commonwealth Avenue if he lived on the opposite side of the alley. He must have followed Max and Brooks home yesterday after they'd visited the atelier. It would have been easy enough to do, now that Max had to walk so slowly. She ought to be grateful that Max was walking at all, she leaned over the table and gave him a rather ferocious kiss.

"I was thinking of taking a run out to Anora's and taking Davy with me, but now I'm not so sure. What do you think, dear?"

"I think you'd better wait to find out whether Anora wants either one of you. They're not having visiting hours at the funeral home, are they?"

"Oh no. Anora wasn't about to let herself in for a pack of sightseers, even if the police hadn't advised against it. She wouldn't even let the undertaker put an obituary notice in the paper, she just got her friends to phone around to people who might have reason to come. There'll be a mob anyway, I suppose. The Protheroes knew everybody."

"So she'll still have a lot to do getting ready for the funeral."

"That's true. It's ten o'clock tomorrow morning at the Church of the Redeemer, we ought to leave here about a quarter past nine. The service will be High Church, I suppose. Anora will want to talk with the vicar. Mrs. Harnett will pick her up, they'll have lunch somewhere. It shouldn't be too bad a day for Anora, considering. What about the office? Do you want me there today, or do I get to stay home with Davy?"

"You get to stay home with Davy. Brooks will be along in a while, and Theonia shouldn't be too late, I hope."

The older couple were both already out on company business. Brooks was with a professional photographer who had the facilities to make multiple prints of the sketch Sarah had made of the stolen primitive. Theonia, with Charles as chauffeur, had gone to call on an elderly gentleman who needed to be politely pried apart from a collection of Staffordshire figurines to which he had no legitimate claim.

Theonia had the advantage, though it hadn't seemed one at the time, of having once been married to a fairly accomplished swindler. Knowing what to expect and how to beat the old rogue at his own game, she'd anticipated being able to wind up the matter over a cozy luncheon at the gentleman's expense, return the figurines to their owner, collect her fee, and be home in time for tea. The family were betting on her to come back with both the figurines and a proposal of marriage.

Anora telephoned at half past nine. It was as Max had predicted: She had her day all organized for her, she didn't need Sarah, she'd see them at the funeral tomorrow morning. They'd be coming back to the house, of course; could she borrow Charles and Mariposa to help with the serving? Phyllis and Cook were both feeling the strain, and naturally they both wanted to attend their long-time employer's funeral.

"Of course," Sarah assured the widow. "They'll be delighted to help. We'll drop them off at your house on our way to the church, if that's all right."

It would mean starting earlier than Sarah had planned and getting a baby-sitter for Davy, but what else could she have said? Anora said that would be fine and hung up because Mrs. Harnett and Mrs. Pratch had arrived to take her to the church. Sarah turned to her trusty henchwoman.

"Mariposa, Anora wonders if you and Charles would be willing to take over at the reception after the funeral? Cook and Phyllis will be too pooped to do anything by the time they get back from the fu-neral, but they'll have organized the buffet in advance. It will be mostly a matter of bartending and passing things around."

"No sweat," said Mariposa. "How about if I bake a couple of my chocolate rum cakes to take with us, just in case?"

"That would be lovely. I'm afraid you'll have to wear that black uniform you don't like and take the orange ribbons off your cap. Anora has old-fashioned ideas about mourning."

"Yeah, sure. Anything for a pal. What'll we do about Davy?"

"I'm going to call Miriam and see if she'd mind coming in for the day."

By marrying Max, Sarah had gained a sister. Miriam Bittersohn Rivkin had many irons of her own in the fire but was never too busy to lend her younger brother and his wife a helping hand. She didn't like driving into Boston, as who in her right mind would, but she could park her car at the Prides Crossing station and come in by train if Sarah needed her; she was always willing to postpone her other engagements in the family's interests. On the other hand, the toys and the crib she kept ready for her only nephew had been too long unused. Why didn't Sarah bring Davy out today and let him sleep over?

Why not, indeed? Davy adored his aunt, his uncle, and particularly his grown-up Cousin Mike. He'd stayed with the Rivkins plenty of times, he wouldn't get homesick, he'd have room to run in their big backyard, he'd probably enjoy the visit more than they would. Now that skinny little men in red jogging suits had started climbing over the back fence at Tulip Street, Davy might be better off in Ireson Town than in Boston.

Sarah thanked Miriam and went to pack her son's blue canvas duffel bag with his toothbrush, a couple of changes of clothing, little boys' habits being what they were, and his stuffed llama who was named for Cousin Dolph Kelling. She needn't wait for Charles to get back with the big car, she could drive herself in the gas-saving compact that had been bought mostly for her and Brooks to use on short trips.

"No swan-boat ride today, Davy. You and I are going out to see Aunt Mimi and Uncle Ira, and you get to stay overnight. See, here's your bag, all packed. Let's phone daddy and tell him we're coming to kiss him good-bye, then we can walk back to the Common Garage and pick up the car."

Once he'd been assured that he could take Dolph along for company, Davy thought that was a great idea. So did Max.

"I'll meet you halfway if I can. At the moment, I've got a guy from Acapulco on the line."

"That's all right," Sarah assured him. "We're starting right now, before Davy has a chance to get dirty. We'll come past the frog pond and take the path that leads to the corner. If we don't find you along the way, we get to ride the elevator up to your office. All right, Davy, time to go."

Sarah buckled her son into his harness, knowing full well that she was going to get a few glances and quite possibly a scolding from some presumably well-meaning person who didn't think children should be treated like animals. Sarah didn't see why a small and particularly precious human being who hadn't yet learned to avoid hurtful and possibly life-threatening situations shouldn't be given as much protection as she'd have given a pedigreed pup. It would have been unthinkable to let Davy run loose in the city, and uncomfortable for his arm to have been kept upstretched for a parent's grasp, for his short legs to be always having to accommodate themselves to a grown-up's longer stride.

The easy-fitting red-webbing harness, with its silvery bells and its six-foot leash, enabled Davy to move freely within a safe radius, to set his own pace, to have both hands free for coaxing a squirrel or waving to a passing pigeon, to enjoy as many small adventures as a very little boy could comfortably handle without being a nuisance to other people or giving his mother heart attacks. Juggling her handbag and his duffel as well as the leash, Sarah couldn't help feeling a tad envious of her happily unencumbered child. When she caught the expected dirty looks, she smiled sweetly back and let Davy go on enjoying his walk while other parents screamed or tugged at their fleeing or whining offspring.

They paused for a minute or two at the frog pond to watch other children playing under the great spray of water, something Sarah hadn't been allowed to do as a little girl and wasn't about to let Davy try at so tender an age. They'd barely turned back to the path when Davy shouted, "Daddy!" and started to run. Fortunately his run was no faster than his mother's trot, so the rendezvous was accomplished without skinned knees.

"Hi, Dave." Max scooped up his son and settled him on the paternal shoulders, holding him by one leg and not seeming to mind being gripped around the neck.

Sarah took hold of Davy's other leg, telling herself that it wasn't far to the garage, that Davy wasn't going to fall, that Max wasn't about to die of strangulation or trip over his cane. They were almost to the garage entrance when a jogger brushed past them, smelling strongly of sweat; as well he might since today was even hotter than yesterday and the man was swathed from neck to ankles in a thick red jogging suit.

"There he goes," said Max. "My God, doesn't that guy ever sleep?"

"Are you sure it's the same one?" Sarah asked.

"Your guess is as good as mine, kid. Maybe the whole Tamil track team's over here training for next year's BAA Marathon. Look, would you like me to ride out to Miriam's with you?"

"Max, you don't really think that man's going to leap on a bicycle and follow us all the way to Ireson Town?"

"More likely I'm the one he's been following. He wouldn't have known what you look like. Only now he does, damn it."

"Not necessarily, unless he's peeking at me from behind a litter basket. Which he isn't, because there he goes. See, up by the Shaw Memorial. He's making very good time, he can't have stopped to look back."

"Maybe he's got a trusty see-back-o-scope, like Charles."

"Well, pooh to him, I'm not scared. Come if you'd like but don't feel you have to. Haven't you rather a full agenda for today?"

"First things first. Brooks will be back pretty soon, he can hold the fort for a couple of hours. I'll phone him from the car."

Now that car telephones were generally available, it would have been unthinkable for so dedicated a phoner as Max Bittersohn not to have one installed even in the little puddle-jumper. He spent a good part of the hour-long ride to the north shore first calling up the office to let Brooks know where he was and why, then checking around with various of his informants in unlikely places. Max's success in his odd profession was due not only to his doctorate in art history, his phenomenal memory, his expert's eye, and his flair for detection; but also to his knack for maintaining an almost worldwide network of useful informants and for never wincing at the size of his telephone bills.

Sarah concentrated on her driving, keeping a sharp eye out for any vehicle that might contain a Dravidian or reasonable facsimile in a red jogging suit, but she didn't see one. Davy was an experienced traveler, he sat back in his car seat and beguiled the time showing his llama the sights along the way, or catching a few winks so as to be fresh and rested for whatever adventures might be awaiting him at Aunt Mimi's.

What awaited them all, of course, was food. Miriam hadn't had time to do more than whip up a batch of prune muffins, a pot of corn chowder, and a magnificent garden salad to keep body and soul together in lieu of what she considered a decent meal. Dessert was a melon sorbet Miriam had made from scratch in her handy home ice-cream freezer, served with pizzelle fresh baked in a remarkably hi-tech reversible waffle iron she'd got for Mother's Day.

"This is marvelous, Miriam," Sarah commented. "And you're an angel to take Davy for us. I only hope we haven't got you into trouble."

Miriam Bittersohn Rivkin was a handsome woman, or could be when she got dressed up. Sartorial elegance was not her top priority, however, her present outfit of a venerable denim wrap skirt and one of her husband's old shirts was about as classy as she generally got around home. Her hair was naturally dark and wavy like Max's, but now showing a fair amount of gray. Another woman of her age might have started touching it up, Miriam believed in taking life as it came. She finished nibbling the spear of endive she'd fished out of the salad bowl and wiped the dressing off her fingers with a cotton-print napkin.

"How, for instance?"

"We don't really know," said Sarah. "There's this little man in a red jogging suit who keeps popping up. Charles saw him in an alley in the Back Bay, he passed us this morning as we were going into the Common Garage. Last night he climbed over our back fence and pounded on the basement door, then ran away. At least we think he was the one, Mariposa only saw the seat of his pants going back over the fence. You tell her, Max. Davy, why don't you eat your chowder with a spoon the way daddy does, instead of picking out the kernels with your fingers?"

"Max ate with his fingers when he was Davy's age," said Miriam. "So did Mike, it's probably hereditary. He'll grow out of it. So what else with the man in the red suit, Max?"

Her brother explained, she nodded. "That's interesting. But he hasn't actually done anything, has he? I mean, you don't seriously suppose he'd have gone running through the Protheroes' yard if he'd been planning to come back and shove a spear into that old man? And you don't really know whether he was the man in the rhubarb leaf, or that he stole Mrs. Percy's painting. Maybe he was trying to keep somebody else from stealing it and they took his clothes to get back at him. Maybe"—Miriam was ever on the side of the underdog —"you should try to make friends with him."

"How?" said Max. "Hold out a fortune cookie and whistle? Hey, Kätzele, not to break up the party, but I promised Brooks I'd be back by half past three. He's got a date with a bird of paradise."

"Well, he'd better not let Theonia know," Sarah replied rather crossly. "All right, then, if we must. Oh, I'll be so glad if we ever get to come home! Thanks for everything, Miriam. Whatever would we do without you?"

"I've often wondered," said her sister-in-law. "See you tomorrow. Or the day after is fine with me. Come on, Davy, let's fill your wading pool and give the llama a drink."

14

"Max," said Sarah, "would you mind if we swung by our house for just a minute?"

"Of course not." Max's glance was both tender and sober. "I feel like a louse for keeping you and Davy in town all summer."

"Darling, don't. Actually it's been rather fun. Some of it, anyway. We've had no problems managing your therapy, as we would have had out here. It proves how right we were to hang on to the Boston house, having a place of our own to stay in has made all the difference. Brooks and Theonia have been marvelous, though I expect they'll be well enough pleased to have the house to themselves when we move back here. It shouldn't be long now, should it?"

"About another three weeks, the doctor thinks."

"Then we'd better get on with finding someone to work full time in the office. I don't intend for either of us to be shuffling back and forth any more than we can help. What a pity Mike didn't decide on an art major."

Max shook his head. "Mike's a great kid, but he'll make a far better engineer than he would a detective. You know, Sarah, crazy as it sounds, that oldest boy of your Cousin Lionel's might not be such a bad assistant if he had the right training."

"Jesse? Are you out of your mind? Anyway, Jesse's not even in college yet and I can't imagine which one would take him. Unless there's a school that offers courses in vandalism and pillage."

"I don't know. I've talked to the kid a few times at those get-togethers your Aunt Appie puts on. He's sharp, he's got imagination, and he's resourceful, to put it mildly."

"Oh yes, Jesse's full of resources. So are his brothers. So were the Visigoths, I believe. I don't know though, Max, you could be right. Remember that time a mob of reporters tried to invade us from the beach and Lionel's boys held them off with a barrage of fish heads? I remember feeling quite proud of them, though not for long. I suppose you could sound Jesse out a bit if you feel up to it. Just be sure to handcuff him to his chair first so that he won't be able to pick your pockets."

"Aren't you being a trifle harsh?"

"Not at all, it's just that I've known those four brats of Lionel's a good deal longer than you have. They're all chips off the old block, unfortunately. Their father's as bad as they are, though Lionel's a lot sharper at not letting his right hand notice what his left hand's up to. Go ahead if you want to, but don't say I didn't warn you."

"Hell, I can outmaneuver a kid his age."

"Jesse's no kid, unless perhaps he's a reincarnation of Billy the Kid, which wouldn't surprise me a bit. We might ask that friend of Theonia's who does past-life readings to check his pedigree. By the way, do you have your key to the house with you? It's just occurred to me that I've left mine in my other handbag."

"It's okay, don't forget I was a Boy Scout once. Hey, how about that? We appear to have a welcoming committee."

A scowling youth in the shortest of cutoffs and the holiest of T-shirts was straddling the drive directly in front of them. "Can't you read the sign?" he was yelling. "This is private property."

Sarah stuck her head out the car window. "Thanks for telling us, Jesse. Whatever are you doing here?"

Without being invited, Jesse opened the back door and climbed in.

"Guarding the premises. What'd you do, Aunt Sarah, rack up the other car? Hi, Max, you still got that bum leg? How come they didn't amputate?"

"How come you weren't exposed on a barren hillside at birth?" Sarah retorted. "What do you mean, you're guarding the premises? Has something happened?"

"Ah, some jerks had a picnic here yesterday. They strewed Chinese food all over the place."

"Chinese food?"

"Well, those boxes they put the take-out in. And broken chopsticks and a couple of fortune cookies. One of them said 'Your luck has run out' and the other said 'Prepare for worse to come.' That was kind of gross, I thought. So Mike told me to keep people off."

"Mike knows you're here?"

"Well, sure." Jesse was all virtue. "I had to ask permission to camp, didn't I? I told him I was your cousin, sort of, and you always let me and my family stay here."

"Since when?"

"Well, grandma does, and we all did, that time when the boat house burned down. I had to go someplace, Vare kicked me out."

"What for?"

"Oh, you know Vare." Lionel and his wife had drilled their children to call them by their first names. Sarah saw this as a way of ducking parental responsibility, which in their case it probably was. "She got mad because I wouldn't go on a slumber party with this dumb kid who's got the hots for me."

"What? Do you mean your mother actually—" Sarah had been aware that such things happened nowadays, but it hadn't dawned on her that they might be occurring among the junior Kellings. "This dumb kid—ah, male or female?"

"Oh, female. Vare's sickeningly conventional in some ways, you know. Anorexic and stupid. Skinny I could have handled, stupid I couldn't. I mean, I can understand where Vare gets off about conforming to the mores of my peer group and all that garbage, but I don't see why I should have to sacrifice the precious pearl of my virginity just to oblige a screwed-up skeleton who can't even look at a pizza without barfing."

Jesse's face had turned the color of a boiled lobster. For the first time in their stormy acquaintance, Sarah saw the boy embarrassed to the point of tears. "I—hell, I suppose this sounds crazy, but I just don't want to do it unless it's with somebody I at least kind of like. And any girl I think I might like never likes me. So here I am, still a virgin at sixteen. Maladjusted, Vare says, maybe she's right for once. I suppose I can't blame my mother for not wanting a nut case around the house setting a bad example to my younger siblings, but a guy's got to march to his own drummer, is how I look at it."

"Buck up, Jess," said Max. "Some day your princess will come. Did you happen to bring any clothes with you?"

"Clothes?"

"You know. Shorts, pants, a jacket, maybe even shoes?"

"Oh, those. I've got Reeboks and Levi's and a sweater. And my sleeping bag. It starts getting cold nights at this time of year. Not that I'm soft, you understand. I just don't want to get sick and be a burden on Mike and Carrie."

"That's thoughtful of you, Jesse." For Max's sake, Sarah tried her level best to sound as though she believed him. "What are you living on? Do you have money for groceries?"

"No, Vare wouldn't give me any."

"Then is Mike feeding you?"

"No! I don't need anybody. I can feed myself. I dig clams and pick berries and stuff. Mike and Carrie did ask me up for pizza a couple of nights, though," the outcast admitted.

"How long have you been here?"

"What day's today?"

"Wednesday."

"Only Wednesday? Then it's five days. I thought it was longer. Time sure flies when you're having fun."

"You haven't been using the house, then?"

"Oh no. Just those two times, and then we ate out on the deck. They don't let anybody into the house, only the woman who comes to clean and Mr. Lomax. They have their own keys because Mike and Carrie are off working all day. I hang out in the lean-to. Remember the one Lionel and we kids built that time?"

Sarah remembered all too well. "But it's falling down."

"Not any more. I've got it fixed good as new. Want to see?"

"We're a little pressed for time just now." Sarah glanced at Max and got a nod. "Would you care to ride back to Boston with us, and spend the night on Tulip Street for a change? You can't live on clams indefinitely, I think we'd better arrange for you and Lionel to have a talk."

"You can't, they've all gone off on the boat."

"When are they coming back?"

"When they get seasick, I guess."

"Is your grandmother with them?"

"Of course. You don't think they'd risk leaving the golden goose without her bodyguard?"

This was disrespectful of Jesse, but Sarah knew it was accurate.

Apollonia Kelling had inherited a great deal of money from her late husband and even more from a deceased friend. The latter and larger legacy had, to Lionel's temporary dismay, turned out to have been left for Appie's lifetime only. Should she fail to spend it all during however many years she had left, the rest would be passed on to the local yacht club.

Lionel was therefore working hard to keep his dear old gray-haired mummy alive and productive for as long as possible. With touching solicitude he shuttled her back and forth in a series of expensive cars from her big old house in Cambridge to her sumptuous new ski lodge in Vermont or her sleek new yacht, selected and captained by her doting only son and manned by her almost as doting daughter-in-law and grandchildren.

Lionel was a passionate sailor, and a good one. They wouldn't be back until he tired of the sea or Vare kicked up a monumental fuss. Sarah could see the handwriting on the wall, but what could she say?

"Then you'd better come with us anyway. Put on your Levi's and we'll borrow one of Mike's shirts for you to wear."

"Can we stop at the garage and tell him where I'm going?"

Ira Rivkin owned Ireson Town's garage and filling station. Mike had been working for his father weekends and summers ever since he was old enough; this probably would be his last year, since he was finishing up his master's degree. Jesse had no doubt begged him not to tell Sarah and Max that he was camping on their property and Mike had, as any warmhearted but conscientious young fellow would do, agreed to keep mum as long as Jesse behaved himself.

Perhaps Vare had done the right thing in shoving her firstborn out to fend for himself, however insane her reason. Away from his hellhound brothers and his weird parents, strapped for cash and not daring to burgle the source of his occasional pizzas, the boy might have been using some of that empty time to do a bit of constructive thinking for a change. Max could even be right about Jesse, he'd turned a few other unlikely characters into reliable members of his far-flung network.

Sarah knew one thing in Jesse's favor, the boy was remarkably fast on his feet. Should the occasion arise, he could probably outrun the little man in the red sweat suit. Thus trying to console herself, she led the way into the house that she'd been missing so much.

Alien groceries in the kitchen were the first blow to her sensibilities: bizarre cereals in hideous boxes, canned soups, an empty take-out fried-chicken box left on the counter, soft drinks in the fridge, things she and Max wouldn't have touched with a ten-foot pole. Mike and Carrie were no doubt trying to keep the house in good order, but their ideas of neatness were not Sarah's. She couldn't suppress a feeling of having been invaded, even though she was truly grateful to the lovers for looking after the place.

Miriam was sending food over, of course. Sarah recognized a Tupperware cake plate with half a cinnamon ring under its clear plastic cover. Jesse was eyeing the pastry with undisguised lust. She took a carton of milk from the fridge and poured him a glass.

"You'd better eat some of this coffee cake before we go, Jesse. We're running behind schedule and shan't be able to stop for food on the way. We'd better just leave a note for Mike, you can phone him this evening from Boston if you like."

The shellfishing and berry picking must not have been all that productive this morning. Jesse finished every crumb of the cinnamon ring and would probably have licked the plate if Sarah hadn't been in the kitchen. He didn't exactly fall on his knees with gratitude over the plain blue knitted polo shirt Max foraged from the bedroom that Mike and Carrie were sharing in accordance with the mores of their peers; but he took it.

"I'll go change and meet you down at the bottom of the driveway."

"At least he's not conspicuously dirty," Sarah remarked as the boy ran off and she picked up the grocery pad to write Mike a note. He and Carrie wouldn't be heartbroken over losing Jesse, she surmised, though they might be rather hard-hit about the coffee cake. "I suppose he's been swimming a lot for want of anything else to do, and sluicing off under the outdoor shower. I shouldn't have minded a swim myself, but there'll be other times."

She finished her note and took out her car keys. "Well, I suppose we'd better go. It's curious, your having mentioned Jesse on the way here and our finding him all moved in. Or is it?"

"Not really," Max confessed. "Mike phoned the other day while you were out with Davy and told me the kid had shown up. I didn't tell you because I know how you feel about Lionel's wrecking crew, but I couldn't help feeling sorry for the little bastard. So I told Mike to keep Jesse out of the house and let me know if he caused any trouble. I figured he wouldn't stay long, I didn't realize that screwball mother of his had shoved him out with no money or clothes. Vare ought to be locked up."

"Many have thought so, dear, myself included. There's your little wanderer now, he must have run all the way. Just understand one thing, Max Bittersohn, this kid's all yours. I took you for better or worse, but not for Jesse Kelling. Oh dear, it's just occurred to me, we'll have to take him with us to the funeral tomorrow. I wouldn't dare leave him in the house by himself."

"God, you're a hard woman."

"You just bet I am. Furthermore, he can't go in dungarees and a borrowed shirt, Anora would be insulted. Charles will have to take him shopping when we get back, and you, my love, will have to shell out the money. Don't think Lionel will reimburse you, either. Aunt Appie might, if Lionel wasn't around to stop her. How long are you planning to keep Jesse?"

"Who knows? He can have one of the third-floor bedrooms, can't he?"

"On the condition that he doesn't set fire to it."

"You're not really sore, are you?" Max was beginning to sound worried.

"Not yet," Sarah answered, "but time will tell. All right, this is the moment of truth."

She hit the brakes, Jesse climbed in with his rolled-up sleeping bag, almost respectable in his borrowed shirt. He'd even remembered to put on his sneakers. Sarah had been expecting Max to get in a little missionary work during the ride, but he didn't say much to either Jesse or herself. He didn't even use the car telephone, she became anxious that he might have overtired himself and started his leg hurting again.

Jesse wasn't talking either, perhaps they were both taking naps. She pushed the little car along as fast as she could without risking a speeding ticket. It rode better with Jesse's extra weight, though he couldn't be adding much over another hundred pounds. He looked like a famine victim; aside from a bath and a haircut and something to wear, that boy's greatest need right now was to get a few decent meals inside him.

"I'll let you two out at the house, Max, and put the car away while you're getting Jesse settled in," she remarked as they were heading down Storrow Drive.

Her husband wasn't having that. "Couldn't you turn off at Arlington and drop me at the corner of Charles and Boylston so that I can walk over to the office? Jesse may as well go on into the garage with you so he'll know where we keep the cars. Do you drive, Jess?"

"When I get the chance. Lionel keeps saying he'll get me a car when my grades pick up, but they're never good enough to suit him. He makes me sick. I'm not going back to school this fall. I'm never going back." Jesse shrugged in self-pity. "So I'll be a dropout and spend the rest of my life doing manual labor and sleeping under bridges. Who cares?"

"You might, some day," said Max. "I'll see you in a while, then, Sarah. Call me at the office if anything comes up."

15

Nothing came up. Sarah led Jesse to the top floor of the high narrow town house, showed him where to park his sleeping bag and perform his ablutions. Then she herded him downstairs and turned him over to Charles, with strict orders about a suit and a haircut.

Mariposa had taken the afternoon off to visit some of her countless relatives. Theonia was out having her fortune told at a tea shop that she suspected of running a sideline in fencing stolen jewelry, some of which she and Brooks had been trying to track down. Sarah found to her astonishment that she had the house to herself.

She caught up on some correspondence, made herself a glass of iced tea, and took it out to Brooks's midget garden along with a book she'd been trying to read for the past two months. She read a few chapters, decided the book wasn't worth finishing, went back inside and telephoned Miriam to make sure Davy was still intact and not missing his parents. He wasn't. A trifle let down, she got dinner started, then went upstairs to shower off the day's accumulations. Feeling a little better, she put on a gauzy caftan and a pair of golden slippers, and swished downstairs to greet her housemates as they straggled in.

Max and Brooks were first. Brooks was chirpy, Max was tired. Sarah administered a therapeutic kiss, made her husband put his leg up on a hassock, and brought him a mild Scotch and water. Theonia came home not long after the men, mildly triumphant. She'd done a little fortune-telling of her own, with the happy result that the proprietor had been scared into forking over the stolen emerald, sapphire, pearl, diamond, and ruby earrings alleged to have been created for Catherine the Great of Russia.

"I've got them right here in my handbag, wrapped in a couple of tea-shop napkins," Theonia crowed. "I thought I'd wait till after the funeral to return them to Mrs. Upscale, I want to be fresh and rested when we start haggling over the fee. She'll lose, needless to say. Want to see?"

With justifiable pride, she unwrapped the ponderous baubles from the tea-shop napkins and held them up. Her husband snorted.

"Preposterous! The empress must have had remarkably sturdy earlobes."

"So have I, my love. I'm going to wear them to dinner. Excuse me while I titivate."

Theonia came back downstairs in her trusty black dinner gown and the empress's earrings, sent Charles into ecstasies, and totally benumbed the newest member of the party. Jesse was looking pretty spiffy himself; when it came to wardrobe, Charles C. Charles was not a man to do the job by halves. In a Brooks Brothers suit, Florsheim shoes, and a Prince Charles haircut, Cousin Lionel's eldest son was a different kettle of clams from the skinny waif in the tattered cutoffs.

Of course Charles hadn't been able to do anything about the Kelling nose. Jesse had inherited his grandmother's looks; Sarah had once observed that Aunt Appie always reminded her of Cyrus Dallin's "Appeal to the Great Spirit." Cousin Mabel had riposted, "Which half, the Indian or the horse?" The question was not unreasonable.

Jesse would grow up to his nose in time, he might even look rather distinguished if he ever got that furtive look out of his eye. All the expensive education Appie was paying for appeared to have left some kind of impression; away from his family Jesse hadn't exactly bloomed but he was giving a pretty fair portrayal of a rational human being. About halfway through the meal, Sarah quit expecting the boy to pocket the silver salt cellars with an eye to clandestine resale or slip a live lizard into the salad bowl out of general nastiness.

Perhaps Jesse hadn't thought to bring a lizard, or perhaps his first genuine meal in what must have seemed a very long time was absorbing his full attention. He ate with enthusiasm but not ferocity, didn't talk with his mouth full or interrupt when someone else was speaking. He asked one or two intelligent questions, particularly of

Theonia with regard to the method she'd employed in getting back the empress's earrings. He was not too appalled to learn that he'd have to attend George Protheroe's funeral in the morning, at least not after he'd learned that the decedent was a victim of murder by spearing.

Except for those two pizza parties with Mike and Carrie, Jesse had had no contact with the outside world during his stay at Ireson's Landing: no radio, no newspapers, no television. He'd stayed clear of the caretaker for reasons associated with certain past incidents. He could hardly be blamed now for craving details of George's melodramatic demise.

"Are you guys working on the case?" he asked avidly.

"Homicide is always handled by the police," Max evaded. "We just happened to become slightly involved because Sarah phoned Mrs. Protheroe and learned that her husband was dead. The Protheroes were old friends of the family, I expect your father would know them, too."

"Oh, were they the people who lived in that big mudflat-colored house with all the junk in it? Don't tell me the guy who got lanced was that fat old drunk who was always trying to tell stories nobody wanted to hear?"

This was the Jesse whom Sarah had known and loathed, she leaped straight down his throat. "George Protheroe was not a fat old drunk. When he was a young man in the Orient, he caught some terrible disease. He almost died, and it left him with serious problems, including a kind of chronic sleeping sickness. Mrs. Protheroe was devoted to her husband and many people, myself included, loved him very much. Kindly bear that in mind tomorrow at the funeral."

"I'm sorry," Jesse mumbled.

"All right, Jesse. But if you're going to be a detective, you'd better learn to get the facts before you start running off at the mouth."

"A detective? Me?"

"Well, possibly. Depending. Max, I seem to have put my foot in it here. Can you help me out?"

Max didn't mind Sarah's having jumped the gun. He knew what a strain she'd been under all summer long, and what she must be feeling now. "Sure, Sarah, no problem. It's just that I've been watching you a little, Jesse, and wondering whether you might sometime be interested in helping us out at the agency. Since you're at loose

ends till school starts, this might be a time to get in a spot of appren-
ticing."

"Me? Well, sure. But what would I have to do?"

"Sweep out the office, answer the phone, wander around the art
museums and antique shops, go out on a few assignments with
whichever of us can use you. Generally get the feel for what we do."

"Do I carry a gun?"

"Not if you're going to work for us. Lethal weapons only invite
trouble. Our protection comes from using our heads all the time and
our feet when necessary."

"I'm a brown belt in judo."

"Bully for you." Max shifted in his chair and winced as his mend-
ing ribs gave him a stab of pain. "I wish I'd been. Does anyone mind
if we go and sit where it's softer? Anyway, Jesse, you might start by
keeping your eyes open tomorrow at the funeral."

"What am I supposed to look for?"

"That's where the detective instinct comes in. You just have to
develop a nose for smelling rats."

Jesse was quite taken with the idea. "So that's what this honker of
mine was designed for. I've often wondered."

Jesse's quip against himself gave them all a chuckle, Sarah began
to feel that Max might have been more perspicacious than anyone
else about the boy's potentialities. That wasn't to say she didn't intend to keep a sharp eye on him for whatever length of time he
might remain in the house. Today had gone better than she'd anticipated. Nevertheless, she went to bed warning herself to beware of
getting too cozy too soon with any child of Lionel's.

During the night an east wind came up, as east winds often do in
Boston. The weather that had been hot and fair all week was damp
and chilly in the morning. Sarah and Theonia both came to the
breakfast table in their robes, asking each other what they ought to
wear to the funeral. Not that it mattered particularly. Few people
bothered about mourning these days, least of all the Old Guard.
Theonia did decide on black because it suited her and because the
outfit she had in mind included a matching jacket that could be left
on or taken off, depending on the weather. Since it looked like rain,
she was going to carry her lovely black-and-white umbrella with the
goose-head handle that Brooks had carved for her, and hoped to
goodness she wouldn't forget and leave it somewhere.

Sarah said then she'd wear her gray silk suit and carry her summer raincoat, just in case. Max and Brooks couldn't help being appropriately dressed since neither of them went in for bright-colored shirts or flashy ties. Jesse got the full treatment and emerged, if not a thing of beauty, at least a credit to Charles's valeting. Charles himself was splendid in his butler outfit, Mariposa had remembered to put on the black uniform and take off the orange ribbons. The two of them looked snappy enough to be raising the curtain at the Wilbur on a British drawing-room comedy.

Seven in one car would have been a squeeze. It was decided that Charles and Mariposa would go in the bug and the rest in the big car, which they'd need for the sad procession to the cemetery after the service. They all walked over to the garage together; Sarah stayed next to Jesse, feeling a slight urge to make up for the heavy-handed way she'd been forced to deal with him in the past.

"What a pity your grandmother has to miss the funeral." Sarah thought she wouldn't mention that Apollonia Kelling liked nothing better than a good cry over a casket. "She and your grandfather were always so fond of George Protheroe."

"Gran loves everybody, grandpa couldn't stand anybody," was Jesse's more accurate rejoinder. "And Lionel and Vare don't do funerals unless there's something in it for them."

"Aren't you being a little bit rough on your parents?" Sarah knew perfectly well he wasn't, but she couldn't let him run on like this in front of people who weren't family. "Nobody's asking you to be a hypocrite, but there are times when it's better to say too little than too much. This is going to be one of them. Many of the agency's clients are people we know, or friends of people we know; we can't let them think any of our staff might go around making rude remarks behind their backs. What it boils down to, Jesse, is that good manners are also good policy, no matter where you are. I don't mean to sound preachy, I know we've dumped a lot on you within an awfully short time. By the end of the week, you may decide you'd rather go back to Ireson's and dig some more clams."

"I doubt it, Sarah, I was getting awfully sick of clams. Do you expect trouble at the funeral?"

"I hope not, for Anora Protheroe's sake, but one never knows. Whenever something sensational happens, there are always ghouls trying to gate-crash. I just hope enough policemen have been put on to keep them out. And I further hope you won't try any judo in that new suit unless it's a real emergency. You look quite nice, by the way. What do you want to bet Cousin Dolph doesn't recognize you?"

Jesse started to offer an opinion about Cousin Dolph, caught Sarah's eye, and grinned. "Okay, I get the message. So what am I supposed to say if anybody starts talking to me?"

"Tell them who you are and that you're staying with us in town for a while. If they ask about your family, say they've gone on a cruise. Don't lie, just tell as much of the truth as you feel comfortable with, then either fade away gracefully or start them talking about themselves. You're entitled to ask questions, too, you know. You could get in some useful practice at extracting information without letting your subject realize he's being pumped. If it gets too boring or too tough, make some excuse to break off."

"Like I have to go to the bathroom?"

"If that's the best you can think of. You'll cope, Jesse. Max wouldn't be interested in working with you if he didn't believe you're worth training."

16

"Too bad it's such a dreary day," Brooks Kelling remarked, "though I suppose the weather's appropriate to the occasion."

Brooks had offered to drive the big car, Sarah was quite willing to let him. She was feeling low in her mind, not so much about fubsy old George, so bizarrely done to death beside his own newel post, as about Anora, abruptly and brutally parted from the man she'd loved and nursed along for more than half a century. What was the poor woman going to do without someone to coddle?

The best she could, no doubt, like everybody else. Sarah had spoken on the phone with Anora earlier this morning; they'd agreed that there was no sense in the Bittersohn-Kelling party's dropping by the house before the service, now that Charles and Mariposa would be coming in the other car. It wasn't as if they were needed; everything was, or appeared to be, under control. Cousin Dolph Kelling and his wife, who also lived in Chestnut Hill, were going to ride in the undertaker's limousine with Anora. Mary Kelling was both kind and capable, Dolph loved a good funeral, the couple could be relied on to do all the right things.

Max was sitting in front with Brooks on account of his stiff leg. Sarah and Theonia had Jesse between them in the back seat, giving him a crash course in the kind of small talk appropriate to the occasion. As they came in sight of the handsome fieldstone church, however, polite conversation turned to murmurs of dismay. They'd expected the local gendarmerie to take security precautions against sensation-seekers, they'd have been greatly disturbed for Anora's sake if the police hadn't acted. They just hadn't quite realized they were going to get stuck in the jam along with everybody else.

A whole cordon of patrol cars were flashing their blue lights in front of the church and the parking lot. Uniformed officers were guarding the entrances, one with a clipboard was stationed at the front door letting some people in, sending others away. Another officer with another clipboard was walking along the ever-lengthening line of idling cars, checking registrations and drivers' licenses, allowing some to stay in the queue for the parking lot, waving the majority off.

Plenty of fur must be flying about this cavalier treatment. Every chance acquaintance who'd so much as bought a white elephant from Anora at a church bazaar twenty years ago, and a good many who hadn't even done that, would feel entitled to attend the obsequies and be furious at getting turned away. It was plain to see that these policemen's lot was not a happy one today.

Sarah and her party could only join the line in meek humility and inch their way along with the rest. It was as well they'd come early. Impeccable as their credentials were, they didn't get parked and inside the church for upward of twenty minutes. Even here, the usher wouldn't seat them until he'd consulted his clipboard. Max was listed as a Kelling but that didn't matter, he was used to it by now. Jesse wasn't on the list; Sarah got him in with a sad and noble tale of how her young relative, as eldest begat of Cousin Lionel Kelling, was representing his family because he was the only one of them not at sea, which was the truth in more ways than one. Touched by the youth's manly bearing and Oxbridge haircut, the usher could not have been more obliging.

"Would you people care to sit down front with the Adolphus Kellings?"

Sarah considered the matter and decided to compromise. "Theonia, why don't you and Brooks go ahead and keep Mary company? Aunt Bodie's by herself, the rest of us may as well slide in with her."

Having to sit next to Boadicea Kelling throughout what would most likely be a long service ought to constitute a valid test of Jesse's ability to show grace under fire. Max would be more comfortable back here, he could sit at the end of the pew and have a chance to stretch his leg out into the aisle without making himself conspicuous. Sarah's own ulterior motive was to see who got past the watchdogs.

Boadicea Kelling acknowledged the advent of her niece's party with a mildly affable nod. Bodie was not given to exuberance at any time, nor did she think a church pew an appropriate place for socializing. Sarah made Jesse go first, slid in after him, and began mentally filling a clipboard of her own.

She was rather surprised to see Leila Lackridge sitting across the aisle with Edgar Merton, she hadn't laid eyes on either of them in ages. Not that she'd missed them or cared about them now, but they had been regular guests at Anora's awful parties and frequent visitors at Tulip Street back when Sarah's first husband and his mother were alive. Edgar was still in the Boston area as far as Sarah knew, but Anora had mentioned a while ago that Leila was living in New York. Leila had never been one to put herself out, it was surprisingly generous of her to have come back for George's funeral.

The time set for the service to begin was fast approaching. About half the pews were filled, a goodly turnout considering how selective Anora had been about letting people in. Sarah could place most of them, Max was also spotting a few.

"See that yellow-faced guy with the stoop sitting in the fourth pew from the front on the opposite side from Dolph?" he muttered.

"The man who looks like a bloodhound with a bad cold? That's one I've never seen at Anora's, who is he?"

"Marcus Nie, the stripper and chipper from Arbalest's atelier. The usher took him right down front, I'm wondering why. Is it possible Nie's a relative?"

"I have no idea. Anora's people are all long gone, but George has a few scattered around. I'll ask Aunt Bodie later."

Boadicea Kelling had never been any great chum of the Protheroes, but she'd know. Family connections were among the many sorts of information Bodie liked to have clearly pinned down. There was no earthly use trying to get anything out of her now, she'd only purse her lips and shake her head. There'd be time enough after the service. Sarah was trying to compose herself into a mood of proper reverence when Max nudged her again.

A middle-aged man, tall, pale, and slightly built though a trifle bulgy around the middle, was trying to persuade a very old man to take his seat in a rear pew. The very old man was insisting in none too *sotto* a voice on sitting down front where he could get a clear view of the open casket.

Max thought open caskets barbarous, he couldn't imagine why anybody would want to look at a corpse. Sarah was more relaxed on the subject. She was used to seeing dead Kellings, they generally looked better laid out than they had in life. Even as a child she'd understood why the family of the deceased, having paid for the embalming, would naturally want to get some value out of it; why some of the relatives would take comfort from a last look at their cherished kinsman; and why others might feel an urge to make sure the dear departed was well and truly gone.

The old man was getting his way. The younger, either his son or his nephew, or so Sarah judged from the resemblance between them, was thrusting forward his goatee and following his elder and the usher with what grace he could muster. Sarah cocked an eyebrow in her husband's direction.

"Dubrec," Max murmured. "The one who sticks things together. That's probably his father. Tell Jesse."

Sarah was not about to start a whispered conversation, not with Aunt Bodie just a glare away. She took out her miniature gold pencil and memorandum book, scribbled, "Keep an eye on those two," and flipped her head meaningfully toward the pair who were at last getting stowed to the elder's satisfaction. Jesse started to say something but she shushed him. The organist, who'd been producing suitably muted and elevating music for the past fifteen minutes had stopped playing.

The rector was taking his place in front of the altar. An old woman in the same gray flannel suit she had been wearing everywhere she'd gone for the last twenty-five years or so and a black velvet toque that could have been a hand-me-down from the late Queen Mary was being led down the aisle by a tall, stout but not fat man wearing a dark gray suit, a black arm band, and the Kelling nose.

Dolph's attire was much more à la mode than Anora's; he'd bought the suit only a decade or so ago for Great-Uncle Frederick Kelling's funeral, either out of respect for his late guardian or in celebration of the old loony's demise, nobody had ever been sure which. Anyway, the suit was wearing well and so was Dolph, bless him. What an impressive undertaker he'd have made, Sarah thought, if only he hadn't got stuck with inheriting Uncle Frederick's millions.

The chief mourner and her escort ought to have been the last ones in, but they weren't. While Dolph and a couple of ushers were getting Anora settled and she was snapping at them to quit their fussing, somebody else slipped into the pew behind Sarah's, the one nearest the door. Simultaneously, the rector stepped up to the lectern and took a firm grip on the sides.

"I am the Resurrection and the Life."

As Sarah had anticipated, Anora had opted for the High Church service. Once begun, it went on and on. Jesse started to fidget; Sarah was about to give the boy a hint to settle down when she realized what was upsetting him. Under cover of the organ's playing, one of the latecomers who'd sat down behind them was crying his or her heart out.

If Jesse were to turn around now, Aunt Bodie would throw a fit as soon as she could properly do so. Under pretense of getting a handkerchief, Sarah fished the little mirror out of her handbag, slipped it between the pages of her hymnal, and handed the book to the new apprentice. Max was right, Jesse was quick on the uptake. Without so much as a sideways glance he palmed the mirror. Presumably he made effective use of it. Sarah didn't catch him doing so and neither, God willing, did Aunt Bodie.

The crying stopped, except for an occasional sigh or snuffle. Who could be feeling such heartbreak over poor old George? Showing emotion in public was not the done thing in the Protheroes' circle. At her own first husband's funeral, Sarah herself had been rebuked for breaking down; Leila Lackridge had been the rebuker. Leila was doing the done thing now, sitting poker-faced in the cushioned pew, sneaking an occasional finger-flicking peek at her wristwatch, no doubt trying to calculate how much longer she'd have to keep a stiff upper lip before she could reasonably expect to find herself within range of a dry martini.

She must have been spending the summer soaking up the sun; her angular profile looked as if it had been snipped out of burnished copper plate by an ill-tempered tinsmith. Except for the tan, Leila hadn't changed a bit that Sarah could see, she'd always been thin as a rake and ugly as sin. It had been in Leila's house that Sarah had first met Max Bittersohn, Sarah wondered whether she knew they'd got married. Probably she did. Leila must have kept in touch with Anora, how else would she have got invited to the funeral?

As if it mattered. Sarah was making a dutiful effort to keep her mind on the lovely service when Jesse nudged her foot ever so gently with his own and handed her back the hymnal. She took out the mirror, screened it with the handkerchief she'd kept in her hand for possible emergency use, caught the reflection from behind her, and almost gave Aunt Bodie cause for umbrage.

The weeper was a portly, middle-aged man wearing a well-cut black broadcloth suit. His face was hidden behind long-fingered, well-manicured hands. Some of his hair was gray, some only grizzled; he seemed to have an unreasonable amount of it. Sarah surmised that the apparent surplus must be a beard. His shoulders were heaving with the sobs that he was beyond trying to suppress.

On the weeper's arm rested a glove. Any glove would have been unusual on a hot summer's day in an era where such once-indispensable niceties as women's hats and gloves had gone the way of flannel petticoats and ruffled corset covers; this would have been no ordinary glove in any weather. It was black kid with white kid inserts between the fingers, it made Sarah think of a pair that Marlene Dietrich had worn as Shanghai Lili in a rerun she'd once seen at the old Brattle Theater.

To the glove was attached an arm, and to the arm a striking brunette ageing gracefully into dowagerhood. She was dressed, like many of the other mourners, in outmoded finery; but she wore hers with a flair: the black redingote with the white revers, the slim-fitting black skirt, the black cartwheel straw chapeau set almost vertically on one side of her sleekly coiffed head. The hand on the arm, should anybody other than Sarah notice it, would probably be taken as a gesture of wifely solicitude. With a gesture of wifely solicitude and a softly murmured "don't faint," Sarah passed her mirror on to Max.

Max Bittersohn was not the fainting type. He only allowed his lips a momentary upward quirk and his head the merest hint of a nod, then passed the mirror back to Sarah. She understood perfectly, up to a point. Yes, the sobber was Bartolo Arbalest. But why was he sobbing? How had he and Lydia Ouspenska got past all those clipboards? Where was their bodyguard? Sarah had already been wondering about Goudge. She'd flipped the mirror this way and that as much as she decently could, she'd scanned the other pews. As far as she could tell, he was nowhere in the church.

Another conundrum to add to the list. Sarah supposed the Resurrection Man must be here because Anora had invited him. Surely not solely on the strength of his having repaired her elephant candlesticks? Why would the widow have drawn the line at so many older acquaintances yet show favor to someone she'd met so recently and knew so slightly?

Old women did get silly about younger men sometimes, Sarah supposed Arbalest might look young to Anora. But Anora just wasn't that sort of person. She must genuinely have loved George to have stuck by him the way she had for so many years; she'd had plenty of men in and out of her house, she'd never shown the slightest inclination to be more than affable toward any of them.

The simplest explanation, and most probably the right one, was that Bartolo Arbalest had approached George not as an old buffer to be humored and put up with for the sake of politeness, but as a sensible man who'd had intelligent things to say on a subject of mutual interest. That must have meant a great deal to Anora. However, it would hardly explain why Arbalest was putting on such an exhibition now.

He couldn't imagine it was the proper thing to do, not in this crowd. But he wasn't one of this crowd. Among the more avant-garde, stiff upper lips were no longer in fashion; men were now permitted to cry if they felt like it. Maybe Arbalest was just moving with the times and letting it all hang out. After the many deaths he'd had to deal with among his former employees and clients, the many funerals he must have been forced to attend, the appalling murder of a recently acquired customer might have been more than the Resurrection Man could handle.

Jesse had borne up better than Sarah had expected, but she was beginning to wonder how much longer he'd last. She was grateful when the rector pronounced the benediction and the organist started the postlude. Anora and Dolph came back up the aisle, both of them decently composed, looking neither to left nor to right. Cook and Phyllis were behind them, being escorted by Mary Kelling and Dr. Harnett. The ushers were monitoring the pews, letting the mourners out row by row. People were moving along rather quickly, evidently Anora had elected not to linger in the vestibule and receive condolences she didn't feel up to accepting.

She wasn't outside on the steps either, she must have got Dolph to shepherd her straight into the undertaker's limousine. By the time Sarah, Max, and Jesse were liberated from their pew, some of those who planned to escort George on his final ride were already getting into their cars and lining up for the cortege to the cemetery.

Boadicea Kelling wasn't going. She'd written her note of condolence, she'd shown her respect by attending the service, she'd done all that was reasonable and could not be expected to waste gasoline on unnecessary junketings. Sarah marveled a bit as to how anybody could refer to a graveside visit as a junket, but she could understand why Aunt Bodie preferred to give it a miss. Aside from duty already done and the inherent grimness of the last rite, Bodie was aware that her 1946 Daimler was not the most fuel-efficient of conveyances, and she still had to drive it all the way back to Wenham. She said the proper things to Sarah and Max, then turned to Jesse, who'd been standing back, maintaining a low profile.

"How do you do, young man? Since my niece has not seen fit to present you to me, permit me to introduce myself. I am Boadicea Kelling."

"But Aunt Bodie, you've met him lots of times," Sarah protested. "This is Lionel's eldest son, Jesse."

"Nonsense, Sarah. Lionel's sons are barbarians. This chap has been a model of deportment all through that unnecessarily lengthy service. His hair is neatly trimmed, he is appropriately and even becomingly dressed. I can only assume that his appearance and behavior are part of a masquerade abetted by certain persons who ought to have known better."

She glared at Max, who was quietly enjoying himself. Sarah started to remonstrate but Boadicea fixed her with another glare and went on. "One realizes, young man, that this must be a ruse to gain you entrance to a private funeral to which is most regrettably attached a taint of sensationalism. Are you or are you not a member of the press?"

Boadicea Kelling put the same degree of misapprobation on the word "press" as she might have done on "leper colony" or "Democratic Party." Jesse faced up to her unflinchingly.

"I'm not a member of the press and I gained entrance because Sarah told the cops I was her nephew. I'm sorry you don't believe me, Aunt Bodie. If you'll wait till my parents come home, I can show you my birth certificate and make Lionel take a blood test."

"Aha! Now you sound like yourself. Very well, Jesse, I apologize for my lack of perspicacity. By way of exculpation, I might remind you that I am a practical-minded person and cannot reasonably be expected to recognize a miracle at first glance."

"That's okay, Aunt Bodie, we all make mistakes. Can I help you out to your car?"

"Don't push it, young man."

But Boadicea Kelling shook hands quite pleasantly with Jesse before she bade them farewell and proceeded with purposeful stride but no unseemly haste out into the parking lot.

17

Jesse looked after his departing relative with his mouth hanging open in a manner that would have evoked Boadicea's reproof if she'd happened to look back. Fortunately for the good impression he'd made, she didn't. "How do you like that?" he said when he could get his voice under control. "Was she trying to be funny, Sarah?"

"Never. Aunt Bodie doesn't believe in fun. You handled her beautifully, Jesse. And now you know how useful protective coloration can be."

"What's protective coloration?"

"Blending in with your surroundings. That suit serves the same purpose as a tiger's stripes or the speckled feathers on a bird. Camouflage, if you prefer. Brooks can tell you all about that. There he is now with Theonia, trying to spot us. Nip over and say we'll meet them at the car, will you? Don't bother coming back, we'll be right along. Max, can you see what's happened to Lydia and Mr. Arbalest? They sneaked out while Bodie was introducing herself to Jesse. Goudge was waiting for them in his uniform, looking quite smashing, I have to say. We ought to talk with them, don't you think?"

"If you say so, Kätzele. What should we talk about?"

"Oh, anything. I'd like to know why Mr. Arbalest was crying. I'd also like to know how he and Lydia got in. Darling, don't you find it a trifle odd that he and three of his artisans are here? Anora must have invited them, or they'd never have got through all those security checks, but why? We discussed the guest list fairly thoroughly on the phone, at least I thought we did. I even made some of the calls for her. Darn it, what does this man want?"

One of the undertaker's assistants was walking toward them, naturally he addressed Max instead of Sarah. "Excuse me, sir, but if you're going to the cemetery, could you please bring your car around and line up with the rest as quickly as possible? Mrs. Protheroe is anxious to get started."

"Yes, sure," said Max. "Ready, Sarah?"

Sarah was ready. "I can see why Anora wants to get it over with, the poor thing must be aching to get her shoes off and lie down for a while. But everybody will flock back to the house afterward and heaven knows when they'll clear out."

Sarah remembered another funeral when people had stayed and stayed until she'd thought she'd go mad. Leila Lackridge had been one of them. Here she came now, driving Edgar Merton's car. Edgar was cowering in the passenger seat beside her, sweating for his paint work. Leila was the kind of terrible driver who was always getting into scrapes and blaming everybody else for her own ineptitude.

"Couldn't Anora have told them not to come?"

"Of course she couldn't. This is the way it's always been done, and Anora wouldn't want George to be slighted. Isn't it odd, Max, how we fuss about what dead people would have wanted? Do you suppose they actually know?"

"There's only one way to find out, kid. Look out!" He pulled her out of the way just in time to avoid a knockdown. "Who the hell is that maniac?"

"Leila Lackridge. How could you ever have forgotten her?"

"Perseverance and positive thinking. What's she doing here? I thought she'd left town."

"She must have come back for the funeral. She's one of Anora's old crowd, she couldn't be left out."

"She could if I were running this show."

"That's not very flattering, I must say. If it hadn't been for Leila and Harry Lackridge, you might never have met me. Worse still, I might never have met you."

"Baloney. Some enchanted evening you'd have seen a stranger across a crowded delicatessen and pop would have gone the weasel. Here they are, full crew aboard. Sorry to keep you waiting, shipmates. God, I'll be glad when I can walk like a mensch."

"You will, Max dear," Theonia cooed. "I saw you in my tea leaves this morning, clear as crystal."

"You're sure it wasn't some other guy?"

"My dear sir, are you impugning my professional ability? Kindly reflect on to whom you are speaking. Brooks darling, aren't you going to call this cad to task?"

"Not at the moment, Theonia. Remind me to issue a formal challenge when I've got us clear of this confounded parking lot, assuming that I ever succeed in doing so. Jesse, you can be my second, Max can have Charles. What do you say, Max, pistols for two and bagels for one at dawn? Or would you prefer bean shooters at twenty paces? I used to shoot a mean bean before I got old and dignified."

"Not bean shooters," said Max firmly. "Those things are dangerous. I've got a wife and kid to think of."

"Cream puffs, then?"

"It's not nice to waste food," Jesse put in virtuously.

"Who's going to waste them?" said Max. "My leg may be bumming, but there's nothing the matter with the old wing. We'll both wear catchers' mitts. Ah, the hell with it, how about if I just apologize? Theonia, is it okay if we put the groveling on hold until I've recovered full use of my right knee?"

"Oh yes, quite all right. I shall expect a first-class grovel at your earliest convenience, however."

"I don't suppose you happen to have any occult information on how early my convenience might be?"

"Not at the moment, I'm afraid. The time of my next forecast will have to depend on whether Anora's cook uses tea bags. Speaking of which, I could certainly use a cup of tea right now. Couldn't you, Sarah?"

"I'd love it. Why do you suppose funerals always make one start thinking about food?"

"Just to prove that one still can eat, perhaps. With that thought in mind, I took the precaution of packing a few little sandwiches and some celery sticks. Anyone for a nibble? Sarah? Jesse, take what you want and pass the rest to those two fire-breathing ruffians in the front seat."

One way and another, they beguiled the tedious crawl. When they were about halfway to the cemetery the rain that had been threatening all morning began to fall, not very hard and not altogether to the displeasure of everyone present. As Jesse observed, the longer the rain, the shorter the service. Max considered that remark less than elevating, he switched on the car radio to station XBIL just in time to catch one of Nehemiah Billingsgate's little homilies. They thus arrived at the graveside in a collectively elevated state of mind, though Jesse's elevation might have been due in some part to the fact that he'd got the lion's share of Theonia's excellent sandwiches.

Here, as at the church, the law was on the alert. A pair of uni- formed policemen had been guarding the cemetery gates and a cou- ple more were here inside, keeping the funeral cortège under strict control. As Brooks pulled over to the verge and parked the car, one of the undertaker's assistants bustled up with an armload of black umbrellas. Max and Brooks were donning their trench coats and hats in traditional private-eye fashion. Sarah had her white silk raincoat and Theonia her elegant bumbershoot with the goose-head handle. Max took a couple of the proffered umbrellas anyway, one on gen- eral principles and one for Jesse, since Charles had somehow ne- glected to include a raincoat in his protégé's new wardrobe. Equipped to brave the elements, they walked across the by now somewhat spongy greensward to where people were gathering, where the handsome gray coffin sat, banked by many flowers, above a carpet of Astroturf that covered a new-dug grave.

Old hand at funerals that she was, Sarah didn't hesitate to lead her little band as close as she could to where Anora was standing. She'd have liked to give Anora a kiss, but the rector was talking to the widow and it would have been awkward. Dolph was still on the job, protecting his charge with one of the black umbrellas; Mary oozed away from his side and came over to say hello.

As usual, she looked just right for the occasion in a blue raincoat the color of her eyes and a little blue hat protected by a clear plastic hood. The hat was a valuable antique; Mary had bought it when her mother was still alive, she'd worn it on her first date with Dolph. She'd never find another hat like this one, naturally she took excel- lent care of it. She greeted her favorite in-laws affectionately but not exuberantly, as the occasion demanded, and shook hands with Jesse as if she was honestly glad to see him.

Overwhelmed by all this affability where he was accustomed to wary looks and instinctive shyings-away, Jesse offered Mary the cour- tesy of his umbrella. She smiled up at the gangling youth as only

Mary could, tucked a hand under his elbow, and composed herself to wait for the opening words of the final rites.

The rector spoke. Sarah cried a little, as she'd known she would. Max made her take hold of the umbrella so that he'd have an arm free to put around her. He still needed the other hand for his cane, standing here in the damp couldn't be doing his leg any good. Sarah hoped for his sake as well as for Anora's that the final rites would be over before this storm got much worse.

The wind was picking up, the bouquets were getting a bit of a tumbling, the head undertaker himself slipped over to retrieve a basket of pink and red carnations that was on the verge of tipping over. Somebody's umbrella blew inside out, somebody else's got away and had to be chased; Theonia was having a tug-of-war with hers. The sky was growing blacker and blacker, off in the distance lightning bolts flashed. After longish pauses, low growls of thunder could be heard above the rector's voice. Brooks would be counting the number of seconds between flash and growl, calculating how fast the storm must be traveling. The rector was cutting it short, consigning George's earthly remains to their last resting place, wishing the real George bon voyage on the long path that he must tread alone, though of course those weren't the words he used.

Now the rain was really driving. The undertaker's assistants, all of them suddenly wearing black slickers and waterproof black-plastic hat protectors, were collecting the black umbrellas and hustling mourners into their cars. The poor policemen were getting their uniforms soaked, they hadn't come prepared for a deluge. Sarah still wished there'd been time to give her old friend a hug and a kiss, that would have to wait till they got to the house.

Dolph was trying to steer Anora along toward the first of the black limousines. The widow wasn't letting herself be rushed, she was standing alone beside the casket, giving the blanket of red roses over it a final pat, sending her last caress to her beloved. Phyllis and Cook were being hustled into the second limousine, though hustling Cook was no mean feat. The yellow-faced man who looked like a weeping bloodhound was getting in with them, Max Bittersohn was intrigued.

"I'll be damned. See that, Sarah? Nie must be going back to the house. How come the VIP treatment, I wonder?"

"Maybe they're just going to let him off somewhere," said Sarah. "There goes Leila, dragging poor Edgar along like a sack of potatoes. She'll try to beat every light between here and Chestnut Hill so she can be first at the bar. Charles had better have a pitcher of martinis mixed and waiting or she'll throw a fit."

Of course mixing a martini for Leila was no great trick. One simply poured gin into a cocktail glass and waved the cork of the vermouth bottle over it once or twice. No ice, no olive, God forbid a pickled onion, Leila had never been much of an eater.

For a moment Sarah was back on the river side of Beacon Hill, at one of the Lackridges' awful dinners. She'd have had a meager helping of some unidentifiable mess in front of her on a Minton china plate inherited from one of Leila's grandmothers. Harry would have been sitting at one end of the table in his grandfather's velvet smoking jacket, Leila at the other end in a caftan covered with squirming dragons. He'd have been running on at great length about nothing in particular, she'd have been breathing fire over the latest stupidity one or another of the city fathers had or had not done or was or was not about to commit. Alexander would have had on the old dress suit that he'd been forced to buy for some function years before and was determined to get the good out of. He'd have been saying next to nothing. His mother would have been beautiful in lace and pearls and saying a great deal, always to the point, never overflowing with the milk of human kindness.

Sarah herself would have been wearing a long blue dress she'd made herself out of a woolen blanket because the Lackridges' house was always freezing cold. The rest would have had enough drinks before dinner to warm them up, she'd have nursed her first one until it was nothing but ice water. She'd have been frozen out of the conversation because the Lackridges had resented Alexander's having inflicted a too-young bride on their cozy long-standing foursome, and because Alexander's deaf and blind mother had demanded his full attention at the Lackridges' as well as everywhere else.

It had been at the last of these dreadful evenings that Sarah had first encountered an enigmatic Mr. Bittersohn who was supposed to be writing a book on antique jewelry for Harry to publish. He'd been courteous, reserved, well and soberly dressed. He'd accepted only one drink and eaten as little as possible. Sarah had found him agreeable, later on she'd found him helpful, eventually he'd become one of her boarders at Tulip Street. It had certainly not been love at first sight, or second, or third. Sarah couldn't have said just when she'd realized she was in love with Max, it had just sneaked up on her gradually until at last she'd realized they were one in all but name and they might as well make it legal.

Was Anora thinking as she was being driven back to her great, cluttered, husbandless house of how she and George had courted and married and carried on their life together? Or was she wondering whether she'd ordered enough ice for the drinks and whether Mariposa had remembered to toss the peeled shrimp in the dill-and-cucumber dressing before she'd stuffed the finger rolls? Men might come and men might go, but the housekeeping had to be coped with regardless. There was that to be said for worrying about the little things, they kept one from having time to grieve over the big ones.

She ought not to be wasting her own time on such private maunderings. "Did anyone notice whether Lydia and Mr. Arbalest were at the grave?" she asked. "I don't recall seeing them."

"Neither do I," said Max, "but Dubrec and his father were. I assume that's his father. It wouldn't surprise me if the old man and George had been business associates back when George was still functioning, I can't think why else they'd have come."

"Nor can I," said Brooks. "They must have been close in some way for Anora to have remembered him all these years. Do you suppose she's invited them back to the house?"

"Surely she must have," Sarah replied. "She'd never slight anybody who cared about George. But nobody saw Mr. Arbalest at the cemetery? Jesse, how about you? I'm talking about that man who sat behind us and cried."

"Yes, I know you are, but I didn't see either him or the woman with the hat. I did see the cops giving the bum's rush to a man in a red jogging suit, though."

"Jesse, you didn't! Where was he?"

"Downhill from the grave. I was beginning to feel sermoned out so I oozed myself to the back of the crowd around the grave and got behind a big tombstone with an angel on it. One of the cops down below noticed me and was starting up the hill to see whether I belonged there, I suppose, but all of a sudden this little guy in a red suit, about my brother James's size only darker, came chugging up the rise, heading straight for where everybody was standing."

"Really? But none of us saw him."

"He never made it to the top, a cop intercepted him. The cop was

trying to make the man understand that he wasn't supposed to go up
there but the man didn't seem to know what he was talking about. It
was as if he didn't speak English, or else he was deaf. Finally the cop
just took him by the arm and led him back down the hill. About then
it started to thunder so I thought I'd better get back to you in case
we had to leave in a hurry. Sorry I couldn't find out what happened
to the guy."

"You did exactly right in the circumstances," said Brooks. "Thank
you, Jesse."

18

Brooks was as expert at driving a car as he was at most other things. He knew every back road, he got his party to Anora's in about a fifth of the time it had taken them to travel the lesser distance from the church to the graveyard. Even so, they weren't the first arrivals. Edgar Merton's car, with a brand-new dent in its left-front fender, was plugging up the driveway, a middle-aged but impeccably dent-free Rolls-Royce had pulled in behind it. Rather than get boxed in, Brooks parked at the curb, right in front of a police car. The arm of the law was still outstretched, he and his passengers were relieved to see.

"Here we are, ladies and gentlemen, I see Leila's beaten us. Why in God's name do you suppose Edgar let her drive his car?"

"One doesn't *let* Leila do anything," Sarah answered, "she just does it. As an educated guess, I'd also say that Alice Merton's long illness must have eaten up more of her estate than Edgar bargained for, whereas Leila has taken excellent care of that wad her father left her."

How easy it was to fall back into the old familiar pattern. What did Sarah Bittersohn really care about either one of them? They might as well marry, Leila'd have someone to browbeat and Edgar'd be relieved of anxiety as to who was going to pay his club dues. Oh, to be back at Ireson's Landing!

But duty before pleasure, there was still Anora to be comforted. Brooks had come around to open the door for the ladies.

"Think you can make it, or shall I nip up to the house and borrow an umbrella?"

"Oh no, we'll be fine," said Theonia. "Jesse can come under mine and you others have your raincoats. It seems to be letting up anyway, I just hope the sun doesn't come blazing out too soon and make everything all hot and steamy."

"The house will be cool enough," Sarah promised, "and you four needn't stick around any longer than you want to. I can ride back later with Mariposa and Charles."

"Let's see how it works out," said Max. "Ah, I see Anora has a new butler."

One of the policemen from the cruiser was standing at the door; no doubt there was another around at the back, nobody cared to go and find out. They had to go through yet another checkoff before they were let in. Mariposa was right there waiting to take the raincoats and park Theonia's goose-handled umbrella in a Chinese porcelain stand with mythical creatures all over it. She looked remarkably sedate, for her, in the high-necked, long-sleeved black uniform with its lace-edged white collar and even lacier white apron, her luxuriant black hair drawn into a heavy roll under her ribbonless white cap. A few old-timers might deem the maid's lipstick a shade too emphatic, her heels an inch too high, the set of her cap a whisker too frisky; the rest would be laying devious plans to lure her away to work for them.

Sarah caught Edgar Merton giving Mariposa a reflective glance. He might be thinking about a spot of luring himself, not that he'd dare try it with Leila around. At the moment Edgar was over by the bar chatting with Lydia Ouspenska. Leila had a martini in her hand, probably not her first, and was laying down the law about something or other to Bartolo Arbalest.

The reason why Lydia and Arbalest hadn't gone to the cemetery had become clear. They must have gone back to Boston so that Goudge could change out of the chauffeur's uniform that had evidently kept him from being let into the church. Now he had on a dark blue blazer and gray flannel slacks, the same outfit Brooks was wearing and that at least four other men would be showing up in any minute now. Protective coloration.

Obviously there hadn't been any standing around and chatting at the graveside, it wasn't long before people were arriving in carloads.

Anora was back home with her two old faithfuls; Cook had headed
for the kitchen without even pausing to take her hat off, Phyllis had
caught one glimpse of Mariposa and hustled away to get into her
own uniform. As soon as she could break a path through her well-
wishers, Anora disappeared too. She was back in about ten minutes
without her toque, her suit, or, Sarah suspected, her corset; wearing
a lovely blue-silk caftan, an Indian silver-lace stole that any serious
collector would have given an eyetooth to own, and a pair of ratty
old brown-felt bedroom slippers with holes worn through at the toes.
She'd lost that wooden-soldier look she'd maintained all through the
long obsequies, she was back in charge.

"Pull up that chair for me, Brooks, before I collapse. Gin and
tonic, Charles, with extra lime and lots of ice. Mariposa, bring me
something to eat, I don't care what. Did you remember the dressing
for the shrimps?"

"Yes'm, Cook had a list all written out. We did everything just like
she said."

"Good. Marcus, come here, you haven't kissed me yet. Sarah, I
want you to meet George's godson. Sarah is Walter Kelling's daughter, Marcus. You remember Walter, you used to go mushrooming
with him."

"Did you really?" Sarah herself had never got to go picking mushrooms with her father. At first she'd been too young, then she'd been
too busy running his household, then he'd died from eating poison-
ous mushrooms and she'd felt no urge to pick up the fallen torch.
"Do you still belong to the Mycological Society?"

She didn't say "Mr. Nie" because Anora hadn't mentioned his last
name. Anyway this wasn't going to be the start of something beautiful. Nie only vouchsafed her one quick, furtive glance, mumbled
something Sarah couldn't catch over the hubbub, gave Anora a peck
on the cheek, and headed for the bar.

Anora seemed satisfied enough. "Poor Marcus, he loathes having
to mix with people he doesn't know. He loved his old godfather,
though. They'd spend hours together, the two of them, just sitting.
George would wake up every so often and ramble on about nothing
in particular, you know how he used to do; Marcus would just smile
and nod and agree with whatever George said. Marcus has quite a
sweet smile, though I don't suppose you'll ever get to see it. I was so

pleased to find out that he's working for Bartolo these days, it's just what he needs. Aren't you having anything to drink?"

"Tea, I hope, when Cook gets around to it."

"Humph. She's probably sat down to rest her feet and fallen asleep. You'd better go wake her up."

Sarah was not about to do any such thing. In the kitchen she stepped carefully around the nodding old woman in the well-cushioned wicker chair, filled the kettle herself, and set it on the stove. The tray was standing ready on the table, trust Mariposa for that. There were extra platters of sandwiches and little cakes too, Sarah lifted the plastic covering on one of them and took a finger roll.

The shrimp was delicious. She was hungrier than she'd realized, she finished the first roll and took another. She might as well wait here for the water to boil. If she went back to the gathering she'd surely get sidetracked talking to somebody and Cook might not wake up in time to rescue the kettle. Besides, Sarah could use a few minutes' quiet time to herself.

How very odd to learn that Marcus Nie had been wont to pick mushrooms with her father. How much odder to discover that he had been George Protheroe's godchild, though why she should feel it so was more than she could explain. Sarah supposed it was just that she herself had never known George except as a member of the familiar circle which had included her own parents and other Kelling connections. She'd thought of the Protheroes more or less as family; it was disconcerting to be made to realize that, all these years, a couple she'd thought she'd known inside out had had so many other facets to their lives.

The small revelation about her father's having known Marcus Nie was less of a jolt. Walter Kelling had been active in the Mycological Society for years, Sarah couldn't recall his ever having evinced that same sense of blood brotherhood toward fellow mushroom enthusiasts as her Uncle Jeremy did toward his Comrades of the Convivial Codfish. Anybody who was interested and had the time could be a mycologist; membership in the Codfish came only by inheritance, and grudgingly at that.

Walter Kelling had been a courteous man but not a particularly gregarious one, except with certain handpicked members of his own family and a few old friends. His best friend had been his distant cousin Alexander; he'd chosen Alexander as his daughter's legal guardian and thus, by a strange chain of events, elected him her first husband. Thank God that father hadn't been best friends with Marcus Nie, Sarah thought a bit wildly. What would have become of her then?

The fact that Walter Kelling had never so much as mentioned Nie's name in his daughter's hearing was not surprising. Neither of her parents had gone in for idle gossip, at least not when their lone chick was around. The two had traveled a good deal. Once Walter's wife had learned she wasn't going to live long, she'd been determined to do all the things on her agenda while she still could; staying home to tend a young daughter was not one of them. Walter Kelling hadn't believed in sending his child to school, Sarah had often been left in the care of a governess or parked with relatives.

Mrs. Kelling completed her agenda when Sarah was twelve and the widower decided his daughter was old enough to take over the housekeeping. His late wife's illness had been costly, Sarah was to manage with a part-time cook-housemaid and a twice-a-week cleaner while Walter worked at the Atheneum on his Kelling family history or pursued his other interests, all of them respectable, none greatly to the taste of a girl just entering into her teens.

Visits to the Protheroes with her parents had been among Sarah's earliest treats. For her the main attraction had been Cook and her big gray cat. Percival had been a placid creature, fat like everybody else in the house except Phyllis, quite willing to be lugged around but too heavy to lug for long, readier to curl up with Sarah in the wicker chair in which Cook was gently snoring right now and to be fed bits of whatever dainty Cook had given Sarah to eat. Food at Walter Kelling's house had tended to be pretty much on the high-minded side, Sarah had relished the goodies she'd got here. She was glad enough to have this brief time alone with her memories.

Then the kettle boiled and duty called. Sarah knew where to find the lapsang souchong: in the ancient black-tin caddy with the half-rubbed-off golden dragons, where Cook had always kept it. She spooned loose leaves into the warmed kitchen pot, a big Brown Betty with a nick in its spout. She remembered the nick from her earliest days, not much had changed around here. Once the tea had got strong enough but not too strong, she'd have to strain it into the good porcelain pot that was waiting on the tray. Anora didn't hold with putting the leaves directly into the good pot and adding more boiling water as the pot got emptied, the tea got weaker and each cupful had to be strained separately. Her way meant a perfect cupful every time.

But nobody got any tea leaves to read. A person could always let the strainer slip, Sarah thought with a shade of the old rebelliousness. No, one couldn't. Cook would find the leaves in the cup when she went to do the washing up, and think she was losing her grip. That would be a sad recompense for all the times Sarah had been let cuddle Percival. She poured herself a cup from the old Brown Betty and was seriously considering a third finger roll when Theonia came into the kitchen.

"Ah, here you are, Sarah. Anora was wondering about the tea."

"It's just ready. Want a cup before I strain it?"

"Why not? Pour me one, I'll take in the tray and come back for the pot."

"No, I'll carry the tray, it's high time I showed my face again. What's going out there?"

"Oh, talk. I've been chatting with Lydia Ouspenska mostly. She's feeling a trifle out of her element."

Theonia herself had adjusted so well to the Kelling ambience that some of the less-collected relatives had come to think of her as a cousin in the third, fourth, or possibly fifth degree; she would never have been so rude as to disillusion them. Anyway, there was always the possibility that it might be true, since her shy young mother had not been bold enough to ask her father what his last name was during their brief but fruitful relationship.

The decibel level in the drawing room was pretty high by now, Leila Lackridge's shrill whine was hardly audible over the general chatter. Lydia Ouspenska wasn't out of her element any more, she was giving Dr. Harnett a lecture on Byzantine icons in a rich assortment of languages ranging from Polish to Hippie. Lydia had been a trifle on the elderly side to have rated as a flower child but that hadn't stopped her from embracing the counterculture of the sixties, nor from continuing to hold the torch alight long after most of her erstwhile comrades had either fried their brains with assorted hallucinogens or retired from the scene to become stockbrokers. Her new persona was better adapted to the current ambience, the men in particular were finding her captivating. Lydia might even have been able to charm George Protheroe into staying awake. What a pity they'd never get to know.

Anora was looking better than she had at the funeral, she'd finished her one highball and was having a cup of Sarah's tea. Mariposa kept bringing her things to eat, people were going over to chat with her. It was a blessing, Sarah thought, that the day was so warm. A fire in the fireplace without George lurking in the inglenook for a chance to tell somebody his bear story would have put a damper on the agreeable party this was turning out to be.

Bartolo Arbalest was all over his weeps, he was fine-tuning his savoir-faire on some of the ladies from Anora's bridge club. Sarah had wondered how Max and Brooks would be able to preserve their incognitos with Jacques Dubrec and Marcus Nie in the room; she needn't have bothered. Instead of trying to dodge the men from the atelier they were deliberately pursuing the acquaintance.

Max was listening intently to the old man who had in fact turned out to be Dubrec *père*. Dubrec *fils* was nodding, smiling, getting a word in when he could, enjoying his father's success in this unfamiliar milieu. Brooks and Marcus Nie were off by themselves in a corner, Nie was sipping from what looked to Sarah like a glassful of straight whiskey with one lone ice cube floating in it. She had a suspicion that this wasn't his first, his yellow complexion had by now changed to a somewhat less unattractive burnt orange. Anyway, the drink was having a tonic effect, Nie was talking quite eagerly about something or other. Brooks was looking ever so impressed, guileful rogue that he was.

Young Jesse had managed to wheedle a highball out of Charles. Soda water and lime with a dash of vodka, most likely. He was sticking to Jacques Dubrec like a burr to a pant leg, Sarah realized this must be her own doing. She'd scribbled that note about keeping an eye on the Dubrecs mainly to give Jesse something to occupy his mind and keep him from annoying Aunt Bodie. He must think the pair still needed watching. Perhaps he was right, Max was certainly in no hurry to leave them alone.

Edgar Merton had managed for the moment to break away from Lydia. He was heading her way, lamenting that he hadn't seen her in ages and wondering what she'd been doing with herself.

"Sarah, you're looking lovely as always. Anora told me you'd remarried, I was hoping I might have the pleasure of meeting your husband. Is he here?"

There was nothing Sarah could do after that except to lead Edgar over to Max and make the introduction, nothing Max could do but be polite to Edgar. Dubrec the younger seized the opportunity to get himself a fresh drink and see what the buffet had to offer, his father seemed not at all loath to turn his attention to Sarah.

Even though the old man had told her he'd lived in America for many years, he spoke with such a heavy French accent that Sarah would have found it a strain to listen, had she not been so intrigued by what he was saying. Long ago when the world was young, he had worked for the Protheroes. He and George had traveled the Orient together, George to buy objects of art and beauty to be taken back to Boston and sold through the family firm, Amadée Dubrec to use his expertise in telling him what was worthy of purchase and what was not. George had held in admiration Amadée's superior knowledge of craftsmanship, Amadée had held in reverence George's magnificent ability to haggle. Always George was courteous, never had he raised his voice, never had he tried to beat the purveyor down below an honest price, equally never had he paid one sou more than the true value of the merchandise. To watch George Protheroe closing a deal had been an experience comparable to seeing Pavlova dance or hearing the great Bernhardt recite the immortal lines of Racine or Corneille. And then there would have been on the other end the profit, always the profit, never once a mistaken purchase; George had known by instinct what would please the market. Madame Bittersohn could take it from Amadée Dubrec, George Protheroe had been a great man.

But then had struck the tragedy. In India, while on the trail of rarities even more exotic than usual, George had been stricken by a terrible disease. It had been Amadée who had walked beside his friend's palanquin to the railroad, Amadée who had flagged down the train and bribed the conductor to provide a private compartment where George could rest, Amadée who had found on the train by a miracle a doctor who had given George treatment and got him to hospital, Amadée who had sat by George's bedside until the crisis at last had passed, Amadée who had sent cablegrams to George's family, Amadée who had sailed with George aboard the steamer that brought him home, Amadée who had visited him faithfully during his long and never-completed convalescence. Amadée took no credit to himself, George would have done the same for him.

When George's father had garnered his final profit and it had become plain that George's infirmity had rendered him unable to carry on the family business, Amadée had received a handsome percentage of the sale price. There had also been a gold watch, with engraving. Mr. Dubrec pulled it out, a handsome hunter, and showed her the engraving on the inside cover: "To Amadée Dubrec in recognition of his inestimable services from his grateful friend George Protheroe."

Sarah felt tears coming, "That's wonderful, Mr. Dubrec. I'm glad you told me. Had you seen George recently?"

"Alas, no, not for many years. You see, I too have suffered from my time in the Orient, though with me it has taken the form of severe rheumatic pains. With my what you might call 'severance pay' I removed myself, my wife, and my then infant son to Arizona. In that more salubrious climate we throve and prospered, but never did I lose touch with my old friend; although of late years, one must understand, communication has been mostly by *carte de Noël*. Upon hearing from my son by long-distance telephone of the macabre demise of my dear friend, I at once telephoned his widow to say that I was coming, which was to her a great solace. She offered at once the hospitality of her home, in which I was of old so frequent a visitor. So I boarded an airplane, me, at ninety-one years, and here I am. It was necessary that I attend, for it is I and I alone who know the secret."

19

Charles and Mariposa had been taking good care of the old man, maybe a little too good, perhaps he'd had more wine than he could comfortably handle. Sarah couldn't tell whether she'd heard him right or whether he was talking through his hat. George Protheroe with a lifelong secret? One that his own wife hadn't known about?

Amadée Dubrec's answer to Sarah's unspoken question was an emphatically Gallic shrug and a moue that would have come across loud and clear in any language. Something, then, that George had been most particular to keep Anora from finding out.

Well, that was possible. George had been young when he and Amadée had traveled the Orient together, rich and reasonably good-looking, judging from the portrait Anora had had painted of him from some of his early photographs. Had some captivating Madame Butterfly or her Tamil equivalent once fluttered into George's life and out again? What difference could that make now? Anora was too old to care, too generous to begrudge, too sensible to be jealous. She might even have a few secrets of her own tucked away. Most people did if they'd lived any sort of life at all.

Sarah felt no great urge to pry into George Protheroe's past, but the elder Dubrec was clearly expecting her to say something. It would be cruel not to oblige him. "A secret?" she replied with the right degree of courteous interest, "then you must have been very close friends indeed."

"Of the closest! It was myself and no other who brought George the pen and the paper to the hospital in his brown Morocco portfolio that had been for so long his companion on our travels and in which he had kept his records of purchase and expense and his diary, *ma foi*, for he was a careful man and trusted nothing to memory. And it was to me that George entrusted on his hospital bed, which we then thought would be his deathbed, that which he had written, bit by bit when his faltering strength would permit, in an envelope to be opened only when he had passed through the gates of heaven to be welcomed by the holy angels, of which there can be no doubt. Who could have thought then that George would survive to a great age? I tell you, that man was a Titan!"

"He was also the husband of a loyal, devoted, and extremely sensible woman." Sarah had no objection to hearing George Protheroe's praises sung, but fair was fair.

Amadée was not at all put out by her reminder. "Ah yes, one sees that Anora is the soul of goodness, a pearl among womankind. Always George spoke of his beloved wife with respect and affection of the utmost. She will be astonished but, one hopes, not desolated."

"I can't imagine anything that would desolate Anora for long, Mr. Dubrec. Then George meant the letter for her?"

"There is, I know, no child of her body. Has the dear lady no brother? No sister? Even perhaps a niece or nephew?"

"No, she was an only child, all her relatives are long gone. George had family, as you must of course know, but that's not quite the same, is it? Anyway, I'm sure Anora will want to be alone when she reads George's letter. Did you bring it with you?"

"But of course. The time had come for me to fulfill my final mission to my dear friend. Was I to be forgetful of the solemn charge he had laid upon me in what he then deemed to be his hour of extremity? One sees that you too, Madame Bittersohn, are despite your youth and beauty a woman of sense and compassion. Is it that you would have the great goodness to advise me?"

"If I can, surely. What is it you want to know, Monsieur Dubrec?"

"It is simply that I am in doubt as to at what time I should present George's letter to our respected Anora. I am, as I mentioned, a guest in this house; therefore I have a choice of opportunities. Would it be less shocking to her, do you think, if I were to approach her later today, after these others are gone and we two are alone together? Or should I delay my mission until tomorrow at breakfast, when she has had time to rest from her ordeal of today?"

Sarah could imagine how much rest Anora would be getting. "As to her resting, I doubt whether Anora will get much of that, unless Dr. Harnett's given her something to take. It might be just as well for you to give her the letter as soon as the other guests leave. If she chooses not to read it until later, that will be her decision. Do you have it with you at the moment?"

"But no, that would not be convenient. The envelope is large and bulky, you understand, fastened with string around two little cardboard buttons and also sealed with glue, not something to put in one's pocket. I have naturally concealed the envelope in a safe place until the moment of revelation shall be at hand."

"I see. How long are you planning to stay?"

"Only until tomorrow morning at eleven o'clock, when I shall be picked up in a limousine commanded by my son Jacques and driven to the airport. Jacques would prefer to accompany me back to Arizona, you understand, for his filial piety knows no bounds; but his sense of duty to Bartolo keeps him here."

Sarah thought Jacques might also consider his duty to his aged parent. "Then you'll be making that long trip all by yourself?" she asked rather sharply.

"Indeed, no. Two of my grandsons accompanied me to Boston. They would not intrude on Madame Protheroe's grief but have elected instead to remain with a friend from their college days and see the sights. It is arranged that we shall meet at the airport. These are sons of my son from my second marriage, not sons of Jacques. He was from my first marriage, he and his sainted sister, Erminie, who was an artisan even more magnificent than Jacques, may her beloved soul rest in peace. Erminie's terrible death was a tragedy of the utmost, it killed her dear mother. But of our own sufferings I must not speak when here in the house of my old friend George is already so deep a mourning."

This was stretching it a bit, Sarah thought. By now any grief most of those present might feel for George Protheroe had to be pretty well numbed. A detached observer would have concluded that the party was going strong, as funeral gatherings so often do. Jacques Dubrec did not appear to be bowed down by weight of woe at having to miss the trip home with his father, he was heading back this way with a fresh glass of wine in each hand and possibly a couple more down his gullet.

Max was over by the bay window, in the Stymphalian clutches of
Leila Lackridge. It would be humane to rescue him, and prudent to
pass him the word about Mr. Dubrec's mysterious mission. Marcus
Nie had Anora to himself at the moment; he was sitting on a foot-
stool at her motherly knee, not exactly laying his head in her lap but
giving the impression that he'd rather like to. Bartolo Arbalest had
temporarily lost Lydia Ouspenska to Dr. Harnett, she was ogling him
over her wineglass as only Lydia could ogle. And he was loving it, the
old rascal.

Bartolo was wandering around by himself, studying various bibelots with an expert's eye, perhaps hoping to pick up another commission from Anora. He drifted through the door and out into the hall.
Sarah half expected Carnaby Goudge to slide out after him, but the
bodyguard seemed not to be present. Where was Goudge, anyway?

Not everybody who'd gone to the grave had come back to the
house. The room was not exactly full, but with so much overstuffed
furniture, so many little tables full of bric-a-brac, and upward of
thirty people milling about, it was not easy to keep the guests sorted
out. Clothing didn't help; except for a few like Theonia and Lydia
Ouspenska they were a fairly nondescript lot. At least half a dozen
men and a couple of the women had on those ubiquitous navy-blue
blazer jackets, all pretty much alike except for the buttons.

Here at least was variety. Sets of blazer buttons were rather an in
thing these days, a suitable gift for the relative who owned a blazer
and perhaps had shed a few of the original buttons with the passage
of time. Some buttons were of brass decorated with anchors, racing
sculls, catboats, schooners; one even had square-riggers under full
sail, which must have been quite a job to get on to so confined an
area as a jacket button. Perhaps there were only dinghies on the
sleeve buttons, Sarah didn't feel it would be polite to ask. A stout
man whose name she couldn't recall had scrimshawed bone buttons
with whaling scenes on them, a thin one had pewter with windmills.
Brooks Kelling's were the handsomest of all: antique silver with a
flock of merganser ducks swimming in neat rows down over his
manly chest and flat tum. Theonia had tried for crested grebes but
had not been able to find any. Apparently grebes had not yet made
the fashion scene.

Looking around the big, dim room, Sarah spied four navy-blue
blazers huddled over behind the huge grand piano at which George,

in his younger and less totally inert days, had sometimes whanged out a few bars of "Chopsticks." Two of the quartet were tallish and thinnish, she assumed that Carnaby Goudge must be one of that pair. They seemed to be engaged in earnest discussion; she had a nasty hunch that they might be planning to break out into "The Whiffenpoof Song" or "Fight Fiercely, Harvard," though she hoped for Anora's sake they wouldn't. Naturally the sun had come poking out as soon as everybody had scurried in out of the rain and Anora had ordered the blinds two-thirds drawn to keep out the heat, so Sarah couldn't see the men's faces well enough to make sure, not that it mattered much.

Jacques Dubrec was steering his old father toward the door. Perhaps they intended to join Bartolo Arbalest on his prowls. More probably, Sarah thought, they were going to deal with the consequences of all that wine. It mightn't be a bad idea to have a word with Cook about strong coffee and another with Charles about weaker drinks before she went to rescue Max from Leila.

Of course Sarah didn't succeed in just darting in and out of the kitchen. She had to spend a few minutes sympathizing with Cook about her years of devoted service to her late master's stomach, with particular reference to the pork roast on the eve of his dreadful demise, and mollifying Phyllis, whose nose was out of joint because Mariposa was doing all the work. What with one thing and another, Sarah was gone perhaps ten minutes. By the time she got back to the drawing room, Max had succeeded in breaking away from Leila un-aided and was talking to Jacques Dubrec.

Amadée was not with his son, Sarah surmised he'd gone to lie down. That lengthy funeral service, the drive to the cemetery, the standing in the rain at the grave, then a roomful of strangers and a skinful of Chardonnay must have been almost too much for a nona-genarian to handle, particularly one with a long flight coming up tomorrow and a secret mission to perform tonight. Whatever could George Protheroe have put in that letter?

That he'd have been able to keep anything a secret from Anora all these years seemed incredible. Perhaps he'd only wanted to express a young husband's love and gratitude to the wife he'd then thought might soon become his widow. What with that devasting fever and the narcolepsy that had plagued him afterward, George had proba-bly forgotten he'd ever written the letter. How touching that

Amadée Dubrec had nevertheless stayed faithful to his trust over all these years, through his own joys and sorrows. Sarah began to feel weepy again; she did the sensible thing and went to see if there were any shrimp rolls left.

By this time most of the guests, mourners no more, had eaten all they wanted. Not so Jesse Kelling, he was still stoking up from those lean days out at Ireson's Landing. Oddly enough he'd found a kindred soul in Lydia Ouspenska. The two of them had the buffet all to themselves; they were standing there pigging out in grand style, talking a mile a minute with their mouths full.

Sarah wondered whether the fact that Bartolo Arbalest was no longer in the room had anything to do with Lydia's reversion to her old habits. No, not quite a reversion; this time Lydia wasn't bundling up whatever she couldn't eat in one of her hostess's napkins to take home for future reference. Anyway, she and the boy were having a lovely time together. Jesse appeared to be pouring out his heart about something, maybe about the girl he hadn't taken to the slumber party, maybe about virginity in general. Lydia might be a trifle rusty on virginity but her general expertise on male-female relationships was certainly far broader than Sarah Kelling Bittersohn's. They'd eaten all the shrimp rolls, there was nothing to keep her here; Sarah eased herself away and went over to see how Max was bearing up.

Jacques Dubrec was an amusing fellow in his quiet way. He and Max were having a fine time trying to decide how a minimalist painting could be achieved with the smallest possible amount of effort. They asked Sarah's opinion.

"Obviously," she replied, "the most minimal thing you could do would be to forget the whole business. I had such an interesting chat with your father, Mr. Dubrec. Is he resting now?"

"Oh no, papa never rests. Or claims he doesn't. He'll be back in a while, he wants to be able to make a full report on the funeral to his old friend George when they meet in the sweet by-and-by. It's very good of Mrs. Protheroe to put him up."

"I'm sure she considers it a privilege and wishes he could stay longer," Sarah replied. "He's leaving tomorrow, your father tells me. I understand you're sending a limousine to pick him up."

Dubrec shrugged. "That's the least I can do. I don't have a car of my own, I haven't driven since my sister—but you don't want to hear about that. So when are you planning to start redesigning the atelier, Mr.—I'm sorry, I didn't quite catch your name the other day."

"Just call me Max, everybody else does. What's up, Sarah? Are you trying to tell me it's time for us to leave?"

"I'm just wondering how much longer Anora's going to hold together. Perhaps if you were to go and round up Theonia and Brooks, some of the others would take the hint and start moving. Oh, I beg your pardon, Mr. Dubrec, I didn't mean you. Naturally you'll want more time with your father if he's going home tomorrow. It's just that Anora's been through such a terrible time these past few days, as you can well imagine. She's pretty well at the end of her rope, though she'd be the last person to admit it. A quiet visit with old friends like you and your father and Mr. Nie, instead of all these people talking at once, would be far more of a comfort to her. Once the party breaks up, I'll stay on just long enough to help Charles and Mariposa pick up the pieces, then we'll clear out and you three can have Anora to yourselves. Is Mr. Nie going to drive you back to Boston?"

Jacques Dubrec shook his head. "I have no idea whether Marcus even owns a car. I never in the world expected to see him here. Marcus doesn't talk, you know."

"Actually I didn't know," Sarah replied. "My parents were friends of the Protheroes'. I've known them all my life and they never once mentioned that George had a godchild. Anora seems fond of Marcus, as she calls him, and he of her."

"Well, I'm glad to know Marcus has got somebody," said Dubrec. "He's not a bad guy, does his work well enough and never bothers anybody else. We have one kook in the atelier who thinks he has to be the life of the party, he never shuts up from morning till night."

"Doesn't that get awfully wearing?"

"Sometimes. Mostly I just tune him out. Coming from a big family, you learn to do that, specially when you have kids of your own."

"You must miss your children."

"Sometimes I do. But you know how it is, they grow up and have lives of their own, they don't need me any more. We talk on the phone fairly often, and write back and forth. The grandkids draw me pictures." His smile was a bit rueful. "But Bartolo has a nice setup here and I really don't mind helping out. He's had such a ghastly

time of—oops, forget I said that, will you? I must have had one too
many."

"There's hot coffee in the urn over there, if you'd like some."

"I guess I'd better. Nice talking to you, Mrs.—"

"Sarah, please. Perhaps we'll meet again before too long."

"That would be great. Well, then—"

20

F ew people would have had the insensate gall to interrupt a social gathering the way Leila Lackridge did. She'd left the drawing room only a minute or so ago, Sarah vaguely recalled having seen her go. Now Leila was back, standing in the exact center of the big double doorway, not having to shout. Her ordinary speaking voice was penetrating enough to carry into every corner.

"Anora, I hate to put a damper on the proceedings, but I do think you ought to know that that old Frenchman who's been lushing it up for the past two hours is lying on the hall floor with his head bashed in. Brains all over the place. Phyllis, go fetch a mop."

"Leila, you crazy drunken bitch, shut up!" Dolph Kelling had never been one to mince his words, it was clear that he'd as soon be mincing Leila. "Max, what do we do now?"

"Stay where you are. That means everybody, including Phyllis. Nobody's to leave this room. Leila, sit down. Charles, get Mrs. Lackridge a drink. I'll go take a look."

Max stepped out into the hall. They heard him say "God!" Then he was calling out to the policeman on guard at the front door. "Come in here, we need you."

Now they were talking. Sarah couldn't catch the words, she had troubles of her own to cope with. Jacques Dubrec had stared blankly at Leila during her shocking announcement, now he'd come alive. As he lunged toward the door, Sarah grabbed his arm. He tried to pull away.

"Let me alone, damn you!"

"No, you mustn't go out there. Dolph, help me."

Hearing his wife's screams, Max darted back. "Steady, Dubrec, there's nothing you can do."

"But my father! I've got to go to him."

"Believe me, it's better that you don't. I'm sorry as hell, Dubrec, but we'll have to wait for the police. Brooks, call Homicide. Jesse, go let the cop at the back door know what's happened. Tell him to stop anybody who tries to leave by the back way. Then alert the guy down front who's directing traffic."

"Gotcha."

Jesse was off like a bandersnatch. Dubrec was still fighting, Max and Dolph wrestled him back into his chair.

"Dr. Harnett, can you take over here?"

"In a minute. Here, Anora, swallow this pill. Water, Charles."

Oh God, thought Sarah, this is all Anora needed, George's oldest friend murdered in her house. "Max," she said, "I'd better go to the kitchen and break the news very carefully. Cook's heart's none too sound either."

"Don't go yet, Sarah, we have to take a nose count." Max raised his voice. "Please, everybody, we need your cooperation. We've all been in and out of this room for various reasons, the policeman who's been on duty at the door says nobody's actually left the house for quite a while. So who's still with the party, but not in here right now?"

Marcus Nie giggled, a horrible high-pitched neigh. "Jacques's father."

Max didn't rise to the bait. "Thanks, Nie, that's a start. Dubrec, you and your father went out together, can you tell us where he was when you left him?"

"He had to go to the bathroom. I took him to that one down the hall a ways and waited till he came out, just to make sure he was all right. Papa's—was a very old man, you know. But anyway, papa came out and told me he wanted to be alone for a while with George. What he meant was, he wanted to go and sit in the den. Papa said that was where he and George always went when they had business to discuss, just the two of them. I could understand. We were always close, papa and I."

"Did you go with him to the den?"

"No, I don't even know where it is. This is a funny laid-out house,

I still haven't caught on to the floor plan. But papa knew, and he didn't want me to go with him. He said I should come back here and talk to the pretty ladies. Papa's been urging me to get married again, the way he did, but I just—oh well. I think papa knew he was going to cry and didn't want anybody to see him. He's a proud man, my—"

Jacques Dubrec himself was crying by now, not caring who saw him. He slumped over in his chair and wiped his face on one of Anora's lace-edged cocktail napkins. Dr. Harnett had Anora under control, she was beginning to react to the sedative; he came over and took hold of Dubrec's other wrist, feeling for a pulse. Dubrec didn't seem to notice.

Leila Lackridge was still raising a ruckus. She hadn't done what she'd gone out for, she still had to go, the old man's body was blocking the way to the powder room, and who did Max Bittersohn think he was? Sarah suggested the facility off the back hall, the one Cook and Phyllis used. Mary Kelling offered to play policewoman. Leila said something disgustingly rude about Irish cops and went with Mary.

One helpful soul in a navy-blue blazer suggested that his Cousin Bud was missing. Another, wearing not only the same kind of jacket but also the same old-school tie, retorted that Bud had been missing on all cylinders ever since the day he was born and a far, far better thing it would be for mankind were Bud to stay missing ad infinitum. Brooks Kelling was delegated to search; he came back to report that Bud was stretched out on the chaise in the sun room, sleeping the sleep of the soused.

One or two other suggestions were put forth with equally frustrating results. "Okay," said Max, wishing to God those laggards from Homicide would get here and take the load off, "who else?"

Sarah had been waiting for a chance to drop her bomb. "Bartolo Arbalest. He was wandering around the house looking at things. He must still be here somewhere, surely he wouldn't have gone off and left Lydia. Mr. Goudge, haven't you seen him?"

Goudge had been leaning up against the grand piano for some time now, with his arms folded across his chest. He raised his head slightly and replied succinctly, "No."

"But why not?"

That was a stupid question, Sarah realized. It deserved a silly answer, and got one. "Because he tol' me to go peddle my papersh."

Brooks was back in the room, having passed the word to Lieutenant Levitan via one of his minions. "Good Lord," he exclaimed, "that man's drunk as a skunk."

"Hell, no, I'm drunker. Lotsh drunker. I can lick any shkunk inna place. Bring 'em on."

Carnaby Goudge flailed at the air, perhaps aiming for some imaginary *Mephitis mephitis*. What he connected with was a small table loaded with bric-a-brac; he, the table, and the bibelots crashed to the floor together. Lydia Ouspenska rushed at him, screaming imprecations in assorted languages.

"Lout! Dummkopf! Xprzsylmbk! *Sacrebleu*, how do we know is Barto maybe murdered by madman in puddle of blood, and here is Carnaby drunk like cage of *singes* with fleas all over, goofing off on job. Get up, get up, *sale cochon*, and go find Barto."

She flipped Goudge over, grabbed his shoulders, and began bouncing him up and down on Anora's precious antique Oriental carpet. He only smiled up at her and tried to pull her down on top of him.

"Come to me, my melancholy bay-hay-bee. Kiss me, Hardy!"

"Hardy who?" demanded one of the other blue blazers, who was fairly well sloshed himself. "What is this fellow, a pouf?"

"No," replied another who appeared to be only mildly elevated, "he must be referring to Tess Hardy. You remember Tess, the boys at Sigma Nu house used to call her Hotcha Hardy. She married one of the d'Urbervilles, as I recall. You'd better quit shaking that chap, Mrs. Ouspenska, or he'll barf all over the Bokhara. What the hell did Anora invite a Yale man for, anyway? You see, this is what comes of being too democratic, if you'll pardon me for using that word in mixed company."

"I thought he'd gone to Dartmouth."

"*Quelle différence?* Here, you," he beckoned in a lordly manner to Charles. "Get this *canaille* out of here. Park him somewhere till he comes to. This is a respectable gathering, *ma foi*, and this is hardly the way to show due respect to a fallen *compère*. Smashing up the widow's antiques and all that. Lowers the tone. *Tout à fait* not *comme il faut*, in my personal opinion."

"And you couldn't be more right, old chap. I mean after all, dash it, men may come and men may go, but Chippendale's a dashed worthwhile investment at any time." The speaker bent with due reverence to pick up the fallen table. His companion watched with detached amusement.

"Chinese export, I believe. Must be something George brought back from one of his earlier buying trips. Well, *chacun à son goût.* Great Scott, I do believe I must be a trifle spifflicated myself. I never talk French when I'm sober. Margaret, don't you think it's time we thought of going home?"

"We shan't be let, Godfrey," replied a weather-beaten matron whom Sarah recognized as the winner of innumerable ladies' amateur golf matches. It was odd to see her not peering out from behind some trophy or other. "One gathers that there's been another incident; it appears the police will want to ask us questions to which I, for one, shall have difficulty offering satisfactory answers. Awfully inconvenient, I'd meant to get in a little practice on my chip shots this afternoon. But there it is, one must play the ball from wherever it lies. Unless one gets a drop, of course. Since we have to stay, I believe I'm going to have a cup of coffee. Would you care to join me?"

"Splendid suggestion, Margaret. I might even venture on one of those pastry affairs, I'm beginning to feel a trifle peckish."

"Then by all means do. Now who's this coming? I thought Anora wasn't admitting any outsiders."

"Perhaps it's the police. They don't all wear uniforms, you know."

"Why no, Godfrey, I didn't realize. How interesting. But then how do we know it isn't the murderer? Oh dear, I do wish I had my five iron with me. Or perhaps a wedge?"

"I'd say the wedge, Margaret. Well, let's have our coffee. I don't suppose the person will mind, whoever he is."

Lieutenant Levitan wasn't begrudging anybody a cup of coffee, he took one himself and appeared to find it good. This modest indulgence, however, did not distract him from the business at hand. He set his empty cup back on the tray, refused a refill, and addressed Anora with due deference but no false humility.

"I'm sorry to have to butt in on you again at a time like this, Mrs. Protheroe, but I need your help and—"

"Leave her alone!" Marcus Nie was on his feet and very nearly at the policeman's throat. "She's sick. She—"

"Hush, Marcus." Anora was still in command. "It's all right, I'll—

oh, I can't think straight. My head's all woozy. Sarah! Where's Sarah?"

"Right here, Anora. Sit down, Marcus. George wouldn't have wanted a fuss. Would he, Anora?"

"No, George hated fuss. You know that, Marcus. It's all right, he's just a policeman. Sorry, officer, I can't think straight. I've taken a pill. Sarah, she'll help you."

"Yes, of course I will. Ask me anything you want, Lieutenant, I'll do my best. I'm Max Bittersohn's wife, remember? We met when—on your previous visit."

"Oh sure, Mrs. Bittersohn. Okay, then. What I'd like to know is, how many of the people here knew Mr. Amadée Dubrec?"

Sarah looked around the room. None of George's oldest friends were here, they were either in wheelchairs or nursing homes or gone before him into the great unknown; these were mostly their sons and daughters. "Actually," she said, "I'm not sure whether anybody here had known Mr. Dubrec before today, except Anora. And his son, of course. Mr. Dubrec was, as his son may have told you, associated with George in the Protheroe family import business until—sometime in the thirties, it must have been."

"Thirty-seven," croaked Anora. "It broke George's heart to sell."

"I know, Anora. But George saw to it that his friend got a handsome settlement, Mr. Dubrec told me that himself. He moved to Arizona on account of his arthritis, or whatever it was. He always meant to come back, but never did. He kept in touch, though, didn't he?"

"He'd write sometimes. I'd write back. George wasn't up to it." Anora was crying effortlessly, noiselessly, just letting the tears roll down her cheeks and splash on Marcus Nie's hand, which was holding hers. "Amadée's with George now. Lucky him."

This couldn't go on. "Lieutenant," said Sarah, "I know we all want to cooperate with you as best we can, but can't we do it in some way that won't be so upsetting to Mrs. Protheroe? Perhaps if you were to go into another room and we could all come to you, one by one?"

"Like in the mystery stories? Sure, why not? Where do I go and who wants to be first?"

"I should think Leila Lackridge would. Mrs. Lackridge is the one who found the body," Sarah explained. Anyway, Leila always wanted to be first. "Go into the morning room, won't you?"

Leila wasn't having the morning room. "Why not the den?"

"Whichever."

There was no earthly use in starting a squabble over so petty a point, Leila was just being Leila, as usual. Sarah saw her and the lieutenant out of the room and went to get herself another cup of coffee. Max came over and put an arm around her waist.

"Tired, Kätzele?"

"Exhausted. Do you suppose it's all right to use the telephone? Miriam will be wondering why she hasn't heard from us."

"No, she won't. I called while I was out in the hall, as soon as I'd realized we were probably going to get stuck here."

"Oh, good. Did you speak to Davy?"

"Sure. He's got a new duck."

"Not a live duck?" Sarah asked in some alarm.

"Perish the thought. A toy one, for him to play with in the wading pool."

"I hope Miriam's not letting him get sunburned."

Max tightened his hold. "She won't, you know that. You just want something to worry about other than Anora."

"How right you are. Max, bend down."

"Like this?" He pulled her still closer and rubbed his lips against her ear. "Now what have you got that nobody's supposed to hear?"

"Mr. Dubrec brought a letter that George wrote ages ago, to be delivered to Anora on his death. He was planning to give it to her after the crowd left."

"Oh boy."

"My feelings exactly. Have they searched Dubrec's body, and his bedroom?"

"I don't know about the body. Levitan sent a man upstairs. The guy found Arbalest prowling around the bedroom. I have a hunch Arbalest's about to be booked on suspicion."

"And I have a hunch that woman from his atelier in Houston who got killed in a car accident will turn out to have been Jacques Dubrec's sister, Erminie."

"You don't say? So what do we do now?"

"Behave ourselves, I suppose. I still haven't broken the news to Cook, I wonder whether anyone's told her yet?"

"Does it matter? She'll find out sooner or later anyway. Won't she come in here to see what's holding up the show?"

"Her? Never. The drawing room is Phyllis's territory, Cook's domain is the kitchen. I just hope Leila didn't go barging in there when she went to the bathroom and blurt it all out. That woman has about as much tact as a power saw. Max, why am I so tired?"

"You're getting old, kid. Cracking up and falling in parts, as my Uncle Hymie would say. Like the rest of us."

"I suppose so. Anyway, Cook's probably asleep in her easy chair and I'm stewing about nothing. Seems to me that's all I've been doing lately. We still haven't done anything much about Anne's painting, either. It's a wonder Percy isn't yammering for his retainer back. Or did he pay one? I can't even remember. Try to think of me as I used to be, dear, before I fell into parts."

21

Levitan must have been working on the principle of age before beauty, it seemed at least one infinity later before Sarah found herself in the den that had also been George Protheroe's bedroom. By now just about everybody else had been questioned, most of them had gone home. Brooks and Theonia had had business to attend to; Sarah had wanted Max to go with them because she could see that he was in pain, but he'd refused to leave her here without him. Rather than miss out on any of the action, wily young Jesse had elected himself a member of the cleanup squad. When last seen, he'd been washing dishes in the kitchen, with Phyllis at his elbow supervising every dip and wipe.

Sarah herself had by no means been idle during the long wait. She'd broken the news to Cook and soothed her with reminiscences of Percival. At Dr. Harnett's insistence she'd helped Anora upstairs, and got her undressed and into bed. She'd then persuaded Marcus Nie not to commit suicide so that he could join his godfather. It would, she'd explained, be rude of him to interrupt George's reunion with Amadée Dubrec before they'd even had time to get caught up. Marcus's turn would come sooner or later, in the meantime Anora still needed him. This had, Sarah realized in retrospect, been a singularly odd conversation. She wondered very much about Marcus Nie.

She'd been under the impression that the artisan hadn't budged from his place at Anora's feet all during the postburial visit, but apparently this was not so. While she was putting Anora to bed, her old friend had mentioned how Marcus had gone alone into the den and knelt by George's empty couch in an agony of tears; at least that was what he'd told Anora when he'd got back. Sarah had tried to pin Anora down as to when this had happened but she'd got nowhere, Anora had been too confused. The incident might not have occurred at all. However, Sarah was inclined to think it had, judging from the way the godson had carried on after Anora had gone upstairs.

She could see why Marcus might have felt a strong attachment to George, the man didn't seem the type to have many friends. She couldn't think why Marcus would have brained Amadée Dubrec, unless out of jealousy for the older man's having been George's close associate before Marcus was ever born. She still didn't know how Marcus had got to be George's godchild; she'd tried to get him to explain their relationship but he'd gone silent again and she'd had to give up. Doubtless Anora knew; it was probably of no consequence in any event, but Sarah still wanted to find out.

At the moment, though, this was Levitan's turn to ask, and hers to answer.

"Mrs. Bittersohn, I suppose you know everybody who's been here today?"

"I've met most of them at various times, in a casual way."

"What about this Mrs. Lackridge? She claims to be a great pal of yours."

"How kind of her." Sarah couldn't quite keep the ice out of her voice. "Actually Leila was more a friend of my late mother-in-law. They were involved together in a number of civic organizations and used to stick me with a good deal of the dog work. My first husband had been a college roommate of her former husband—she and Harry Lackridge were still married then—so we naturally saw a good deal of one another while Alexander and Aunt Caroline were both alive. Afterward, Leila and I had no interests in common and didn't bother to keep in touch. But you know how it is with people one's known for a long time. I suppose one does feel a certain tie."

"I get it. But you say you've worked with Mrs. Lackridge on various projects. What sort of witness do you think she'd make?"

"Arrogant, abrasive, and biased, but not consciously untruthful, if that's what you want to know."

"So she was right when she said she hadn't been away from the party more than a few seconds before she found Mr. Dubrec's body?"

"Oh yes, I saw her leave the room myself. Leila hadn't been gone any time at all before she was back with the gory news. She wasn't particularly tactful about it."

"What did she say?"

"She said the drunken old Frenchman was lying in front of the downstairs bathroom with his brains all over the floor. Those weren't her exact words, but that's the gist. So then my husband went out to check, brought in one of the policemen, had my cousin telephone you, and told everybody else to stay put. I assume you know all that."

"Right. Mrs. Lackridge told me she'd never met either of the Dubrecs before. Is that right?"

"Probably. I don't think most of the others had, either. I certainly hadn't. I expect the son told you about his father's former connection with the Protheroe family?"

"Oh yes. Mrs. Lackridge claimed she hadn't known anything about that."

"I don't suppose she did, it was all so long ago. Leila got to know the Protheroes more or less by inheritance, as I did. Her father was in George's class at Harvard. But then he went into his family's publishing firm. I doubt whether he'd ever have shown much interest in the Protheroes' importing business, and he certainly wouldn't have cared to know any of their employees."

"That kind, eh?"

"Very much that kind. Lieutenant, do you have anything else you want to ask me? Because I have something you ought to know."

"Terrific. Go ahead, Mrs. Bittersohn."

"As I mentioned, I'd never met either of the Dubrecs before and couldn't think why they'd shown up at the funeral. I did know Anora must have invited them; otherwise they wouldn't have been let in, as you know. So naturally I was curious. When I got the chance I went over and spoke to them, as one does at these affairs. The three of us chatted a bit, then the son wandered off and I was alone with the father."

"And so?" Levitan prompted.

"I have a feeling Mr. Dubrec took me for some relative of Anora's, or it may have been just that he'd had a little too much wine," said Sarah. "Anyway, he became quite confiding. He explained to me that he was here on a secret mission. Years ago, while he and George Protheroe were together in the Orient on a buying trip, George became terribly ill and wasn't expected to live. In the hospital, he'd written a letter to be opened by Anora after his death. He'd given Mr. Dubrec the letter to keep until the time came for Anora to have it. Of course, as you know, George actually lived for many years afterward, but all this time Mr. Dubrec had held on to the letter as a sacred trust. That's why he'd come back for George's funeral. A man in his nineties, imagine!"

"Did Dubrec tell you what was in the letter?"

"Oh no, it was no business of mine. I don't suppose he knew himself, Mr. Dubrec hardly seemed the type to read somebody else's mail. However, he and George had been the closest of friends and it's quite possible that, without actually having seen the contents, he had a pretty good idea of what George might have written about. I should say that it's also possible Anora already knows. George was in a high fever for quite some time after Dubrec brought him back from the Orient, and she was right with him night and day. He might very likely have babbled his secret, if there really was one, in a fit of delirium. Anyway, that's my story."

"Uh-huh. Dubrec didn't tell you where he was keeping the letter? It wasn't on him when we searched his clothes, do you think the killer could have taken it?"

"Not from his body. Mr. Dubrec told me the envelope was too big to carry around, and quite bulky. Have you searched the room he was sleeping in?"

"Not thoroughly, yet. When was Dubrec planning to hand over the letter to Mrs. Protheroe? Did he mention that to you?"

"Yes. He asked my advice as to whether he should do it tonight or wait until after breakfast. He was planning to leave late tomorrow morning, I expect the son told you that."

"What did you tell him?"

"I suggested he do it as soon as the others left, and get it over with. So it looks as though somebody overheard me and decided they'd better kill him right away to keep Anora from getting the envelope. I wish to heaven I'd kept my mouth shut."

"No sense blaming yourself, Mrs. Bittersohn. Who was close enough to eavesdrop on you?"

"I didn't think anybody was, but you know how it is at these affairs, people wander around. I shouldn't be surprised if there were a few lip-readers present, now that I think of it. So many of Anora's friends are elderly, some of them may have hearing problems."

"Huh. And you don't think the son knew about the letter? Why not? Didn't he and the father get along?"

"I don't know whether the son knew anything about his father's secret mission, I only know Jacques Dubrec wasn't present when the father and I discussed it. As to their getting along, they seemed to be genuinely fond of each other. The son became terribly upset when he realized Leila Lackridge was talking about his father, he tried to rush out into the hall. I held him back."

Levitan found this amusing. "You held him back? Jacques Dubrec's a big man, Mrs. Bittersohn."

"I know. It was only for a second, my husband and my cousin Dolph came to help me. Then Jacques sat down and talked quietly enough about how he'd taken his father to the bathroom and intended to walk him back, but the father had said not to wait, he'd rather come in here and be by himself alone with George for a while. This is where they'd used to talk over their business. It was," Sarah lost her voice for a moment, "rather touching. Then the son broke down and started to cry and Dr. Harnett gave him something to quiet him down. You've heard all this, I suppose."

"That's okay. Come on, let's go look for the envelope."

"Just so we don't waken Anora. Her bedroom's directly at the top of the front stairs. We'd better slide up the back way."

"You know this house pretty well, do you, Mrs. Bittersohn?"

"Oh yes. As a child I used to stay here overnight sometimes when my parents went away. Anora and George were always very kind to me."

"Treated you like a daughter, did they? Childless couple, maybe Protheroe left you something in his will?"

Sarah was not amused. "That's rather unsubtle of you, Lieutenant. The answer is no, I did not murder George in order to collect an inheritance. He and Anora did not treat me like a daughter, they treated me like a nice child who'd come to visit. When they got tired of me, they'd send me out to the kitchen to play with Cook's pussycat. They've given me nice presents on appropriate occasions, as they have to the daughters and sons of their other friends. George Protheroe was quite aware that my parents could and would provide for me; also that I have a husband and many relatives, with few paupers among them."

"Okay, Mrs. Bittersohn, you can't blame me for trying. What about his friends the Dubrecs?"

"George made a very handsome settlement on Amadée Dubrec at the time the business was sold. Mr. Dubrec told me that he'd used the money to establish himself in business in Arizona and done very well. They kept in touch, so George must have known that his friend was prospering and didn't need any more help from him. I hadn't known about Marcus Nie until today, but Anora says Marcus and George were devoted to each other, so George may have made some provision for his godson. Unless Marcus already has money of his own, which is quite possible. He works for Bartolo Arbalest, did he tell you that? He and Jacques Dubrec both. But anyway, my guess is that George left most of whatever hasn't been spent by now to Anora for her lifetime and then to his niece and her children."

None of whom was among those present. Levitan glanced down the list of people he'd been interrogating.

"I don't remember talking to any relatives except the godson, if you can call him a relative."

"He might actually be one, I wouldn't know. George's niece wasn't able to come; she's sick herself, Anora told me. Her son and daughter and the daughter's fiancé attended the funeral and went to the grave, but didn't come to the house. I believe they all had jobs to get back to."

Or something. At least they weren't hypocrites. The niece and her husband, when he was alive, had been faithful enough in their visits, but their offspring had never overwhelmed George with attention. Sarah supposed one shouldn't blame them too much, George in his later years had been the dullest man alive and Anora's parties weren't much livelier. She'd ducked a few herself. She didn't want to stay in this room any longer, she stood up.

"I thought we were going to hunt for that envelope."

"We are." Levitan got up too, and waved her out the door. "Which way?"

"Through here."

The back stairway was poky, closed in by oaken doors below and above. The walls above the golden-oak wainscot were plastered but had never been papered, sometime or other they'd been painted a

less-than-heartwarming shade of tan. Sarah couldn't remember them
any way but this. The whole house needed redoing. Anora wouldn't
bother, Sarah didn't think the widow would care to live much longer
without George to fuss over. She was relieved when Levitan spoke
again.

"You said it's a big envelope. How big?"

"Mr. Dubrec didn't say, exactly. I automatically visualized it as the
standard nine-by-twelve file size. He said it was brown and quite
bulky; I wondered if perhaps George had put in some kind of present for Anora, possibly a joke such as a portrait of himself dressed
up as a rajah. George had a rather childlike sense of humor. Oh
dear, I'm going to miss him."

Levitan had no time for mulligrubs. He looked down the hall, all
the doors were closed. "Which room?"

"Good question. Let's just keep trying till we come to a suitcase."

And perhaps an unmade bed; Phyllis might not have had time to
straighten up the bedrooms before she'd left for the funeral. Sarah
opened the door at the end of the back hallway. This was where
she'd slept those few times when Anora and George had baby-sat
her. Nothing here except a made-up bed and a film of dust on the
dresser, poor Phyllis didn't get around to things as briskly as she used
to. The next room, the one directly opposite the back stairway, was
occupied. Carnaby Goudge was sleeping it off. Fortunately whoever'd put him to bed had remembered to remove his shoes.

"Who's this guy?" Levitan asked.

"His name is Carnaby Goudge, and he's a professional bodyguard,
currently working for Bartolo Arbalest. Or has been, until now,"
Sarah amended. "I don't know how well his getting smashed at a
client's funeral is going to set with Mr. Arbalest. But then I don't
know why Anora invited any of them to the funeral."

"Who's them?"

"Arbalest himself, Mr. Goudge, and Lydia Ouspenska. Counting
Jacques Dubrec and Marcus Nie, that makes five members of Arbalest's atelier present."

"Atelier? Means workshop, doesn't it? Why shouldn't Mrs.
Protheroe have invited them?"

"Well, naturally Anora was entitled to ask anybody she wanted.
It's just that there are a good many other people whom she'd known
far longer, who'd expected to be asked but weren't."

"What do you mean by longer, Mrs. Bittersohn? How long had Mrs. Protheroe known Arbalest?"

"Do you know, Lieutenant, that's a good question. To the best of my knowledge, they'd only met a couple of months ago. He calls himself the Resurrection Man; he and his employees specialize in repairing works of art, including what I suppose you'd call high-class bric-a-brac. Anora and George had a pair of filigreed Indian silver candlesticks that they wanted to give George's great-niece for a wedding present. The pieces needed to be cleaned and repaired first and a friend recommended Mr. Arbalest, so they called him in. Anora told Max and me that George and Mr. Arbalest had hit it off like old friends and had a long conversation about Asian art. She said George hadn't been so animated in ages. Perhaps that's the reason she asked Mr. Arbalest to the funeral, because he'd been nice to George."

"But why the bodyguard?"

"Because for the past twenty years or so, Bartolo Arbalest has been plagued by a series of disasters. Not to himself, oddly enough, but to the artisans who've worked for him. Several of them have died in various unexpected ways and the word's got around, with the result that he's had a terrible time finding expert craftsmen who are willing to join his atelier. He tried to hire my Cousin Brooks once, that was in New York. But Brooks didn't want the job and neither did anybody else, so Mr. Arbalest moved to Los Angeles until disaster struck again, then to Houston with the same result. Now he's back on the East Coast. This time he has all his artisans living with him, in a house on Marlborough Street with grilles on all the doors and windows and Mr. Goudge as resident security officer."

"How did you find out about him?"

"Through Lydia Ouspenska, indirectly. We've known Lydia for some time. My husband happened to run into her a few days ago and she told him she was working for Barto, as she called him. She was shopping for truffles; Barto's quite a gourmet cook, she says, and prepares the artisans' meals himself. I suppose that's to keep them from being poisoned. One can hardly blame him for taking precautions, all things considered."

22

Levitan nodded. "I can see where Arbalest might be a little twitchy by now. What else did Mrs. Ouspenska tell your husband?"

"She claims the whole operation is highly top-secret. Mr. Arbalest never lets anybody come to the atelier, he goes out to visit the clients. In a Rolls-Royce with Goudge as a uniformed chauffeur, we later found out. Lydia wouldn't even tell Max where the house was. Naturally he got to wondering what she might have let herself in for, so after she'd gone along on her errand, he called me and we put a tail on her."

"That's when you found out about the house on Marlborough Street?"

"Yes," said Sarah. "That same evening, Mr. Goudge showed up at our house on Tulip Street. He'd been bodyguarding Lydia, it transpired, at Arbalest's orders. He thought he'd better let us know the setup so that we wouldn't be making extra work for ourselves, which of course was his polite way of warning us off. But we couldn't let go because right after that a cousin of mine called us about a painting of his wife's that had been stolen. Arbalest had just returned it to them, after doing a very nice job of cleaning and reframing. Furthermore, it was right after Arbalest had brought back the Protheroes' candlesticks that George was murdered."

"That doesn't exactly prove the crimes were related."

"We are not amateurs, Lieutenant," Sarah reminded him in her best Aunt Emma tone. "We did have a little more to go on than coincidence. After he'd tracked Lydia to Arbalest's atelier, our man went around through the alley to find out whether the back is as well-protected as the front, which it is. He came upon a small Asian-looking man in a heavy red sweat suit doing exercises in the alley, directly behind Arbalest's house. When Max and Brooks visited Arbalest the following day, the maid told them that Mr. Arbalest got upset whenever he saw the man."

"Did she say why?"

"No, evidently she's not very bright. But anyway, we ourselves saw the fellow in the red suit, or someone like him, yesterday when we were going to get our car from the Common Garage. He ran right in front of us quite deliberately, we thought. And when I went out to see my cousin's wife, Anne, that afternoon about the painting that had been stolen, Anne told me an odd little story of having come upon a small, thin, Asian-looking man behind a bush in her garden on the morning after the robbery."

"Wearing a red sweat suit, was he?"

"No, he was wearing a rhubarb leaf."

That got a smile out of Levitan. "For God's sake! Did he explain why?"

"He didn't explain anything, he was trying to hide from her. This was very early, before she'd discovered that the painting was missing. Anne knew that her husband, my Cousin Percy Kelling, would hit the ceiling if she told him there was a naked man in the garden, so she took out an old pair of dungarees and a T-shirt, dropped them casually on the ground near the bush, and went in to get breakfast. When she looked out the window, the clothes were gone and so was the man."

"And the painting?"

"Oh yes, but they didn't know until Percy discovered it missing a little while later. He called the police and then rang us up, wanting our help in getting it back. That's what we do, you know. So I went to check things out and found that a vent duct in the greenhouse had been unscrewed. The house had been locked up and protected by an alarm system, this seemed to be the only way a burglar could have got in. The hole wasn't very big; he'd have had to be somebody small and thin, so we assumed it must have been the man with the rhubarb leaf. We surmised that either he'd torn his clothes to ribbons trying to squirm through or else he'd taken them off first and left them outside, and that either a person or an animal had gone off with them."

"But you don't have any concrete evidence," Levitan insisted.

"No, we don't. However, you may be interested to hear a little story Anora told me that same afternoon. She said that the day before George was killed, he and she had been sitting out on the veranda. She'd gone into the house for a few minutes and when she came back, George was standing up looking out over the railing. He told her he'd got up to watch a little brown man in a red jogging suit run across the lawn and into the backyard. George thought the man looked like a Tamil."

"Why Tamil?"

"George was familiar with Asian physical characteristics, he'd traveled in the Orient a great deal when he was an importer. He could even speak a little Tamil, Anora told me. I might add that it would have taken something pretty special to haul George out of his rocking chair, considering his age and weight and general inertness. I know this doesn't count as solid evidence either, but you must admit it's somewhat thought-provoking."

Sarah opened another door and closed it again. "Anora must have put Mr. Dubrec in George's room, the one he used when he could still climb stairs. Ah, here we are."

"Well," said Levitan, "what do you know? This is where we found Arbalest."

"Really? What was he doing?"

"He was down on his knees looking under the bed. He claimed he'd dropped his fountain pen."

"And had he?"

"Who knows? He had one in his hand when he got up. I asked what he'd been writing and he said he was taking notes. I asked to see them and he said he hadn't actually written any yet, he'd been just about to when he'd dropped his pen."

Sarah shrugged. "Well, as you said yourself, Lieutenant, you can't blame a person for trying. If he was looking for the envelope, he apparently hadn't found it. Or else he had, and didn't want to be caught with it. Did you look up under the mattress? I expect the old-fashioned bedsprings are still there, Anora never gets anything new unless she absolutely has to. They're easier than a box spring for hiding things in, you don't risk messing up the bed. I used to hide my coloring books that way when I stayed here, I don't know why. Shall I peek?"

Levitan grinned. "Allow me."

It wasn't quite that easy. They poked around a bit, then Sarah remembered that sturdy old dressers tend to have extra space under their bottom drawers.

"This must be it." The file-size envelope was exactly as she'd pictured it: yellowish brown with age, the little red cardboard discs and the string twisted around them faded to a melancholy russet. Sarah felt a surge of something like panic.

"We'll have to wait till Anora wakes up. It's her letter."

Levitan wasn't buying that. "Mrs. Bittersohn, we've just had a second murder here in four days. Mrs. Protheroe's under sedation, we don't know how long she'll sleep. By the time she wakes up we could have another corpse on our hands, for God's sake. I'm not going to stand on formality when I may be holding the solution right here. Now do you want to open this envelope or would you rather I did it myself?"

Much as she hated to, Sarah yielded. "All right, Lieutenant. If it has to be done, I expect Anora would rather have me than a stranger, but I'd feel less awful if my husband were with us. Could we go back to the den?"

"Sure, why not? Want me to call in one of my men as an additional witness?"

"I'd rather you didn't. I can trust myself and Max not to repeat whatever may be in that letter, and I sincerely hope we can also trust you, but I do think we should keep it among ourselves till Anora's had her chance."

"Fair enough." Levitan tucked the envelope under his arm and followed her downstairs, the front staircase this time.

Max was prowling back and forth between the open drawing-room doors, he stopped pacing when he caught sight of Sarah. "What took you so long? Where the hell have you been?"

"You'll find out. Come on, darling, we need you. At least I do," Sarah amended. She had a feeling that Levitan would as soon have left Max to prowl.

That was his problem, not hers. She was not at all happy to see Levitan sitting at George's desk, unwinding that faded old string, reaching into the bulky envelope, drawing out what was there. The bulk was a padded folder covered in fine green leather, with a photograph inside. The letter was many sheets torn from a lined writing tablet.

Sarah recognized the clerkly script, she and George had played word games sometimes. He'd always kept score, writing their two names neatly at the top of the score pad, jotting down the rows of figures in absolute symmetry. George could add in his head quick as lightning, Sarah had always marveled at that because he'd done everything else so slowly. Oh, God! She hoped he hadn't had time to see that spear coming at him!

"Go ahead," she snapped, "read the letter."

Levitan didn't want to. "Maybe you'd better, Mrs. Bittersohn. You're her friend."

"I'm sorry, I just can't. Max, please, you read it."

"Okay, Kätzele."

Max had succumbed to reading glasses. He pulled out a pair of tortoise-rimmed half eyes and stuck them partway down his nose, adjusted the pages to reading distance, and began.

My dearest Anora,

I don't know how much longer the doctors are going to keep me around before the undertaker gets me, so I thought I had better tell you something that has been on my mind since I left India. Amadée knows but he won't tell anybody, I am going to give this to him to keep until after I die. If I get better I can always tear it up but if I don't you may have to do something for me. It is an odd thing to ask a wife but I know I can trust you to do what is right. As you know, I am not much good at voicing my feelings, but I want you to know I count every day blessed that I am with you, even though I know I don't deserve you. I only hope I can be spared long enough to pay you back for a little of the joy you have given me.

I hope you can read this. I can write just so long, then I get too weak to hold the pen and have to stop for a while. So I will cut it short though not sweet. As you know, I started going on shopping trips with Amadée right after college. I was green about the Orient and everything else then and I got into the usual kind of trouble.

Her name was Medea. That should have tipped me off but it

didn't. She was very beautiful, with black hair and green eyes. She said she was the daughter of a Russian prince and an opera star but I suspect she was lying. Amadée said she was something I won't quote and was probably right but I wouldn't listen. So one thing led to another until she told me she was in a certain condition.

I was all for marrying her at once but Amadée said I had better not be precipitate because father would be very upset, to say the least. Medea herself was not eager, she said there was something that had to be done first. She told me that her own father's family had once owned a fabulous jewel, a diamond as big as an egg. She didn't say what kind of egg, but it was as big as a hen's, roughly speaking. Some Indian monks or lamas or something had stolen the jewel from her father's great-great-grandfather and put it in the forehead of an idol they had in their temple, which was not far from where Medea and I had both been staying; that was how we'd happened to meet.

Medea told me that since then all the male heads of the family had tried one after another to get the diamond back and had all met terrible deaths. She said she could not marry me and give our child a legitimate father until the stone was restored to its rightful owner, which would be the son she was carrying as she was the only one left and had gone to India for that very purpose but been distracted from her mission by falling madly in love with me. So it now became my duty to help her get the jewel back.

As you can understand, this put me in an awkward position. Not being head of the Russian family, I had no personal inclination to court a terrible death but as the father of the child (I had of course no idea whether the child would turn out to be a boy or a girl but did not deem that to be an honorable reason for ducking my responsibility) I thought it my duty to see Medea through what she considered to be her family obligation. I never did find out what the family's name was as she didn't use any name but Medea all through our alliance, though I suppose you would think *misalliance* the more appropriate term.

Anyway, I went along with the adventure, as it seemed at the time. I will not bore you with the details, you would think me a fool for taking the risks I did, with Medea egging me on. (That was not meant as a pun, dear, forgive me.) Those monks or lamas or whatever (you must remember I was new to the Orient at that time) had been, as seemed to be the local custom, pledged to kill anybody who desecrated their sacred idol and were quite serious about honoring their vows. I had a couple of near misses, then one night Medea somehow managed to slip powdered opium into their begging bowls and they all fell asleep sitting in a semicircle around the idol.

This made it fairly simple for me to swarm up. The idol was set on a high pedestal and was itself about ten feet tall so the climb was not a short one but the pedestal was carved with elephants and other beasts in high relief and the idol had a good many arms and legs sticking out in all directions so between the trunks and tusks and assorted limbs plus my experience in rock-climbing as an undergraduate I did not have much trouble. Prizing the gem out of the idol's forehead without dropping it on a sleeping lama was the hard part. It was quite dark up there and I couldn't see very well, but I managed and got down with the diamond weighing down my shirt pocket. It was surprisingly heavy.

I never did get a really good look at the jewel. Medea immediately demanded that I hand it over to her, which I did very gladly as I was anxious to leave before the lamas or monks (or priests, whichever they were) woke up. Instead of making a quick getaway as I had anticipated, however, Medea started around the circle with a cutthroat razor in her hand, calmly slitting each throat. My remonstrances were in vain. She wouldn't quit until she'd slaughtered every one of those poor fellows who had been, after all, only doing their duty. From that moment, the veil of infatuation (if that isn't too high-flown a phrase) fell from my eyes. I saw Medea as she really was and I can honestly say I did not like what I saw.

As it turned out, Medea was pretty sick of me, too. After we'd finally got away from the temple (or shrine) she told me that all was over between us, that I was a dull stick and a fool to boot and that she didn't need me any more because while I was climbing the idol she had busied herself prying rubies out of the elephants' eyes and would be able to take care of herself quite nicely from then on, which I didn't doubt for a minute.

I told Amadée the whole story because I had to give him some explanation as to why I thought we'd better get away from where we were (even now I don't want to say where it was as I believe those Asiatic men of the cloth can be very persistent over that desecration business) and he said the best thing for me to do was go home and marry some nice girl of my own class. As you know, I took his excellent advice and only wish I'd had sense enough to do it sooner.

So now you know my sordid secret, dear, and I hope you will not judge too harshly of a dull stick who loves you as he never loved before, and I am not just quoting the song. I will only add that on this last trip I ran into Medea in Bangalore, of all places. She was dressed to the teeth and had an ayah walking behind her with a little boy by the hand. I have to admit the boy was the spitting image of myself. Even Amadée, who was with me, noticed it at once.

I wanted to speak with the boy but Medea sent him off with the ayah and suggested that I get rid of Amadée and that she and I have a drink somewhere and discuss our son's future. I felt it only decent to comply although I insisted that Amadée accompany us and that she bring the boy so that I could get to know him. She acquiesced to Amadée's presence but said she did not want me to meet the child because he now had a stepfather and it would only upset them both. She was eager for me to start a fund for the boy's education and wanted a down payment of a thousand dollars American. I said I would get it to her but she must first give me a photograph of the boy and send another photograph each time she asked for further funds, which I would pay through our Bangalore agent directly into a trust fund in the boy's name because I did not trust her an inch.

The next morning the ayah came around to my hotel with a very nicely hand-colored photograph in a leather folder and I gave her the money to take back to Medea. That's the last I've heard so far. I am putting the photograph in the envelope so that you will at least know what the boy looks like if you are approached to accept any responsibility for him. If so, you had better investigate carefully to make sure Medea isn't up to one of her games, but if you find that there is a real need, I beg you to care for the boy. Not as your own, I can't ask that of you, but

as the son whom your husband might have loved if he'd ever got
the chance to know him.

> Yours always, no matter what happens,
> George

Max laid down the letter. "Well, that's it. Poor bastard. I wonder
what happened to the kid?"

23

Let's have a look at the photograph." Levitan opened the elegant leather folder. "Huh, pretty fancy. Hand colored, I suppose. Nice job. How about it, Mrs. Bittersohn, does this kid look like George Protheroe?"

"Oh yes, no question, the likeness couldn't be missed. Oddly enough, though, he also reminds me of somebody else. I can't think who."

"The great-nephew, maybe?"

"No, George's sister's children took after the other side of the family. Furthermore, none of the Protheroes ever had green eyes, definitely not George. His were pale blue."

"He says in his letter that the girl friend's eyes were green," Levitan reminded Sarah.

"Oh yes, so he does, the boy must have got them from the mother. But this other person whose name I can't think of has green eyes too, and that same little bump at the tip of the nose. Max, you're better· than I at faces, can you help us out?"

"Hell, yes," Max replied after a moment's study. "It's Bartolo Arbalest. You can't mistake the nose, or the shape of the eye sockets. So that's why he was crying at the funeral, poor bastard. What have you done with him, Levitan?"

"He's in the dining room with one of my men. I haven't charged Arbalest with anything yet, but on the strength of this evidence, I think I'm about to."

"Would you mind holding off long enough for my wife and me to have a little talk with him?"

"Not without my being present."

"Of course not, I know the rules. I was just thinking we might be able to supply a little more background, maybe speed things up so we can all get out of here. Sarah and I still have to drive out to Ireson Town and pick up our own kid before he drives my sister nuts."

"Okay, Bittersohn, just so you don't try sticking the department with a bill for your services. Stay here, I'll go get Arbalest."

He'd left the photograph lying exposed on the desk. When Arbalest caught sight of it, he fell apart again.

"Then it's true. Oh God, why is this curse come upon me? Why? Why?"

Max got a chair under the hysterical Resurrection Man before his knees had quite finished buckling. "Take it easy, Arbalest. Want a drink of water? Brandy?"

"No, no, I—where did you get that photograph?"

"You know who it is?"

"Of course I know. I had to sit frying under a ghastly great light while the photographer fiddled around, then my ayah took me back the next day before the sun was even up. I had to sit still forever and ever while somebody else painted in the colors. I'd no idea what it was all about. I was five, I think. That was right after we'd seen the man, I remember distinctly. How could I forget?"

"What man was this?" barked Levitan.

"The one who wanted to talk with me and my mother wouldn't let him. And I wanted him to!"

"You can remember that from when you were five?"

"Of course I can, I remember things from when I was three. There were two men, both of them tall. I don't remember much about the other one except that he was thin. I just remember the big, nice one who looked like me. I wanted so much to run to him, but my ayah gripped hold of my hand and wouldn't let me. Then my mother took the man by the arm and led him away and I felt—I don't know—lost. It was bad, I dreamed about him for a long time. I still do, sometimes. And then that night, when Carnaby and I came to pick up the elephant candlesticks, here he was, old and fat and getting ready to die, but kind and good, and mine."

Arbalest fought for control. "I could feel the goodness all around me like a warm, woolly blanket. I looked into Mr. Protheroe's face and it was the face in my dreams. I saw my own face in his and knew this had to be my father."

"Did you tell Mr. Protheroe who you were?"

"With his wife sitting right there beside him? What was I to say? Here's your long-lost bastard, come home to roost? I know I'm naive about some things, Lieutenant, but I'm not quite that big a fool. I just sat here and made small talk and—loved him. For the first time in my life, I was experiencing perfect happiness. I think my father felt something too. And it was even better when Carnaby and I brought back the candlesticks, because my father and I knew each other a little by then."

"And Mrs. Protheroe had no inkling of what was going on?"

"I'm quite sure she didn't. I think she was just pleased to watch her husband enjoying himself. I wanted to stay on and on, but I could see my father was getting sleepy and knew I mustn't wear out my welcome. They both said I must be sure to drop in again next time I came out this way. Now here I am and—"

Arbalest's face contorted, he couldn't go on. Sarah went and got him a glass of soda water, and a couple of napkins to wipe his streaming face. She wanted to ask how he'd got on the list for the funeral, but decided a change of subject might be more therapeutic.

"Where did you learn your skills, Mr. Arbalest?"

"In India, mostly. My ayah's brothers were all fine artisans, they had a workshop not far from where mother and I lived. Ayah used to take me there almost every day, she'd go off to chat with their wives and leave me to watch them working. I was totally fascinated, I'd sit by the hour, hardly daring to move for fear they'd chase me away. When the brothers realized how absorbed I was, they began teaching me things and giving me small jobs to do. I seemed to have a natural aptitude, I learned quickly. Before long I'd become so useful to them that they'd scold me if I didn't show up early enough."

"Were they paying you?"

"Heavens, no, they'd never have dreamed of anything like that. Children were slave labor. I didn't care. It was enough that they wanted me around, for whatever reason. My mother didn't know what was going on and didn't care, so long as I was out of her way and not spoiling my clothes. My ayah used to undress me and make me put on a loincloth as soon as we got to the workshop, she'd clean me up and dress me again before we went back to the house."

"Didn't you ever go to school?" Sarah asked him.

"Oh yes, in a manner of speaking. My ayah could read and write English after a fashion, she taught me the rudiments. Aside from my looks, my mother was only concerned about my manners and accent. When I was nine she put me in a snotty little day-school for the sons of gentlemen. Meaning, of course, British sahibs. In fact, most of the boys were like myself, half-castes of one sort or another whose parents had big ideas and enough money to pay the fees. They taught us virtually nothing except how to aspirate our vowels and snub the lower orders. I didn't spend much time at classes, I'd slip off to the workshop whenever I got the chance. The headmaster didn't seem to miss me, he was drunk a good deal of the time. We boys all learned to speak with a hint of a hiccup."

"What fun for you. Your mother was fairly well-off, then?"

"I don't know. It seems to me we lived quite lavishly when I was small. Then things got a bit tight for a while and I had a couple of stepfathers—or was told I had—in quick succession. Neither of them ever paid the slightest attention to me, which was probably just as well. Finally there was Roderick."

"Another stepfather?" asked Max.

"No, a neighbor. He rented the bungalow next to ours shortly after the second stepfather decamped. He had a son who was known as Barn. I don't know if that was the boy's real name or a nickname but he went to my school and was rather a swell. Roderick was a cousin or something to the head, I believe. Barn was two forms above me, so of course he didn't even recognize me on the rare occasions when we met. As I mentioned, I wasn't around much. I tended to show up only on days when there were art lessons."

"Art lessons? What sort?"

"Oh, mostly just looking at prints and getting short preachments about the chaps who'd done them. We young gentlemen were supposed to absorb a little culture along with the cricket. Which I detested, I must admit. Keeping a straight bat was never one of my priorities. But I did like the art master, I suppose I turned him into some sort of father figure. Actually the poor chap was a drug addict, he died of an overdose during my third and, as it turned out, final year. Or so the story ran; we pupils weren't supposed to know, but of course we did. Or thought we did."

Arbalest drank some more of the soda water Sarah had brought him. "I was having drug problems myself by then, in a manner of speaking; my mother was high as a kite most of the time. I think Roderick was supplying her, though I can't accuse him of having got her started. Looking back, I believe mother had probably picked up the habit years before. She'd always been volatile in her moods, I never knew from moment to moment what sort of temper she'd be in. Sometimes she'd forget I even existed, sometimes she'd berate me for hours at a time over nothing at all, sometimes she'd be sweet as honey. During the sweet times, she'd spin me grand stories about her noble father, who'd been a Russian prince and lived in a palace until the wicked Bolsheviks killed him and stole all his fortune except the one great family treasure of which I would some day be custodian. But I shouldn't be telling you this."

"On the contrary, Arbalest, I think you should," said Max. "We have reason to believe your own father knew a lot more about this family treasure than your mother ever told you."

"But how?"

"Trust us, Arbalest. We'll explain in due time. What happened to your mother, and where's the treasure now? Do you know?"

"Yes, of course I do. I had to know. I got home from school one afternoon—it must have been an art day—and found my mother on the floor, terribly bruised and bloody, trying to crawl to the sofa. Roderick had been there, and had beaten her so badly she couldn't even stand up. I think both her legs may have been broken, she screamed when I tried to raise her. He'd been trying to get the treasure from her, he was coming back soon to kill her if she didn't tell him where it was hidden."

"Good God!" gasped Sarah. "What did you do?"

"I brought water and tried to wash the blood off mother's face, I couldn't stand seeing her like that. But she was a raging fury. She pushed my hand away, she would not be mastered, she was ready to die first. I must take the treasure from where she'd hidden it—she told me where—and escape with it, and guard it with my life forevermore. She grabbed my hand—hers was all sticky with the blood, it was dreadful—and pressed it to her heart and made me swear that I'd keep faith with her, or the gods of her forefathers would wreak a terrible vengeance on me. She scared the hell out of me, not to put too fine a point on it. She still does."

"I can imagine," said Max. "So what happened after that?"

"I went and got the treasure and stuffed it down my undershirt. I brought her a drink and tried to make her more comfortable, though there wasn't much I could do. I knew it was no use calling the police, not that she'd have let me anyway. Then Roderick came storming back across the yard between the bungalows. Mother shoved me away and told me to run for it. The last I saw of her as I jumped out the window, she'd taken a cutthroat razor out from under a sofa cushion. She had it open in her hand, and was staring at the door with her lips drawn back in a snarl, her long black hair all tangled around her face and her eyes flashing green fire. I don't know which of them died first, I never went back to find out."

"Where was the ayah?" Sarah wanted to know. "Did she escape?"

"She'd been gone before I ever got home. I'm sure her relatives were hiding her, I ran to the workshop and they wouldn't let me in. They told me to go away and stay away. I could understand. These were poor people trying to make a living, they couldn't risk having their shop wrecked by a murdering madman. I apologized and left. One chap who'd always been kind to me did slip me a few annas and a couple of chapattis for the road."

Arbalest tilted his glass to catch the last of the soda water. Sarah offered mutely to get more, he shook his head. "I'm all right now. Shall I go on?"

"Yes, please. What did you do next?"

"Ate my chapattis and thought a bit. I was wearing my school uniform, that would make me an easy target for Roderick to spot. I went to the old-clothes bazaar and traded my fine feathers for a ragged shirt, dirty shorts, and a pair of worn-out sandals. I got skinned on the trade, of course, but I was in no shape to haggle. I did persuade the merchant to throw in a pair of battered old sunglasses. I was deeply tanned pretty much all over from working so much in just a loincloth, my hair was black, I could pass for an Indian except for my green eyes. That was why I insisted on the sunglasses. I made him give me a scrap of rag to clean them with. Once I got away from there I wound a bit of the rag around one temple and scratched up the lenses a little more to make them look as if I'd found them on a trash heap. It wasn't a bad disguise, Roderick was snob enough himself not to believe a boy of my alleged caste would demean himself by dressing down to the level of the street."

"But this treasure of yours," said Sarah, "how could you keep it hidden in such a skimpy outfit?"

Arbalest smiled. "Easily enough. Mother had put it in a little leather bag. Lots of Indian people wear charm bags around their necks; I just ripped off another piece of rag, covered the bag with that, and added a clove of garlic I pinched out of a peddler's basket to keep the evil spirits away. I still wear it, without the rag, of course. See?"

The necktie he wore was sober enough in color but wider than ordinary in shape. He slid the knot down, opened the top buttons of his shirt, and revealed a small soft leather bag hanging on a slender gold chain. "It's somewhat like having a misplaced goiter, but I've grown so used to the bag after all these years that I don't feel dressed without it."

Levitan was getting restless. "Could we see your treasure, please?"

"But I—I've never shown it to anyone, ever," stammered the Resurrection Man.

"Look, Mr. Arbalest, you as much as saw your own mother killed over this thing you're wearing. Now we've got two more murders on our hands, most likely with the same motive behind them. One victim was your father, the other his best friend. Open the bag, Mr. Arbalest."

24

Moving slowly and mechanically, like a man in shock, as he quite likely was, Bartolo Arbalest pulled the golden chain up over his head and laid his charm bag on the desk in front of Max.

"You open it," he said. "I can't."

"Why not?" said Max. "You must have done it often enough."

"No, never. Not once. I've tried a few times, but I always see mother's face, the way she looked when she handed me the bag, and I—I just can't. Please, Mr. Bittersohn."

Max shrugged, fumbling for a moment with the time-stiffened puckers at the mouth, then held the bag upside down and let the heavy stone slide out onto George Protheroe's blotter pad. It was in fact the size and shape of a large hen's egg; its many facets gathered the rays from the desk lamp into a cool, still interplay of light and shadow, of color and no color.

"Very pretty," said Max.

Sarah was staring at the great jewel as if mesmerized. "It's so clear, so still. What is it, Max?"

"Rock crystal. Mid-eighteenth century, as a guess. Probably cut for some nabob's bedroom doorknob."

"What's it worth?" barked Levitan.

"In dollars? A couple of thousand, more or less. Sorry, Arbalest."

"No! Oh, my God! All that for—mother, father, Erminie, Mr. Dubrec, all those others, killed for a crystal doorknob. Take it away, for God's sake! Throw it in the ocean. Throw me in, while you're about it. I'm not fit to live."

"Oh, come on, Mr. Arbalest," said Levitan. "You'll be okay. Get him that brandy, somebody. I may as well keep this—what do I call it? Crystal doorknob?—for evidence. I'll give you a receipt."

"I don't want one."

"Sorry, it's in the rules. You wouldn't want to get me fired."

Levitan tore a sheet off a memo pad that was lying on George's desk and began to write, in a surprisingly beautiful hand. Sarah slipped out to fetch the brandy, and also a glass of soda water just in case. When she returned, Max was asking Arbalest, "Was it on account of the stone that you decided to hire yourself a bodyguard?"

Arbalest shrugged. "I suppose so. Indirectly, anyway. So many awful things had happened, and they've been going on so long. Erminie Dubrec was the great love of my life. I wanted desperately to marry her, but I didn't dare ask. There'd been others before her, you see. Anybody I got close to, man or woman—I'm a sociable person by nature, I need to have people around me. I suppose a psychiatrist would call it a holdover from my ayah's brothers' workshop. I drift into friendships, I can't help it. I form ties, and suddenly they're horribly, hideously broken. It's as though I put a curse on anybody who lets me get too near."

He was crying again. "I have so much love to give, and I'm poison wherever I give it. I've signed so many death warrants just by caring for people. Oh, God! I can't stand any more. I want to die and be with my father."

That made three who'd loved George Protheroe, all lining themselves up for Charon's ferry, not counting Anora. Fat old George, of all people. Who would have thought he meant so much to so many? Sarah couldn't bear to stand here listening to the Resurrection Man's sobs, she went back to the bar for more soda water. By the time she returned to the den, Arbalest had himself in hand and was answering somebody's question, probably Max's.

"No, I didn't tell Goudge about the crystal when I hired him, I saw no reason why I should. The catastrophic record among my former artisans was reason enough."

"Have you ever told anybody else?" That was Levitan.

"No, not even Erminie. Nobody has ever known, unless Roderick's still alive. I can't imagine my mother survived their last encounter, she'd have been after me to get back her so-called treasure. She'd truly convinced herself that it was a real diamond, you know. One had to believe her, she was so sure. I never doubted her, not for a moment. I'm sure Roderick didn't either. One believes what one wants to, of course."

"How would she have known where to find you?" Max asked him.

"I don't know, but she'd have managed. I used to wonder sometimes if mother was a witch. Anyway, I didn't get far away those first days. I'd only my feet for transportation, my few annas wouldn't have taken me any great distance on the train, and I did have to eat. Food has always been a top priority with me, as you can see."

None of his hearers gave a rap about Arbalest's *embonpoint*, they waited for him to go on. He was too courteous not to oblige.

"I wasn't much worried about Roderick, oddly enough. I kept remembering how mother had looked with that razor in her hand; I felt fairly confident that even if he killed her, she'd have managed to do him some serious damage first. Even if she didn't hurt him too badly, he'd have wasted a good deal of time tearing our bungalow apart piece by piece with his bare hands, looking for mother's secret cache before it occurred to him that I might have run off with the boodle. Roderick wasn't all that swift a thinker."

"What about his son?" asked Max.

"By Jove! You know, Mr. Bittersohn, I've never once in all these years thought about the son's possibly getting involved. Stupid of me, Barn was a sneaky young devil. I remember coming home from the workshop one time and catching him lurking under mother's bedroom window with a camera in his hand.

"What did you do?"

"Oh, nothing, of course. Barn was older than I, you know. I just slipped into the shrubbery and waited till he'd got tired of snooping and went home. God knows what the poor kid's life must have been like, now that I think of it. I've no idea whether Roderick was taking drugs as well as dealing in them, but he obviously did drink a lot, though never into oblivion, unfortunately. Mother and I could always tell when he was drunk. We'd hear him bellowing at his servants, calling them filthy names, accusing them of stealing things. They didn't care, he paid well enough and they didn't half understand what he was saying. Then of course Roderick was American so he didn't count as a sahib."

"Where was Roderick from in America?" asked Max.

"I've no idea. He'd no particularly marked regional accent, that I can recall. He talked the way Carnaby does. Where is Carnaby, by the way?"

"Upstairs taking a nap," said Levitan. "He's got a bodyguard of his own, you may be interested to know. We didn't think it was smart to leave the man up there by himself, considering what's been happening around here. Does he have a drinking problem?"

Arbalest conjured the ghost of a smile. "Oh dear, no, he finds it no problem at all. Carnaby could empty the Heidelberg tun without getting even slightly squiffed. There's a trick to holding one's liquor, he says; he picked up the knack from bodyguarding all those Texas oil barons. He's always having to pose as something he isn't, you know, and often the role puts him in a position where he can't avoid keeping up with the party without making himself conspicuous. Why do you ask about a drinking problem?"

"Because he's drunk. He passed out."

"Surely not. You don't suppose he can have been drugged?"

"He didn't act drugged when I saw him," said Sarah. "He was singing 'Melancholy Baby' and trying to get frisky with Lydia. Max, wait! Don't you go up there."

"Sit still, Bittersohn, this is a job for Supercop." Levitan was already on his feet, checking his shoulder holster, rushing toward the stairway.

Bartolo Arbalest looked after him in amazement. "Is he going to arrest Carnaby for being rude to Madame Ouspenska?"

"Who knows?" Max wasn't happy at being held back. "What was this Roderick's last name, Arbalest?"

"I can't remember. I must have known, but it's escaped me. One of Freud's repressions, I suppose. I disliked both him and his son so intensely, even before—God! How could I have been such a coward, leaving mother there helpless on the floor, with that madman coming to kill her?"

The dutiful son hadn't heard about George Protheroe's climb up the many-limbed idol, or the circle of monks Medea had left lying around it with their throats all slit. Medea must have realized her chances of surviving Roderick's second attack were nil, or she wouldn't have given up the diamond, even to her son, Sarah thought. Evidently the woman had drugged herself into believing her own fairy tale about the noble Russian family, and filled her son's head with it. How else could Arbalest have persevered in honoring his vow after so many years and so many tragedies? If ever the sins of the parents were visited on the child! Now what was this ruckus?

In through the door came an odd assemblage of arms and legs that turned out to be Jesse Kelling dragging a little man in a red jogging suit. The man was trying to kick his captor in the shins, but Jesse hadn't roughhoused with his three bloodthirsty brothers for nothing.

"I got him, Max!"

"I'll be damned! How?"

"Saw him coming across the yard, jumped out the kitchen window, and landed on his back. We can get him for trespassing, can't we?"

"And he can get you for unprovoked bodily assault. Nice going, Jesse. Okay, comrade, whoever you are, what's with the red suit and the athletics?"

Jesse's captive made an unintelligible noise; unintelligible except to Bartolo Arbalest, who made similar noises back. The little man quit trying to kick Jesse and made other noises suggestive of entreaty. Arbalest nodded and turned to Max.

"He says please let him go, he was only doing his job. He says if we hurt him, my boss will be angry."

"His boss?"

"No, mine. Isn't that intriguing?"

Arbalest emitted more sounds and got a spate of frenzied outpourings in return. "He says I am a bad and ungrateful servant and need to be taught a severe lesson. He says he is going to tell my boss on me for consorting with persons of bad character. He says this woman here is too beautiful to be virtuous, she belongs in a zenana. He didn't exactly say zenana. I do beg your pardon, Mrs. Bittersohn."

"Not at all. Ask him your boss's name. By the way, what language are you speaking, Hindustani?"

"No, by Jove, Tamil. That's interesting. I thought I'd forgotten how, but out it popped. Odd how things come back to one. I can't ask this fellow my alleged boss's name, Mrs. Bittersohn, he'd think I'd gone mad. Perhaps I have. What's he doing here?"

"I don't know, but your father saw him running across the yard the day before he was killed. George said the man looked like a Tamil."

"How bright of father, what a marvelous man he must have been! Good heavens, what's going on upstairs?"

"I'll go see." Jesse crouched for the sprint.

Max barred the way with his cane. "The hell you will. Two cops with guns are up there, they don't need you. Does Goudge go armed, Arbalest?"

"Now that you mention it, I shouldn't be surprised if he does. I've never asked because I preferred not to know, I loathe guns. Not much of a credit to my father, am I?"

Sarah wasn't about to let him start crying again. "I shouldn't say that, I don't believe George ever touched a gun in his life."

"Oh, Mrs. Bittersohn, you relieve my mind immensely! But Carnaby—I'm all confused. Don't you think we ought to go up?"

"No," said Max. "How did you happen to hire Goudge instead of somebody else?"

"Through a concatenation of circumstances, as one might say. Back in New York, when I first started out in my own business as an art restorer—I'd worked my way from Madras to New York on a tramp steamer as assistant cook—this was some years after I'd escaped from Roderick. I'd been working here and there in India and also in New York for a while before getting up courage to launch out on my own. But I mustn't digress, must I? Anyway, there was this little coffee shop where I used to go and this chap would come in."

"So you got to know him?"

"Not really, one doesn't go accosting strangers in New York unless one's a mugger. But one does begin to recognize faces. He usually had a camera with him, I assumed he was a professional photographer of some sort. Then I ran into problems, as Brooks may have told you, and moved to the West Coast. On my very first day in Los Angeles, whom should I see but this same chap?"

"Did you speak to him?"

"No, I nodded but I don't think he noticed. Then I didn't see him again for a long time. I ran into more problems in Los Angeles and relocated to Houston. That was where I met Erminie, but I can't talk about that. After she—after the accident, I was sitting on a park bench one day wondering whether to kill myself when he came walking by again. He stopped and looked at me, then he said, 'Don't I know you from somewhere?'

"I said yes, in a manner of speaking, we'd seen each other fairly often in New York years ago. So then we got to chatting about what a small world it was and finally decided to go and have a drink together. I'm a person who needs company, as I mentioned before. By then my Texas artisans had learned about my previous fiascos; they'd walked out on me, all except Jacques and he was busy consoling his family. The Dubrecs were badly broken up about Erminie, of course, as who wasn't?"

"So you finally got acquainted with Goudge," Max prodded. "Did he talk about himself?"

"Yes, he said he hadn't had much luck in photography so he'd given it up to become a professional bodyguard. He'd been guarding a Texas oilman who'd got into some kind of difficulty, but that was all straightened out and he was at liberty. Like myself, he was trying to decide what to do next. He said he'd come from the east and would like to get back but didn't have any connections left in these parts."

Arbalest sighed. "So that gave me my bright idea. I could set up a maximum-security atelier with a resident bodyguard and keep my artisans from getting killed. I asked Carnaby if he'd be interested. I warned him that I couldn't pay the high fees he'd been getting from the oil barons, but he said that wouldn't matter. He was a bachelor, he'd nobody but himself to support, he came from a well-to-do family and didn't really have to work at all. He merely preferred having something to do, and he liked my idea. Maybe living communally with a group of artists would stimulate him to get back to his photography."

"And that's how it happened?"

"Yes, just like that. Carnaby and I flew east together. He helped me find a house and get a security system set up. Grilles on all the windows, an intercom system, locks and safety catches everywhere, it was most reassuring. I began interviewing artisans and picked out a few who were ready to go along with my concept—you've met them—then I sent for Jacques, who'd promised to join me as soon as I got set up, and here I am. And there, I suppose, I go. But where?"

"You never once suspected that Goudge might have been stalking you all these years?"

"Oh no." Arbalest was shocked. "Why should he?"

"You could ask," said Max. "Here they come."

25

Barnaby Rudge!" howled Arbalest. "I know you now, Barn. You've had plastic surgery, but I ought to have recognized those mean little eyes. You're Roderick Rudge's son. He murdered my mother!"

The man who'd been calling himself Carnaby Goudge smiled a mean little smile. "*Au contraire*, Barty, old bean. She murdered my father. Slashed his throat from ear to ear. Prettiest job I've ever seen, I got some lovely photos. I never did care much for old Roddy."

"Then what happened to my mother?"

"Nothing much, for a while. She and I got rid of Roddy's body, I don't suppose you'd care for the details. I made my servants mop up the gore since Medea's had sloped off, as so often happens just when one needs them most urgently. Then I moved in with her. Our own bungalow was rather a shambles by that time. Roddy had had this impetuous habit of tearing out walls and floorboards when he got into one of his moods."

"You mean you and she—"

"Oh yes, Medea could be quite good company, in her way. Had a temper, of course. She was really pissed at you for running off with her diamond, Barty. Made me swear to track you to the ends of the earth and take revenge on you for your perfidious betrayal of her trust and so forth. Medea had quite a gift of rhetoric, as you surely know."

"But mother gave it to me herself! She knew Roderick was coming back to kill her, she told me to flee from the doom that o'ershadowed her and guard the family jewel with my life, as a sacred trust."

"Did she really? That would seem to put a somewhat different complexion on the matter then, wouldn't it? And did you keep faith?"

"Of course."

"Good lad. That was what Medea couldn't stand about you, Barty, she used to go on about how damnably nice you were; she said you were just like your father. I must say that after spending so much time in your cozy little ashram, I've developed a deeper understanding of what she meant. You're a bloody bore, Barty."

The Resurrection Man lifted his shoulders and let them fall. "I'm sorry you haven't been happy with us, Carnaby. Or Barn, if you prefer. I did try so hard. But then you haven't made me all that happy either, have you? Am I to infer that the terrible string of tragedies that have plagued me ever since I got to America have been your way of honoring the oath you swore to my mother?"

"Well, yes, in a way. And it was something to do. One does like to keep busy. That was what attracted me to Medea, she always could think of something to do. She had this simply marvelous scheme all worked out: We'd find a temple that contained an idol with a truly impressive jewel in its forehead, drug the monks who were guarding it, pry out the jewel, and slash the monks' throats as a farewell gesture. Rather clever, don't you think?"

"It's been done before," said Max Bittersohn.

"Really? Well, anyway, while we were still scouting around, trying to find a suitable idol, Medea got knocked down and killed by a very large Bengalese on a motorbike. Call me sentimental if you like, but I hadn't the heart to pursue the matter without her. I was only fourteen at the time, you understand, though quite mature for my age. So I decided to come back to the States and get on with the revenge as a tribute to her memory."

"How did you manage the trip?" Jesse Kelling was all set to take notes.

"Quite easily," replied Goudge. "Money was no problem. Roderick had done quite well out of his drug-running enterprise; he'd completely carpeted the space under the floor of our bungalow with wads of rupees done up in aluminum foil to keep the bugs out, a fact I'd never happened to mention to Medea. I beguiled the time for a week or two exchanging them for travelers' checks and American dollars, then attached myself to a nice American gentleman who agreed for certain considerations to pass me off as his son, and booked a flight to New York under a forged passport."

"Why a forged passport?" said Levitan.

"The man who wanted to adopt me thought we'd better both use the same name. He was a bit sensitive about being suspected of evil designs. I ditched him as soon as I got off the plane and headed for Connecticut, where Roddy's parents were still living at the time. I presented myself on their doorstep with my fingernails cleaned and my hair slicked down and broke the news of how Roddy had sacrificed his own life to rescue a tiny tot from the jaws of a crocodile on the banks of the great gray-green greasy Brahmaputra River far away. I further explained that their devoted son's last words had been (a) Mater! and (b) Pater! It was that sort of family, you see. So of course they were overjoyed to see me and lost not a moment in shoving me off to the right sort of prep school and thence to the right sort of college, where I acquired the old-school-tie manner that has stood me in such good stead as a bodyguard."

Goudge smiled benignly at the little group who were hanging on his words, all except the man in the red suit, who seemed only bewildered. "Having thus won my grandparents' hearts and made sure they'd revised their wills in my favor, I gave them a really splendid double funeral and decided it was time to get on with the revenge, for want of more pressing business. You can fill in what happened after that, can't you, Barty old pal? Now if you minions of the law would kindly uncuff yourselves from my person and direct me to a competent bail bondsman—"

"Not a chance," said Levitan. "Not after the way I caught you trying to strangle Officer Greenaway. How's the neck, Greenaway?"

"Awk," replied the lesser minion.

"Let me get you something to drink." Sarah felt she ought to be making herself useful and there didn't seem to be much else that needed doing just now. "Hot tea? Coffee? Soda water? Perhaps a spot of whiskey for medicinal purposes?"

"Awk!" said Greenaway.

"Soda water," growled the lieutenant, "with plenty of ice. Why did you off George Protheroe, Goudge? Or Rudge, or whoever you are?"

"Goudge is the family patronymic, Barnaby Rudge was just Roddy's bit of fun. Offing dear George was my own little treat. Do bear in mind that I'd had to stand at attention for two long, long evenings watching him and Barty play verbal patty-cake. It was obvious to the discerning onlooker, namely me, that they had to be father and son, and that Barty was coming down with a serious case of filial piety. One could hardly let that sort of thing go unchecked, could one? Furthermore, Mrs. Protheroe had been quite insistent that we drop in again when we were out this way, it would have been uncivil not to take her up on the invitation. I may add that this house is quite immorally easy to break into. You really ought to drop the old duck a cautionary word about getting a locksmith out here, Mrs. Bittersohn."

"Thank you, I'll do that. And what was your rationale for stabbing Mr. Dubrec?"

"Not upon me be the onus, dear lady, that was your fault. I'm fairly clever at eavesdropping without being noticed, cad that I am. I overheard Monsieur Dubrec burbling on to you about his secret mission and it crossed my mind that George might have fobbed off a lump of glass on Medea and been letting Dubrec baby-sit the real diamond all these years, though I couldn't imagine why. Anyway, I thought I might as well give it the old school try. Unfortunately, there was nothing in Dubrec's pockets worth pinching except a gold toothpick and the ancestral silver corkscrew. Quite a nice one, actually; I'd be glad to show it to you if I weren't wearing these handcuffs."

"So you went and searched his room, right?" said Levitan.

"Bang on, Your Worship. I didn't dare take the time to do a thorough job. I'd planned to go back once my good samaritans left me alone and I'd recovered from my drunken stupor, but you botched that for me by planting—Greenaway, is it?—at my bedside. I do apologize for my clumsiness in not finishing you off, Mr. Greenaway. I'm not usually so inept."

"That's okay, I don't mind." Officer Greenaway was still croaky, but the soda water was helping.

"Thank you," said Goudge. "That's very generous of you. I also regret not being allowed to finish my search, however. I can't help thinking the diamond may still be up there."

"No, it isn't." Bartolo Arbalest patted his necktie. "I've had mother's little treasure right here, under my shirt. You've been guarding the idol's eye ever since I hired you, Carnaby, and didn't know it."

"Curses! Foiled again. How wily of you, Barty. I suppose now you're going to evict me from the atelier."

"Don't worry about that, Mr. Goudge," consoled Levitan. "We've got a nice, cozy cell all ready and waiting. Would you mind phoning the station, Bittersohn? Ask the dispatcher to send along a stretch limo instead of the meat wagon, Mr. Goudge is used to traveling in style."

"That's awfully kind of you, Lieutenant," said his prisoner, "but please don't bother about the limo. Now that I seem to have run out of things to do, you may as well have them bring back that hearse."

"Well," said Max after he'd helped Levitan and Greenaway unshackle themselves from Goudge's corpse, "that was thoughtful and considerate. He must have had a cyanide capsule parked behind his bridgework."

"Crazy as a bedbug." Officer Greenaway's articulation was much improved, Anora must have bought top-quality soda water. The policeman started to say something else, but his words were drowned out by the loud wails of the little brown man in the bright-red suit.

"What's the matter with him?" cried Sarah above the tumult. "Can he be mourning that ghastly murderer?"

"No," said Arbalest, "he's lamenting the fact that Goudge has died without having paid him the money he was supposed to get for all those clever tricks he's been playing. He says running around Boston in that red suit is worse than being downwind of a burning ghat. Poor fellow."

Arbalest shouted a few words in Tamil, the ululations turned to what could only be an outpouring of gratitude. Sarah thought perhaps a round of soda water might help. She was on her way to get some when she met Anora, waddling through the hall in a lurid yellow-and-magenta chenille bathrobe and her brown felt slippers.

"Anora! What are you doing up? I thought the doctor had given you a sleeping pill."

"So did he. What's going on down here? Who's doing all that howling?"

"The man in the red suit, the one George saw running across the yard. He's all right now. It's a long story, Anora. Are you sure you feel up to hearing it?"

"No, but I will be once I get something into me. Phyllis, quit fluttering around like a wet hen. Go tell Cook to make a fresh pot of tea and heat up some soup, I'm starving. Who's here? Sarah, what are you looking at me like that for? Don't tell me there's been another murder?"

"Not exactly, this last one's a suicide."

"Who?"

"That man Goudge, who drove the car for Mr. Arbalest."

"The fellow with the mean little eyes? I caught him staring at George that second night they came here, he gave me a funny feeling. Was he the one who speared my George?"

"Yes, Anora."

"Too bad he killed himself," Anora grunted. "I'd gladly have done it for him. Where's Max?"

"In the den with the policemen and the body. He's called an ambulance."

"Good. Tell him I said thanks. What happened to Marcus?"

"He and Lydia Ouspenska drove back to Boston with Brooks and Theonia," Sarah explained. "He said to tell you he'd be out next Sunday and to phone the atelier between times if you want him for anything."

"Well, that was quite a speech for Marcus, bless his heart. Is Amadée's son still here?"

"No, he went in the other ambulance with his father's body. Jacques is going to let you know about the arrangements."

"They'll have Amadée cremated here and hold the funeral in Arizona, I suppose, it's the only practical way these days. I'll have to go, if I live that long. He did as much for me. Not much else to live for, now that George is gone."

"Don't be too sure of that, Anora. Go sit down before you fall down. I'll tell Max you're here, he wants to see you." Sarah hurried to the den. "Max, Anora's downstairs. Would you bring George's letter, and the photograph? Mr. Arbalest, you may as well come too. And the Tamil man, does he have a name?"

"Why—yes." Arbalest got rather uncertainly to his feet. "It's Cijay, he says, Cijay Cattahoochee, if I've got it right. It's so long since I've spoken Tamil. Cijay's really a nice fellow, we've been chatting a bit. He's in the country illegally, as you may have guessed. Carnaby found him wandering around the waterfront a few weeks ago, scared him into thinking he was in immediate danger of being sent to jail forever, and offered to become his protector. Translated, that appears to have meant using him as a slave, which was a terrible shame because he's quite a bright, sociable fellow. He says he knows a little English but he can't speak it well enough because Carnaby wouldn't teach him and warned him against talking to anybody else."

"Did he tell why Goudge made him do all that running around?" asked Levitan.

"He believes his master was a very strange man. He doesn't understand why he's been made to wear that red suit and do monkey tricks. He thinks Carnaby may have been slightly off in the head."

"It never occurred to him that Goudge might have been trying to make him look crazy, with the object of pinning him for George's murder?" said Max. "Well, it's water over the dam now. Come on, we'd better get straightened out with Anora."

"I hope Mrs. Protheroe isn't too—oh, well, we'd better go and get it over with. Perhaps if I just lurk in the background?" The Resurrection Man was scared stiff, why wouldn't he be?

"Whatever you feel comfortable with," Sarah told him.

She let Max lead the way carrying the leather portfolio and the fateful letter, and laid her hand on Arbalest's arm. He needed all the moral support he could get, she could feel him trembling. Anora was in her big armchair, her hands resting on its rubbed-bare plush arms, her eyes on nothing at all. She barely turned her head when they came in. Max opened the portfolio and held it up for her to see.

"Good Lord, that's George! Where did you get that photo, Max? I've never seen it before." She fumbled a tissue out of her bathrobe pocket and blew her nose. "Very nice. Except that the eyes are wrong. Whatever possessed whoever took the picture to color them green?"

"That isn't George, Anora." Max handed her the letter. "You'd better read this."

Now he had her full and undivided attention. "Max, this is George's writing. Where did you find it?"

"Amadée Dubrec brought it with him. George wrote to you years ago in the hospital, when he was so sick and expecting to die. He gave the letter to Dubrec, who was supposed to hand it over to you after the funeral. As it turned out, Dubrec had to wait a lot longer than he'd bargained for. He was intending to give you this tonight, after the rest of us had cleared out."

"Hand me my reading glasses, Sarah, they're on the mantelpiece."

Anora put them on and read through the yellowed pages, taking her time. At last she folded the sheets together, took off her glasses, laid them very carefully on the small table beside her.

"Well! All these years, and I never had a notion. What happened to the boy, I wonder?"

"I'm here."

Bartolo Arbalest's voice was low and shaky. He knelt down before the widow either in supplication or because he had no strength left to stand.

"I knew who he was as soon as I saw him, Mrs. Protheroe. I sensed it, just from being near him. And I had the feeling he knew me, and was glad to see me. I realize you'll never want to see me again, I just want you to know how desperately sorry I am to have been the reason why he died. I'd far rather have died for him. Oh, God, if only I had!"

"There, there." Anora was patting his shoulder, smoothing his grizzled hair. "Don't cry, laddie, it wasn't your fault. Let's go and have some nice hot soup, just the two of us. You'll forgive us, won't you, Sarah? My stepson and I have some things to talk over. For one thing, George, I'm not sure Marcus is taking his medication regularly. You'll have to lean on him about that. You don't mind my calling you after your father, do you? You're so like him, I'm bound to keep forgetting and saying George anyway. Before we eat, I want you to shave off that bush so I can see your face. And what are we to do with this chap in the red suit? Can he garden?"

"I'm sure he can do lots of things, once he gets the chance. His name is Cijay Cattahoochee. He says he knows how to drive a car, he can bring Marcus out to visit you on weekends. And me too, if you want me."

"What do you mean, if? This is your home, George. And somebody's got to keep the place from falling to pieces. You can't expect me to do everything, not at my age. Does Cijay have anything to wear besides that silly red suit? You'll have to get him fitted out. Where's he been living?"

Arbalest said something in Tamil, the other smiled for the first time and said something back.

"Cijay's been living in an apartment Carnaby rented across the alley from the atelier. I've seen him out there several times, he's always upset me because he reminded me of so many things I'd rather forget. He says he has some other clothes that a kind lady gave him last week."

"Anne," exclaimed Sarah, "my Cousin Percy's wife. Ask him what he did with the painting of the girl holding the parrot."

"Oh yes, that nice little primitive." More words were exchanged, Cijay looked worried. Arbalest didn't.

"He says the painting's in the apartment. He's sorry he stole it but his master made him. His master took his clothes away and made him go naked down through the vent in the greenhouse. He handed the painting out the window to his master, then got stuck trying to get back up through the vent. He couldn't get loose for a long time, his master got impatient and drove off without him and he had no clothes. Then the kind lady brought him some and he walked back to Boston. I'm afraid Carnaby hasn't been treating him very well."

"Phyllis," said Anora, "take this man out to the kitchen and give him something to eat. His name's Cijay and he's going to be working for us till we find him something better. He can have the room over the garage. And this is my stepson George, whom Marcus works for. They'll both be coming to Sunday dinner tomorrow. How are you going to manage without a chauffeur, George?"

"I can drive, mother. Oh, it feels so good to say that! Mrs. Bittersohn, Mr. Bittersohn, Mr.—I'm sorry, I don't know this young man's name."

"He's Jesse Kelling," said Sarah. "And I'm Sarah and my husband is Max. And we'll call you George too, if you don't mind."

"I'll be delighted. Quite frankly, I've never cared much for the name my mother gave me, though I suppose I'll have to keep it for professional reasons. You're off then?"

"Yes, we have things to do."

"Tell Cijay I hope I didn't hurt him too much when I jumped him," said Jesse.

"It was in a good cause, Cijay will understand. I do want you all to understand how deeply I appreciate your good offices on my behalf. And Brooks's too, of course. I must drop him a note. I'll see that you get Mrs. Percy Kelling's painting back tomorrow and I'd be delighted to entertain everyone at the atelier as soon as we can fix a date and mother feels up to traveling. I'm afraid all this has taken a lot out of you, mother. Perhaps we'd better go get that soup."

"I thought you were going to shave first," said Anora.

Over the newly christened George Protheroe's face spread a smile of ineffable delight. "Isn't she wonderful? She's bullying me already."

Max Bittersohn shrugged and grinned. "So what's a mother for? Come on, Sarah, let's take Jesse back to Tulip Street and go pick up our kid."